Voltaris

By Corrina Westfall

For the eternal seekers of knowledge,
there is always possibility when we look to the light.

VOLTARIS

First edition. February 4, 2026.
Copyright © 2026 Corrina Westfall.

ISBN: 979-8994572214

Written by Corrina Westfall.

Table of Contents

Chapter 1: Anomalies

Ember's dark hair fell across her face as she hovered over the data from their quantum encoding experiment she'd collected that morning. Something was not right, and her patience was holding on by a thread. She *knew* the answer was there. Why couldn't she see it?

Their experiments had not been going as planned, but *that* was not the source of her frustrations. She was frustrated because she couldn't get clear data about *why* they weren't going as planned. Ember wanted answers, and she knew that was the key—*the why*.

Ember Quinn was a graduate fellow in physics at Edmondston University. She'd grown up in Landings, the town surrounding Edmondston, and had known of the school's elevated position in the world of quantum physics since she was a kid. She felt honored to work in this cutting-edge laboratory where she had daily access to the insight of the world-renowned Dr. Alena Voss.

Their current research was focused on encoding information in photons, experimenting with how pulses of light could carry data through quantum states without degrading. Despite her years of study, Ember felt like she was just getting her feet wet in the weeds of quantum mechanics. She knew there was a lifetime of work ahead of her—at least equal to what felt like the lifetime she'd invested already.

Her interest in physics had started when she was incredibly young, and now, as she approached the defense of her thesis, Ember felt stuck. She couldn't shake the feeling that something was really wrong in her work.

It didn't appear to be her research. Though she was frustrated, the peculiar data results were not the most concerning uncertainties on her mind. No, the real issue was deeper. It tugged at her consciousness.

The discomfort stirred in her gut, making it hard for Ember to pay attention to the materials before her. The dis-ease was too familiar—a nervous ache that spun and grew in her stomach, agitated by the steady cyclone in her mind. How, after all this time and all this investment, was she still questioning her competence?

Ember had known since childhood that she would be a scientist. But here she was, on the verge of the very accomplishment that would set her up for a lifetime of research and discovery, and she felt uncertain, unsettled, and unfulfilled. Because it wasn't just about her.

Whatever it was that was tugging at her drew from a place deep within her, stirring her to do something—anything—about the unfolding chaos in the world. Tension was escalating among the global superpowers, and the pressure was only getting stronger. Strained relations crossed continents and threatened safety in even the most autonomous regions. Historically, the U.S. had always positioned itself to be outside of the conflict, but recent decisions had put the people and place she loved at great risk as global war became more and more likely.

It felt eerily as though history was, in fact, repeating itself. Ember feared that the world was on the precipice of destruction, and few truly understood what was at stake. Not only famine, pandemic, and violent destruction, the nuclear arms race had far surpassed the daunting contest of the Cold War. Despite the constant chatter of news anchors and media personalities, Ember knew that the threats were real. In any hands, the misuse of power would bring unimaginable consequences.

This laboratory was a haven, though. Ember's research benefited from the leaps and bounds physicists had made since Einstein. Albert Einstein's discovery of quanta in light and his exploration of entanglement had evolved into a modern frontier. In her graduate studies, Ember was soaking up new references and resources regarding quantum computing, quantum communication, and the search for unifying theories. It was inspiring to find that the same phenomena Einstein questioned now powered real technologies: photons carrying information, particles entangled across distance, and matter behaving as both wave and code.

Ember's studies in quantum mechanics revealed a reality in which time (as people tend to think about it) didn't exist, but the urgency of a single lifetime still burdened her.

Yes, of course, she contemplated her existence in the future and the past. But some days she simply couldn't handle the immensity of her existence *here and now*. It was all too complicated, really. When she started to get caught up, she'd just remind herself of the facts.

She was a normal person—she carried neither the brilliance of her inspirational heroes like Einstein nor the worldly savvy of her mentor, Dr. Voss. Ember's wish was simple: to somehow make an impact; to understand the crises of the world and find some way to contribute. Okay, maybe it wasn't all that simple. But Ember was clear. She wanted to find out what one person could do—someone dedicated, curious, and passionate, someone who knew there was more to learn.

She wanted to change the world.

As she sat on the tall stool reviewing her notes, though, Ember couldn't deny that her work invited further interrogation. She had to wonder if her ambitions might ultimately be thwarted not by the state of the world but by the research results laid out before her. She was confronted yet again with the unsettling reality that was only becoming more and more evident: there were anomalies in her experiments, and Ember had no idea how to explain them.

Her coworkers had been teasing her. They'd suggested *she* was somehow influencing the results. But how? She'd watched both of them in process and knew she wasn't doing a single thing any differently from either of them.

Today, though, she finally had enough material to see that the pattern they had identified (and had teased her about) was measurable. They were right! The experiment results changed dramatically depending on who took the measurements.

When one of her colleagues took measurements, the results were murky, uncertain, and generally unhelpful. But when Ember took the measurements, she got precise information.

Ember really couldn't imagine she was somehow the only one doing it right. It made more sense—to her, at least—that she was doing something wrong. (She was certainly more inclined to criticize herself than her colleagues.) According to the other grad assistants, though, either Ember had some sort of incredible luck to be getting such fine data, or *she* was somehow altering the experiment.

Ember always worried she was somehow contaminating the experiment—any experiment. Now, their results seemed to reinforce her suspicion.

Being a physicist was all she'd ever wanted, but maybe she really wasn't cut out for this level of work. She couldn't consider her research intact if she was coming up with skewed results.

She didn't just want a career in physics; she wanted to make discoveries that would uphold the power of science as a force for good in the world. She was ambitious enough to aim for real global impact. She'd been fostering her scientific ambitions for more than two decades, and getting hung up by distorted outcomes was not the direction she hoped for.

Her mind had fully turned against her. She was spinning now. How could she be so presumptuous as to think she might be able to contribute at the level of the brilliant minds she so admired? Was her passion for physics enough?

She had to wonder if completing her doctorate was really the best thing. But she couldn't see herself leaving such an amazing opportunity as she had now, working with the luminous, brilliant Dr. Alena Voss.

Ember sighed, lifting her head from her hand, where she'd been resting it for more some time now. She wasn't going to make any rash decisions today. She was committed to her work in the lab.

Dr. Voss had given Ember a unique opportunity to develop quantum memory vials. And Ember knew there was real potential here. This was, truly, her first chance at meaningful contribution.

Her mood started to lift. If she didn't give up, she could discover something important; she could contribute to advances in improving quantum memory. Her visions held intricate new systems that could store information like light and other data, even thought-like patterns, beyond seconds into days or even weeks.

That would be a game-changer.

●

Focus, Ember thought, reorienting herself to the possibilities on the table here. Maybe her innovations would one day not only provide stable long-term storage for quantum computers but also lead to breakthroughs in neuroscience and consciousness.

Ember heard heels clicking down the hall outside the laboratory and turned just in time to see Dr. Voss stride purposefully through the door. She was an elegant scientist—none of that mousy presentation she'd thought of when envisioning women scientists as a kid.

Dr. Voss showed up in a room with the most powerful composure. She wore chic professional attire, sharp makeup, and elegant hairstyles. Her presence was fierce. She carried the cunning and wisdom of someone far older but, looking at her, Ember was certain Dr. Voss couldn't be more than 50 years old.

Today, Dr. Voss wore a skirt, vest, blazer, and deep red lipstick; her dark curls flowed like water over her shoulders. She clutched several folders tightly to her chest, and her long fingers stretched across the folds and tucked into the fine red cloth of her blazer.

Ember felt nothing but admiration for this woman whose brilliance was reflected in every facet of her life. Dr. Voss seemed to be able to hold it all together in every way, and Ember only wished some of her mentor's finesse would rub off on her.

Dr. Voss had been spending less time in the laboratory lately. She'd brought her three new grad students on at the lab around the same time, and over the past year, she'd seemed quite comfortable entrusting them to pursue their particular avenues of research. Everything in the lab fell under her jurisdiction, of course, but she seemed preoccupied with tasks outside of the laboratory.

Her university office was through the laboratory, though, so even when she wasn't involved in their experiments, she made an appearance in the lab most every day. Sometimes she just passed through and didn't even speak to them.

Dr. Voss scanned the room, and Ember suddenly remembered she was meant to be working. She tucked her chin and looked back down at her data. She at least wanted to look the part of a dedicated scientist, even if today her thoughts were elsewhere.

Upon noticing no one else was there, Dr. Voss strode across the laboratory towards Ember.

"Good morning, Ember," Dr. Voss said, a sly smile spreading across her lips. "How is that new data? I'd love to get some updates this week when you have time."

"Of course," Ember's voice caught. She wasn't excited to report her findings to Dr. Voss, but she couldn't avoid it any longer. Besides, maybe Dr. Voss would see something in the data she had missed. Still, she hesitated.

As Dr. Voss looked down at the report Ember was reviewing, she set her folders on the counter beside them. She began to speak, then abruptly stopped herself and grabbed the folders back to her chest.

"Oh," she said to herself, clutching the stack tightly again, almost as if she were guarding them.

Dr. Voss was always a bit strange with her research. The students were never invited to review her notes, though Ember was certain her mentor's insights would be illuminating. Ember had talked with her colleagues about it, but ultimately it didn't appear any stranger than Dr. Voss herself. It just fit with Dr. Voss's other unusual behaviors.

This seemed a rare moment of awkwardness, though, as Dr. Voss fumbled their conversation and left Ember mid-thought. The elegant physicist strode away and into her office just as Max and Olive appeared in the doorway. Their jovial presence was a welcome shift to Ember's nervous mind.

Max was bragging boisterously to Olive about his entanglement encryption project. He'd been working on a particular dimension of Dr. Voss's interests, linking detectors across the lab to test secure entangled channels.

Dr. Voss was clearly proud of Max's investigations. She often explained his research to visitors. "This technology could revolutionize communication," she'd say.

Ember wasn't quite sure why that point about Max's research always sparked her mentor's enthusiasm so dramatically, but it certainly filled Max's cup to have Dr. Voss's approval.

Ember smiled familiarly at her colleagues, but she knew she was in need of a break. She'd been at it for six hours and was getting nowhere. She needed to clear her head.

She cleared her workspace, stuffed a few specific resources, including her laptop and notebook, into her bag, and said her goodbyes.

●

Opening her front door was like entering a cocoon. Ember dropped her jacket and bag at the door, slid off her shoes, and crumpled onto the couch. She reached towards her current novel resting on the side table, but as she curled up to read, the pair of women on the cover— an elder and a teenager—sent her deep into her memories.

She couldn't help but wonder what it would've been like to have her Momo's influence in her teenage years.

Ember had begun to call her grandmother "Momo" as soon as she could form sounds, but the name stuck her whole life long. Even now, Ember's friends knew of her grandmother as "Momo." It suited her somehow.

Momo had been a woman of knowledge and insight, ranging from the practical to the personal, the tangible to the spiritual, and beyond. And she told the most amazing stories.

Most of what Ember knew of the world and what was beyond it came first through Momo's eyes. She had spoken to Ember of botany and ecology, astronomy and meteorology. She talked about the details of what they could see and the possibilities of those liminal spaces, the realms unseen. They talked about the origins of life and the origins of Earth itself. They talked about death, too.

Ember remembered it so clearly, how sometimes, in hushed tones, Momo would suggest, in one way or another, that the boundaries between the living and the dead were not as rigid as most people believed.

There were no bounds for Momo, and Ember learned that doubt was usually nothing more than the shape of her own fears.

No matter the subject, Ember was captivated by every word her grandmother spoke. It was as though she was imparting the wisdom of the world as it had been passed down through generations. Momo's stories meant just as much as the scientific theories she devoured.

Momo always had her nose in a book and studied widely. She especially had a firm grasp on the major scientific discoveries of her time, and she was deeply curious about quantum physics well before it held any ground in the mainstream lens. She often gave Ember the impression that Momo knew more about a subject than she was letting on. She especially reveled in Einstein's discoveries and how he used imagination to go beyond the limits of knowledge and conventional experiments.

Looking back, Ember could tell that Momo's retelling of Einstein's stories was not dry history; rather, they held qualities of myth, as though they were inventive retellings, not dissimilar to the historical novels Ember loved.

Momo talked about Einstein as a real person—first, a boy and then, a brilliant man—who asked impossible questions about light and time and all instances of matter.

"In daring to imagine," Momo would say, "that man reshaped the universe."

It was as though Momo had had a glimpse into the realities of Einstein's life, as though his influence had affected her personally. Ember had thought what great friends they would've made—her grandmother and the great Albert Einstein.

Even now, long after Momo's death and well into Ember's own studies in physics, Einstein's influence persisted in her mind. She could not forget how often Momo said, "Imagination is our most powerful tool."

Afternoon had turned to evening as Ember followed the course of her memories. She looked up to see the sunlight fading and stretched her arms above her head to shake the cobwebs from her mind. She needed to make dinner—something simple, surely. She had too much on her mind to follow a recipe. But after she ate, she felt restored, and she thought, before she took a shower, she'd look at those notes just one more time.

Maybe, with a fresh lens, she could find the clue that seemed to be eluding her. She wanted to know where the anomalies were coming from.

She reached into her backpack for her lab notes, once again entrenched in the drama of her day. What if this was all some mistake? Could the answer be that she's been messing things up over and over again? She spread the printed materials across her kitchen table.

Ember's eyes scanned the inexplicable results before her. Now, looking over the pages, a feeling of alarm was rising through her. She'd missed the most important question.

What if her results were *true?*

If her experiments were turning up accurate results, then this research—the research she was piloting—was showing them more than just (*Really?* she thought to herself—*Just?*) the potential to store light, data, and thought-like patterns as quantum memory in photons...

Was this really possible?

The research was showing them that the photons were sentient.

Chapter 2: The Inkwell

Ember opened her eyes with a start. Her heart raced, and beads of sweat formed on her forehead and across her chest.

It was a dream. It was only a dream.

The realization relieved her stress, and she settled back into the comfort of her bed.

All she remembered was the very end. It had seemed like a pivotal moment. She remembered reaching for a book, but it was not any book from her memory—not one of her journals or anything she recognized from Momo's extensive library. It wasn't a textbook or something she would find among her physics nerd friends either.

She couldn't place it. An old, red book with rough-cut pages and well-worn corners. It was strange—why would a book have her nervous system all charged up? Even in the dream, though, the book had piqued her interest.

Ember turned to check her phone for the time. 6:59. One minute before her alarm would sound. Time to greet the day.

She was preparing for a day of refined focus in the laboratory. She *had* to figure out what was really going on with the quantum encoding data.

Dutifully, Ember rose from the bed and shuffled to her dresser. Jeans, a silk tank, and a professional button-down. Chunky socks and her dark red boots. She was thankful the season was finally shifting. She was ready for cooler weather, for wool sweaters and cozy evenings by the fire. There was more to life than science...

Ha, she thought. *Yeah, right.* Nothing would compare to the feeling she had when she found the right formula or revealed a new answer about the world. She felt like physics gave her the ability to touch the unseen, to make the imperceptible tangible. She gathered the papers still strewn across the kitchen table and tucked them tidily into her backpack, then pulled a jacket from the hooks by the door and was on her way.

The anxiety of the book dream followed Ember to the lab. As she checked over the lab equipment, her imagination started rolling. Momo had always told her,

Science and wonder are the same.

She tried to remember that. When things stopped making sense, following the direction of her vision, or providing intelligent outcomes, she channeled Momo's spirit—her spontaneity, her joy, and her reverent respect for what she knew *and especially* what she didn't know.

But in the lab that day, wonder took a backseat to the parade of memories distracting Ember. She couldn't stop thinking about her earliest memories with her grandmother.

Those were her first lessons in arts and sciences. She couldn't have been older than five or six when Momo introduced her to the scientific method and then Einstein and, eventually, quantum theory. Ember's mind wrestled with those advanced subjects as though they were her playmates and Momo, her very best friend. According to Momo, quantum oddities were the closest thing to magic humans could apprehend. Ember remembered her spinning a web of story around the idea of entanglement.

Momo said entanglement was like two particles that existed on opposite sides of the universe instantaneously feeling the slightest change in the other, as if they were connected by an invisible thread in a place where time and distance didn't exist.

Ember didn't understand it then, but today the concept of entanglement drew her into a world of potential. She could get lost for hours in spirals of inquiry.

Since those first lessons with Momo, Ember had spent decades as a student. She'd found, unsurprisingly, a keen interest in scientific thinking, experimentation, and research; but lately she felt her memories with Momo were blurring the stark boundaries she had drawn between science and magic. More and more was coming back to her:

Science doesn't kill magic; it reveals it.

"Contrary to popular belief," Momo had said. "Because scientists often doubt magic is real, and they try to stifle it. To stamp it out. But it is as obvious to the curious observer as the hair on my chin!" Ember remembered it clearly—Momo had pointed to a tiny coarse hair that grew from her chin. "When you really understand the science," she said, "you can't help but find the magic."

Ember smiled at the memory and wondered—was there some reason that Momo's insight kept coming back to her over these past few days?

Ember shook off the last wisps of Momo's story, blinking as the fluorescent lights of the lab settled back into focus. She was finally sitting down when Max sidled up to her stool. "Any insight into the mysterious data?" he asked, inquisitive but also a bit teasing in his tone.

Ember leaned over to get yesterday's collection of notes from her backpack. "I don't know what you want me to say."

Olive joined the conversation. "I see you took the notes home with you last night. Are you still bent out of shape about these anomalies? I really think you have to run them again, Ember," she said encouragingly. Olive was always supportive, and this was no different, but her suffocating encouragement would sometimes take Ember over the edge.

"I can't, Olive," Ember said with exasperation behind her voice. "I have gathered the data from this experiment more times than the both of you combined, and my results are consistent, just not with yours." It was true—and no one knew why.

"I have to figure out where the change is happening. I do have some ideas, but..." her voice trailed off.

She wasn't quite ready to tell them what she was thinking—that the photons—the most fundamental of particles of energy might be sentient.

Ember could imagine the looks that would cross both of their faces, and she just couldn't deal with that today. If they thought the anomalies were noise, she'd just have to deal with that for a bit longer. Because the other option—well, it truly seemed impossible.

But what if the impossible is simply undiscovered?

Momo's voice echoed again in her mind. But Ember wondered—had her grandmother ever said anything like that? She couldn't remember exactly, but she didn't know where else it would have come from. No matter. It was something to think about. What if the impossible is simply undiscovered?

It's been true before, Ember thought to herself.

She decided to take the conversation in a different direction. "Honestly, I'm feeling overwhelmed—a bit bent out of shape—about the state of things. Every time I open the news, it's something else. Another international standoff, supply chains falling apart, governments denying problems that they have so obviously created. Half the world seems to be bracing for something, and no one can agree on what it even is."

She shook her head, a frustrated laugh slipping out. "And meanwhile, I'm sitting in a lab all day trying to make heads or tails of these readouts, staring at photon noise and coherence times, feeling light-years away from being able to contribute anything meaningful to society. It's like... the stakes feel enormous out there, and I'm stuck squinting at data."

It wasn't untrue, though that was only *part* of what was bugging Ember at the moment.

A conversation ensued between the trio of graduate assistants. Max and Olive had plenty to say about what was worrying them in the world.

Max was particularly animated about a timely podcast. "I was listening to an interview with Charles Hadden on my walk over," he said. "He was talking about data integrity and global security—how fragile information systems are right now. He actually mentioned Dr. Voss by name."

Olive looked up. "Seriously? Dr. Alena Voss?"

"Yeah," Max said. "He praised her work on photon-based encryption and error-resistant communication. He said it was the kind of research that could set a new standard for trust in scientific and economic systems. Coming from him, that's... not nothing."

Ember felt a small flicker of surprise, though she kept her expression neutral. Dr. Voss's public work was impressive—elegant, even—but hearing it framed as globally consequential, as something already on the radar of people like Hadden, made it feel heavier somehow.

It wasn't difficult to imagine how easily good science, developed with the best intentions, could be pulled into the orbit of larger forces once it caught the attention of people in power. It was easy for all three of them to imagine how previous generations, especially the ones who lived through global wars, would respond to present circumstances.

Like so many mornings before, they were swept into conversation about historical context for the moment, especially about physicists and other scientists before them who had made significant contributions that ultimately influenced the course of history, including war.

Marie Curie was an obvious subject—when she discovered polonium and then radium, she created new avenues for healthcare *and* warfare. Her radiology and X-ray contributions were crucial during the first world war, but then her pioneering research was likely the cause of her own death. And it also made possible the future development of the atomic bomb. She pursued her work diligently, nonetheless.

Then of course, there was Ember's beloved Einstein. She loved to discuss his most well-known discovery—that a small amount of mass could be converted into a huge amount of energy. That life-changing revelation altered the course of physics and eventually led to one of the most destructive acts of war in written history, one he was alive to witness.

"We're staring down the same problem, in some ways, at least," Max said, quieter now. "Every real step forward we make in this lab—every new way of manipulating information, energy, or uncertainty—can be repurposed. Even if we start with the best intentions, there is no guarantee our discoveries remain neutral. If they get folded into systems of power and dominance, the consequences can outlive us."

Ember and Olive knew he was right. None of them had entered this work without that awareness.

But even with their good intentions, controlling the potential outcomes was certainly beyond them. Ember had to face the fact that her idealism, especially her ambition to have a meaningful impact in the world, might not play out as she hoped.

Ember wanted to turn the conversation around. She needed some momentum. "I want to be more open to the unexpected. I'm feeling stuck—in my studies, in my experiments... I feel like I need some inspiration."

"A good dose of imagination," Olive offered.

"I know Einstein used his imagination to realize his breakthroughs..." Ember's voice trailed off. Her imagination *had been* playing a role lately. But should she tell them?

She gulped down her worry as she looked at Max and Olive. What did she have to lose?

"I've been dreaming," Ember said sheepishly, as though admitting some sort of fault.

Max's eyes began to glaze over at the mere mention of dreaming, but a spark glimmered in Olive's eye. "Dreaming, like envisioning something, or dreaming, like having experiences in your sleep?"

"Well," Ember wasn't sure exactly how to respond. "I guess the latter. I've been having dreams. I've been waking up and remembering most of them."

Max promptly grew bored and barely tried to hide his disinterest as he spun from one side to the other on his stool, like a schoolboy. Within a minute, he'd not-so-stealthily snuck away to do his own lab work.

Ember glanced over at him. Was he still listening? He certainly hadn't contributed anything helpful on the dream front. Olive had lots to say, though. She started spewing information at Ember about the intersections between dreams and quantum physics, about superposition and entanglement and the many worlds interpretation. She went on and on, and eventually Ember forgot the details of the dream she meant to share.

Vague shapes remained in her mind. There had been a book of some sort, and the feeling she'd somehow found the answers she'd been looking for...

Ember shook the cobwebs from her memory. It didn't seem to matter. By the time Olive finished talking, Ember was saturated, exhausted from listening and unclear again about the meaning of the many layers precipitating in her own mind.

When Olive finally let her be, Ember realized she could use a minute to gather her thoughts. She looked around and saw the bookshelf.

A good time to be inspired, she thought. She took a book from the shelf—the first volume of *The Feynman Lectures on Physics*—and sat back down on the tall stool to let her mind wander.

Maybe this would feed her imagination. A bit of wandering to get her back on track.

●

Max and Olive packed up for their ritual after work drinks just after five, but Ember stayed at the laboratory a bit longer. Her reading had proven very interesting and relevant to her work at the moment. She wanted to stay with it while she had the compulsion.

And it was Friday and her turn to clean up from the week. When she finally closed *The Feynman Lectures* volume and put it back up on the shelf, she scoped the lab. It wasn't in terrible shape, but she should give it a bit of attention.

Ember mindlessly went about the cleaning tasks, shuffling records into their rightful files and cabinets, placing instruments in their safe storage, and at last, she wandered to the back corner to grab the broom and dustpan. She reached mindlessly for the broom and startled herself when she nearly knocked something off the countertop.

What was this? It was some sort of vessel—nothing she had ever used before. A thick glass container, shaped to capture liquid, or light? It seemed a bit dated for their modern experiments. Maybe it was just an odd vase. But here in the laboratory? There was no reason for flowers here.

She really couldn't tell what the vessel was, or where it belonged. She picked it up to get a closer look, but before she could lift it to her face, the vessel was gone.

The laboratory was gone too.

Ember stood over a wooden desk in the center of a small room, like an office. Books lined the walls, and the desk itself was covered in papers and weighty books open to full pages. A pipe lay on its side at the corner of the desk, loose tobacco strewn around it.

Where was she?

A scientific journal lay at the center of the desk, open to the first page of an article. The title caught her eye: "The Translation of Energy at Death: An Exploration of Quantum Dynamics Beyond Life."

Those words lit her up with excitement, but somehow—strangely—she knew the excitement didn't belong to her.

Ember felt drawn to this piece as though she knew it on some fundamental level. She felt a sense of longing around it.

This was what she had been searching for—someone whose interest in physics extended beyond the terrors of war, into the questions of reality and existence. There was a sense of justice here.

Ember wanted to return to the article, to see what was there, but some other part of her was controlling her actions. That part was leading her motions... and her thoughts. Not just leading—it was as though another mind dwelled within her, compelling her every idea, her every action.

Now an insatiable curiosity stirred as she took a seat at the desk, pushed the book and the stack of others beneath it aside, and withdrew from the top drawer a leather folder. She opened it to select a single piece of parchment and placed it purposefully before her. Then she lifted the fountain pen beside it to write.

"Dear esteemed colleague—"

The letters drifted easefully onto the parchment as her hands—but not her hands—moved the pen. Her fingers were wider, weightier, and... hairier.

"I am delighted to encounter your recent article in the publication Of Time and Consequence. *I find your process compelling, your ideas imaginative and potentiating, and your writing superior. I myself am—"*

The ink was running thin. She looked around the room—where was that bottle? And then she spotted it. A fine glass vessel with a simple label: Sharp's.

With urgency, she rose from the table to reach for it, but she stood so quickly the chair knocked into the wall behind her and fell to its side on the floor. Flustered, she took a deep breath, bent to reposition her seat, and saw again the stunning title: "The Translation of Energy at Death." Just the site of it grounded her. Here was a companion in wonder.

As she reached again for the glass bottle, the room started to blur, as though the very particles that made it up were dissolving before her.

Ember found herself back in the laboratory, inkwell in hand.

She scanned the room, hoping that no one had seen. But of course she was there alone.

She could see her face reflected in the glass pane window of the back cabinets. Yep, that was her. She looked down at her hands. Familiar, thin fingers, no visible hairs from this point of view.

What a strange experience, she thought to herself. *Was it even real?* She barely believed it. First dreams, and now this?

"I need to get more rest," she whispered aloud.

Ember caught the time on her watch and realized Max and Olive had been waiting on her at the bar for nearly an hour now. She did a quick scan of the laboratory and determined it was, in fact, clean enough. In the odd case that Dr. Voss was the first one in on Monday, Ember doubted she would notice a rare bit of dust on the floor. And who would doubt that the dust hadn't just collected over the weekend?

Ember set the broom upright back in the corner and grabbed her backpack. As she slung the lightweight bag over her shoulder, something on the ground caught her eye.

Damnit, she thought. *Maybe the place does need a sweep.*

She bent down to grab it and realized it was not a piece of trash but a full sheet of paper with some sort of graph and several paragraphs of writing.

Ember drew the paper out from under the cabinet and stood beneath the light to get a better look. This wasn't her research, or Max and Olive's, but it was definitely physics material. Could it be Dr. Voss's?

Maybe she dropped it, Ember thought, remembering how Dr. Voss had been holding a stack of folders when she came in yesterday. And they had slipped... But Ember couldn't remember if anything hit the floor.

The page was covered in complex equations. These were not simple subjects. It seemed the material was about the curvature of spacetime... and the distribution of matter and energy...

Ember felt uncertain.

The equations were interlaced with symbols she didn't recognize— curved, looping shapes that look more like sigils than letters. Was this some archaic notation? No, not that.

The longer Ember stared, the more she realized—the math on the page wasn't any sort of science she was used to. It seemed to be describing consciousness as a measurable field, as if the equation was solving for... soul.

No reputable physicist would have taken this seriously. Yet, the math *was* rigorous. If this were Dr. Voss's, why would she hide it? If it were accurate, this information would have a profound influence in their field.

Ember didn't know why Dr. Voss would keep it secret, but she also couldn't understand *how* this research was happening. Obviously, it went well beyond the work they were doing in the university laboratory. Where were these experiments taking place? What were her reasons for keeping this project separate from her team?

After such a long day contemplating her own anomalous results, Ember was surprised to find data that seemed so much more outrageous than her encoding details.

Ember felt a prickling down her spine.

Upon further examination, the math wasn't just outrageous—it was impossible.

It was impossible not because it was wrong but because it was too complete, too integrated.

It did include their own datasets, but it was also laced with symbols that didn't belong to any scientific notation she knew. As it became clearer in her mind, Ember realized it looked as if someone had taken Max's coherence work, folded in her photon-encoding results, and carried the equations far past the boundaries of known physics.

The realization descended upon her dramatically: these weren't hypotheses. These were derived results, the output of experiments she and her team had never run.

And tucked between the lines—those looping sigils, those non-human forms—was something even more unsettling. The equations didn't feel written by a single mind. They felt generated by a system she couldn't identify.

Whatever Dr. Voss was doing, she was working with a breakthrough so volatile it could never appear in a journal. Something that governments would classify instantly. Something that could change the world, or fracture it.

Ember swallowed hard.

This wasn't eccentric research.

It was a warning.

Voltaris

Chapter 3: The Laboratory

The bar was more packed than usual, and Ember pushed through the crowd gathering to order drinks with an anxious smile. She was bursting with excitement and a strong dose of panic, anxious to tell Max and Olive what she had found. Worry thrummed through her chest.

Before she left the lab, Ember had tucked the document that she'd found beneath the cabinet into a fresh manila folder, then she tucked the folder into her backpack. As she moved through the busy bar, she tried to keep her cool, to hold her backpack casually. But she felt like she was carrying an enormous secret. She needed her friends' insight.

Max and Olive lounged in their usual booth in the corner. Ember pressed through a few more students and scooted onto the bench beside Olive.

They were talking shop. Olive was teasing Max that his simulations were eating up all the lab's computing time, and Max was whole-heartedly defending himself. "I want to revolutionize communication!" he said emphatically. "If we can keep coherence longer—"

She did not have time for Max's quantum musings. Ember interrupted him: "You guys, I have something to show you." She pulled the folder from her backpack and threw the paper down on the table dramatically. But she didn't mean to come on so strongly; she tried to soften her tone a bit. "I just found this in the lab."

She looked critically at her friends—her colleagues—her eyes entreating. "Do you know what this is about?"

Max and Olive studied the strange notes. "Well," Max started, "I mean, this looks like my research, I think..." He pointed to one of the equations on the page. "But the rest of it... I have no idea. I've never seen anything like it. What's it from?" he asked.

Olive drew the paper closer and hovered above it, clearly reading every detail. "This goes way beyond your work, Max." She looked up at him. "It's just... so far beyond." She promptly returned her attention to the page. "This is impressive and truly strange." There was too much to take it in all at once.

"That's what I thought," Ember said, relieved at their candor. It did seem this was news to them too.

"Olive, let me take another look." Max turned the paper back towards him and analyzed the other equations on the page. "You found this in the lab, Ember? Where? I don't..." he stuttered. "Why does it have my research? And... well, who is doing these other experiments?"

He turned the paper towards Ember and Olive again, pointing midway down the page.

"This—this is what I've been working on," he said. "But here..." his fingers traveled along the other equations and the strange sigil-like characters, "The data clearly go deeper. I honestly don't know if I would believe all of this. I'm not sure it's realistic, nor am I sure this is safe. If this is real, it could take the work we're doing in the lab in a really dangerous direction.

"Okay, here," he went on, pausing to look up at Ember and Olive, his eyes incredulous. "This expands on my work on entangled states and memory stability.

"Then this bit here is familiar—" he pointed further down. "The math describing quantum coherence beyond normal decay times. But then it goes further, well past what's generally accepted in academia, even in fringe circles."

Ember's face showed focus; all of her attention was pointed at Max. Could her discovery really be so big as all this?

"The notes are equally disturbing." Max looked just as puzzled as Ember felt. He was clearly struggling to keep it together. "They're literally talking about 'persistence beyond collapse.' Do you see this bit about 'information/essence transfer'? It's like someone took my work and applied it to... consciousness."

He sat back, and the three friends looked at each other, trying to integrate the implications of what lay before them.

It was starting to land for Ember. For the first time since she'd arrived at the bar, Ember took the paper in her hands. "If I'm understanding correctly, these equations suggest..." She paused, checking her commitment to the comment she was about to make. But she knew she had to say it out loud.

"If these equations are accurate, they're not just preserving quantum information, they're preserving the 'pattern' of living consciousness." Another breath. "In theory, that means you could capture someone's thoughts, their memories, even their identity."

31

The table was totally quiet in the otherwise noisy establishment, each of them taking in the implications of the equations. A growing disease had overwhelmed the previously carefree conversation.

Ember's mind wandered to detailed eventualities. If this data was real, then they were looking at groundbreaking material.

They were holding proof that someone had already taken their research and carried it somewhere far beyond what any of them intended.

The implications were enormous.

This knowledge would give its wielder inexplicable power over others. It would be devastating in the wrong hands: political institutions, economic systems, social movements, and especially the global leaders who shaped them could be subject to the influence of a single entity.

Worse still, the equations weren't speculative; they looked like results. Someone was already running trials on consciousness and using their work without their consent. It wasn't difficult to parse out the details, but Ember was finding such a reality truly hard to imagine.

"Hmm," Olive murmured, stirring Ember from her spiral. Olive closed her eyes as she spoke, finally naming the severity of this discovery aloud. "We're talking about capturing the essence of an entity. We're talking about harnessing a person's soul."

She looked between Ember and Max, locking eyes with both of them, one after the other. "This could have world-changing consequences."

Just what Ember had been thinking. The heaviness that had settled over the friends brought with it a sense of urgency. Was there something they could—something they should—do to ensure the safety of their research?

"There's one question we must answer first," Max said.

The statement lingered in the air. They were all thinking the same thing: Where had this paper come from?

Ember was the only one with a real answer.

"It had to be Dr. Voss," with such an apologetic tone they might have thought she was admitting to doing the research herself. "I think she dropped it in the lab. It could have been yesterday, when she came in with a big stack of papers..."

Ember's statement certainly felt to her like a confession, as though she was at some sort of fault for considering Dr. Voss could be culpable of this. But then, Ember knew Dr. Voss was the only reasonable source.

She wondered for a moment, though, about Dr. Milton. He was a mousy, nervous scientist who had worked with Dr. Voss for years before their cohort of graduate assistants arrived. He came around at least every day or two to review their work; but he'd been absent for over a week now.

If he'd been in and dropped the paper, someone would have found it days ago. So, Dr. Voss was the only real suspect. Unless...

Ember's eyes widened at the direction her mind was taking. *Unless it was one of them*, she thought.

Ember looked across the table at Max who was studying the paper intently, then beside her to where Olive's jaw was clenched tight. No, her friends remained just as shocked as she was. They were curious, investigating, unsettled. No, it couldn't be one of them. At least she didn't need to worry about that.

Olive interrupted Ember's thoughts. "Surely there's more to this. There must be something we don't know yet." Ember watched her friend struggle to get her point across. "I just... I just want to give Alena the benefit of the doubt."

Olive had a bad habit of referring to their boss by her first name. In this circumstance, though, it seemed purposeful. She was trying to humanize their mentor *and*, in promising Dr. Voss's good intentions, salvage their own work.

They'd just been talking about the ill-effects of their predecessors' inventions that morning. Ember knew they were all concerned about contributing to something that would cause more suffering in the world. With this, the concern became even more immediate that their research could be being applied without their knowledge or their consent.

"I don't know who else would have been in the lab this week," Ember responded. "But honestly, I can't understand why Dr. Voss would hide something like this from us. We're her assistants. Shouldn't we know how she plans to use our research?

"She's a professional, a world-renowned physicist," Ember went on. "If this new research is valid, why isn't she talking about it? Why isn't she publishing it?" Urgency was building behind her questions. And she wasn't the only one whose stress was growing.

"And, if it's not valid," Max added, "Why pursue it at all?" He flipped the paper over, but the reverse side was blank. "Did you look around for other papers?" His eyes widened at the thought that there might be more information to help them figure out this evolving mystery.

Ember thought back to that moment when she'd first seen the paper. She'd studied it closely, then put the paper safely in her bag and run out the door. She hadn't even turned out the lights in the lab.

"No," she said, "but I need to go back. I forgot the lights. I may not have even locked the door."

"I want to see if there are any other clues," Max said. "I'm coming with you."

"Me too," Olive chimed. That was that. Max and Olive drained what's left of their drinks. A group of undergraduate students who'd been hovering nearby slid quickly into their booth as the three hurried out of the bar and back to the lab.

●

It was well after six, so Ember swiped her keycard to get them back into the physics building. Though it wasn't unusual for any of them to work late, they might raise eyebrows if someone were to catch all three of them entering the building together at this time of day.

They hurried to Dr. Voss's lab. Ember turned the knob. Unlocked. *Oh, well*, she thought. *They were here now. No harm done.* She hoped not, at least. Max dimmed the lights to low so as to attract less attention, and Olive locked the door behind them.

The lab was like a comfort zone, and Ember began to let her guard down as she scanned the room. Max put his lab coat on and pulled his recent materials out of the cabinet so as to look like he was working, then he promptly dropped to his hands and knees, using his phone as a flashlight. He searched beneath the counters, looking for more papers.

"Where was the one you found?" he asked Ember.

"Under the cabinets down by my station," Ember responded. She was rifling through a stack of papers on the giant lab table at the center of the room, looking for anything unfamiliar, keeping a special eye out for images like those sigils.

Olive seemed to be following some intuitive compulsion. She searched through drawers and opened cabinets, one after the other, around the exterior of the room.

"Nothing yet," Max was crawling along the floor, looking thoroughly but frantically under all the equipment and every shelf, cabinet, and workbench. Ember found herself drawn to Dr. Voss's office. The open doorway felt like an invitation she must follow.

She rarely had a reason to enter Dr. Voss's office, but tonight she had a feeling that she might find a hint, some sort of clue, inside that door. Max must've finished his ground-level investigation, because he followed her in. The two of them looked meticulously around the office—not just for papers, but for anything that might resemble the research they'd seen.

They were quietly opening closet doors, gingerly looking through stacks of books and inside drawers, careful to put things back in the precise position they'd found them.

She had a whole library of books in her office, but Dr. Voss also kept a small collection of trinkets and antiques amidst the books on her shelves. Max lifted a tiny wooden box and gently opened the lid.

"Here's a key," he said, lifting the old-fashioned instrument for them to see.

So far, that was the most exciting thing they'd found, and it felt like a win.

It was probably just one of Dr. Voss's antique pieces, though. Maybe it went to a piece of furniture. If it were more important, surely it would be kept more securely than that, in the kind of box Ember might use to stash trinkets and treasures at home.

Max tried the key in the filing cabinets and then Dr. Voss's desk, but its aged structure didn't fit any of the modern keyholes that decorated the office.

Ember kept looking. Maybe there was still a real clue here to find—something with sigils or some reference to the other research. She scanned the bookshelves, running her finger along the books. Three fell to the side, revealing a home for their strange key.

"Here! There's a keyhole in the wall!" Ember sounded just as surprised as she felt.

"There's a keyhole in the bookcase?"

Olive had finally joined them in Dr. Voss's office. Ember was glad the door was locked now. Dr. Voss wouldn't be here on a Friday night, but it would be a bad look to be seen snooping around her office by anyone at that time of the evening.

Max brought the key around to the wall. Click.

"Wow!" Max shouted, then more softly repeated, "Wow..."

The key was a fit. He turned it to the right, and the three graduate assistants watched as the whole bookcase shifted smoothly forward and then to the side.

Before them was a wide, white door made of metal, not at all cohesive to the old infrastructure of the physics building. Shock registered across each of their faces.

Ember peered at the screen beside the door. It seemed to be some form of face-reading technology, or maybe it was an eye scanner, like the ones she'd seen on TV shows. She was wondering how they would get through when the door opened on its own.

Had the security system recognized her? Had this secret door just opened to her face?

Neither Max nor Olive seemed to notice or care how Ember had mysteriously opened the door. They wanted to see what was on the other side. Ember peered through the opening to see a stairwell that led down in a stark-white spiral.

"Shall we?" Max said, the levity in his voice doing little to mask the seriousness of the situation. The trio had thought they were looking for clues, but a secret doorway—that was so much more than they had expected.

Cautiously, the students agreed to go down the stairs.

"But slowly," Olive warned.

She closed the office door and followed Ember and Max into the unknown.

●

At the bottom of what felt like a hundred or more stairs, the trio found another locked door with another security reader. The screen flashed with a place for five fingerpads, and Ember lifted her hand to the reader. If it worked for her before, why not now?

Max and Olive watched in awe as the heavy metal door slid to the left, revealing a space glowing with the green-white of fluorescent lights. It was easily three times bigger than the laboratory, maybe as big as the physics building itself.

Without moving a muscle, the students could see into a massive central room with at least eight doors around its edges. A giant boardroom table stood in the far corner. There were no windows this far underground and the greenish hue of the many fluorescent lights added an eerie starkness.

What was this strange place?

At the center of the room, a massive screen showed what must've been a livestream of the world right outside. They could see the lamps that lined the lawn and the old classroom building across the way. Along the bottom of the screen, though, was somewhere else, for sure. The series of miniature views looked like... laboratories?

"Do you see the feeds on the screen?" Max asked. "There's our lab, and then... CERN? and I think that's a shot from Fermilab. They're all familiar." He broke his focus on the screen to scan the room again. "What *is* this place?"

Ember was still hypnotized by the technology. Beneath the laboratory views, she could see lines of code scrolling past: photon counts, coherence times, entanglement registers. This was data, the same data they ran upstairs. She was trying to take it all in.

Finally, Olive spoke. "It's like some sort of command center," she said. "It's tracking what we're doing upstairs and also what is happening around the globe." Her voice quivered as she admitted her concern: "Do you think Dr. Voss could be part of this?"

"It definitely seems like it to me," Max responded. "We got here through her office! I don't know what she's up to, but this setup means she can keep an eye on what is happening in all of these labs across the country and around the world."

He paused for a moment, and his friends could almost see by his expression, the speed of the thoughts running through his mind.

"If she does have some sort of evil intention, this technology means she could co-opt or even sabotage other work. She could definitely use this to stay ahead of the game. I'm starting to feel like we really don't know her at all..."

Just then, a door on the other side of the conference table at the far end of the space began to open.

The students didn't wait to see who came through. At once, all three of them turned and raced to the entrance they'd come through just moments before. They ran rapidly up the stairs, and Ember could just see Dr. Voss's office when the security door—the one she'd somehow opened with her face—began to shut.

Max and Olive stumbled into the office in front of her, and Ember tripped over the last step as she squeezed through. She caught herself before her knees hit the ground and rolled over to catch her breath.

Her shoelaces had come untied, and the lace of her left shoe was broken. Had it snapped in the door? She looked back at the security door, but there was no sign of it. She tied a double knot in the waxy laces for good measure. "We better keep moving," she said, hoping she hadn't left a piece of her red shoelace as an obvious trail behind them.

Olive pushed against the bookcase and watched as it easefully moved back into its original position and clicked into place. Max returned the key to the box and shut the lid. Ember did one scan of the room before the three left the office, leaving the door propped as Dr. Voss usually would.

She had had enough for tonight. "I think we should get out of here," Ember said, warily.

"I agree." Max was already gathering his things.

"I'll get the lights... and the door." Olive closed up as they filed out of the laboratory.

Was it still a laboratory? Ember was exhausted. At minimum, she needed a nap. But she knew there was much more for them to sort out.

It seemed undeniable that Dr. Voss was running some kind of underground operation. She had clearly gone to great lengths to keep it from them *and* everyone else. What was her extracurricular research really about?

Just this morning Ember had been a good-hearted graduate assistant with big ambitions, following in the footsteps of Einstein. And now, she was confronted with the daunting reality that she might be involved in a pernicious conspiracy.

She hadn't signed up for this.

Chapter 4: The Chosen

The antique clock above the fireplace showed 11:15. It was late into the night already but well before Alena would lay down to rest for the meager four hours her body required lately.

She was in her apothecary, her sanctuary.

This space held the origins of her evolutionary mind. Here, she reveled in the comfort of her earliest practices, like her childhood affinity for numerology and her adolescent interest in reading tea leaves.

Alena had been keen to experiment throughout her youth. She'd gathered ingredients as raw materials, blending them, heating them, and eventually treating them through other elements, devising her own alchemical interpretations. In her twenties, alongside her scientific studies, Alena had delved deep into hypnotism and telepathy.

There wasn't much she hadn't tried. Memories of her early work compelled her attention as the night wore on. It was almost inevitable in this special place.

The dark green walls of her apothecary were marked by seemingly infinite wooden shelves, each of them stacked with abundant resources—ancient and new—that informed her wise perspective. Among the voices of influence were Galileo's *Dialogo sopra i due massimi sistemi del mondo* and Newton's *Philosophiæ Naturalis Principia Mathematica*. They sat amidst works from physicists, scientists, mathematicians, and philosophers known and unknown. Some of them were even Alena's own friends. Her beloved Einstein's

Relativity and *The Evolution of Physics* were there, always within reach. And there were so many more.

One book sat apart, though. Though she'd tucked it into the far shelf alongside her other now ancient tomes, Alena held this book in highest esteem. Well, that wasn't quite the right word.

This book was the source of it all.

It truly was *The Book*.

It stood out on the shelf, its crimson cover loose at the edges, unappealing, and yet... it spoke to her. She'd tucked it on the shelf next to other treasures lately, to protect its binding. It was far older than she and far wiser too. Alena was lucky to have this tome. It had shaped her visions, her choices, her life:

The Book of Aeons.

She had built her apothecary around it, using the knowledge she had garnered from *The Book*'s companionship.

She had consulted *The Book* at every turn, using its strange combination of science and spells to develop her truly unique understanding of quantum mechanics. It was not just experimentation, it was magic that had shaped her knowledge.

Most importantly of all, *The Book* had allowed her to shape the apothecary into the laboratory for her most elaborate experiment.

It was here in this small room that she initiated the conquest of intellect. It was here she learned how to harness the souls of those she most admired and where she held them captive, within reach for her every whim and aspiration.

Over time, Alena came to think of her library of souls as her Collection: a repository of the most profound discoveries and the genius that conceived them. *The Book* housed them. With *The Book* in her hands, she had access to potential beyond any one person's wildest dreams.

This was the reason *The Book of Aeons* remained her greatest treasure—through it, through her, genius was immortal. This was the reason she could never let it out of her grasp.

Time had enchanted Alena, and tonight she had thrust her hands into her own history.

As she tried to stimulate the deepest parts of her mind, she recognized the significance of this endeavor. This was certainly her most significant project yet. This was her life's work.

Alena's professional role as a scientist was only enhanced by her decades of magical practice. Her present efforts stretched far beyond the bounds of scientific progress. In truth, they stretched beyond human aspiration and into the mystical. For Alena cared not for immortality, that vain motivation; nor did she endeavor to claim the Nobel Prize, though she would not dismiss the award if it came her way.

Her ambition was much more comprehensive than any one thing.

Alena wanted to become the singularity. She wanted to experience the fullness of reality and then *become* it.

Alena envisioned herself not as a person or even as a soul but as a force of nature—a living black hole of intellect and willpower—with the capacity to bend the future *around herself.*

This was her ultimate ambition. But the road was long. To accomplish her goal, she would need to tether the ends of her worlds together. At one end, she was in passionate pursuit of scientific progress. Scientific research was an avenue of "work" that proved much more acceptable to the world.

In this vein, Alena was always working to grow her position in greater and more powerful contexts, from the scientific to the political, and thus create demand for her research.

The work she was pursuing would address the global struggle for advancements across all sectors: military, education, technology, and economy. But this was not her only work.

The other end of her tether veered deeply into the magic of *The Book.* For generations, Alena had been harvesting the brilliant wisdom and imaginations rising in the world around her. She gathered from scientists of all sorts, but she found physics most enticing. One by one, she used these wise and curious minds to become stronger—stronger than she could ever be on her own. Stronger than any force in history. Her ambitions would support nothing less.

Alena had been making speedy progress on the practical fronts. Her newest research was evolving quickly. Her laboratory at the university was thriving, especially with Ember, Max, and Olive's unwitting contributions. And her *other* project, the deeper research, was moving right along. She was pleased in all regards.

There was yet one more jewel in Alena's life at this time, and she found it most promising.

•

Ember. Alena's most promising, perhaps most unexpected treasure, was Ember Quinn.

At first, Alena had meant to do nothing more than keep a close eye on her. But once Ember began work toward her dissertation, Alena realized that she was an even more potent investment than she originally imagined.

The day Ember was born, Alena made note. Her existence was not familiar because of any premonition or magical notions. No, Alena's knowledge of the child was based solely on proximity. Alena was very, very close to Ember's origins.

Alena had watched Ember's life attentively, wondering who the unusual child would become. It was clear from the start that she was bright. And Alena thought it entirely likely that the child would grow to be unique, unusual, even gifted. Alena had missed her chance with the child's grandmother when she decided *not* to steal her soul. She hoped that Ember's existence might make that mistake worthwhile.

In truth, Alena's loss of Mabel's soul had felt less like a mistake and more like a failure.

Mabel's brilliance had been a meaningful match for Alena. She had found it so difficult to find true friends or even colleagues among the women she met in her early career. So Alena liked to think she'd let Mabel live out of respect. But her witch's intuition reminded her often that Alena simply wasn't certain that she *could* have stolen Mabel's soul. Mabel Quinn was extraordinary.

It was not strength or talent or luck that positioned Mabel apart. It was something much deeper—something innate, a rare attunement to the unseen structure of reality.

Mabel perceived patterns before they emerged; she felt currents of information moving beneath ordinary phenomena; and she could coax clarity from chaos in ways that defied explanation. Mabel called it intuition. Alena knew better.

By the time Mabel became a parent, she had accumulated knowledge that even her closest colleagues didn't fully grasp. Though she adored her daughter, the girl had no interest in the sciences, choosing instead a quieter, more conventional life. Mabel accepted this, but even from afar—for, by then, their paths had parted—Alena saw it differently.

She believed Mabel carried a legacy in her blood. An inheritance of perception, insight, and something that brushed the edge of magic was alive in Mabel, and Alena was determined to discover it.

So when Mabel's daughter had a child of her own, Alena paid attention. A new life meant a new possibility. If Mabel's gift was hereditary, the grandchild might be the one to inherit it.

Alena watched closely, certain the child was destined to be extraordinary, and equally certain that whatever Mabel had kept hidden might come to light in her relationship with Ember.

Mabel cared strongly for the girl, and Ember took an affinity to her grandmother. From the start, Alena had seen in Ember the same spark that she'd recognized in Mabel all those years before.

Now, years and years later, long after Mabel's soul had left her body for no reason aside from the passage of time, Alena was still connected.

She had not only followed the grandchild Ember throughout her life; she had also garnered her way into that life. And she was proud of her witty insertions. After a decade of watching the young Ember dabble in sciences and decide to pursue physics, Alena had coaxed the budding physicist into her own laboratory.

Now she had access to every one of Ember's developments. Alena was excited not only for her potential insights but also the undiscovered magic Alena knew was in the young woman. Ember had no idea how much she resembled Mabel when she concentrated, how the same quiet intensity gathered behind her eyes.

It seemed more and more likely to Alena that she would have an opportunity to recover the loss of Mabel's soul *through her granddaughter*. If Ember proved to be as bright as her grandmother, if she held even a touch of her predecessor's ingenuity and wisdom, Alena wouldn't risk the loss. The magic of the Quinn family finally felt within reach.

When the time came, Alena would add Ember's soul to her Collection, without hesitation.

In the meantime, Ember and the other graduate assistants were moving her research forward. Olive and Max were quite smart and natural additions to her team. Each of them brought, from Alena's perspective, the perfect amount of ambition: They focused their interests on work. They were high achievers intellectually but not publicly. They kept their heads down and aimed to please her.

While Alena did hope Olive and Max would contribute meaningfully to her university research—and so far, they certainly had—she felt comfort in knowing that she could keep them in the lab, where they belonged. They wouldn't interfere with her larger scientific and political interests. No part of these young minds would overpower her bigger plan.

The sweetest part of her charade was that Ember fit so effortlessly with Olive and Max. Alena encouraged the trio's closeness—it kept suspicion low and the work flowing. But beyond their genial academic rapport, Alena's thoughts remained fixed on Ember.

There was a resonance in the young woman—a rare harmonic she had sensed only twice before in her lifetime.

The university saw a promising researcher.

Olive and Max saw a friend.

Ember saw a mentor.

Only Alena saw the truth: The girl was an unopened door. And when the time came to open it, Ember would offer more than data or even insight. She would offer passage.

Voltaris

Chapter 5: Science or Magic

One by one, Alena returned the tools she'd been using in their places. She'd gathered fire (a candle), water (a bowl filled from the town's old well), and time (the antique clock that sat on the mantle). She'd gotten quite distracted, though, and it really had gotten late. Alena was ready for sleep.

An old-fashioned alarm trilled in the apothecary, riling Alena from her thoughtful stupor: briiiing! Someone in the lab was calling on the emergency line. She answered abruptly, spurted brief responses to the caller, and angrily hung up the phone.

Fury rose in her body, and Alena's face grew hot. She was incensed. How the students discovered her laboratory, she had no idea, but her plans were clearly thwarted.

Alena had been doing her research in secret. She couldn't risk it getting discovered. These studies went well beyond the physics she was doing upstairs in the university laboratory, and no one could know about her underground project.

She had hoped to let Ember in on some part of her secret soon.

She knew she needed to build trust with her mentee, to develop rapport. Their present dynamic was stale, mundane. Alena wanted to be sure Ember believed in her. She needed Ember to confide in her, entrust her spirit to her.

Despite Ember's magical background, Alena sensed the young woman didn't realize her own power. Thus, from Alena's point of view, Ember posed little threat to her magical secrets for the present moment.

What she needed, though, was to move their relationship along so she could find out how much Ember really knew. Just to be sure.

It seemed to her that if she offered some vulnerability—for example, divulging an important secret (even one draped in disguise) about her unstructured research—it might strengthen her relationship with the young woman.

Still, though Alena was considering letting Ember in on the underground research, she had not intended for anyone else—Olive and Max, especially—to find out.

The whole project was really risky. She couldn't have her upstairs research, the university-approved labwork, compromised by this situation.

If Ember, Olive, and Max had witnessed any part of her doings, Alena would have to come back to *The Book*. The memory spell. She hadn't needed the memory spell in quite some time.

She grabbed her satchel from the nearby table and turned to the bookcase beside the fireplace. She pressed the books to one side and peered into the security panel. Her personal access to the underground facility opened automatically, and she descended the stairs to the tunnel.

●

Alena's underground network spanned nearly the length of Landings' tiny downtown, so the entrance through her apothecary required a bit of a trek to reach the laboratory doors. She passed through two distinct security checkpoints before entering a quiet office where her colleague, now entirely rattled, Dr. Marcus Milton, was waiting to meet her.

Milton repositioned his wide-brimmed hat and then his thin-rimmed glasses. He was clearly too nervous to speak.

"Come then," Alena encouraged urgently. "Let's have it. What happened?"

Her vocabulary shifted when she was anxious or upset. She became a different version of herself—a much earlier, unrefined version. It was unbecoming, but Alena hoped her youthful face disguised it.

Milton handed Alena the three-ring binder.

It was an analog but effective full plan for facility compromise. Among its pages were recommended steps ranging from circumstances of mild exposure to full public knowledge. In the case that the secret laboratory was discovered by a lay person, Alena was prepared to handle whatever might come—press that would sensationalize the facility's secrecy, or even national and international news that would make the lab a target and put the town at risk. Operating under cover was as much a necessity as securing any threats and mobilizing a response.

"They were here. The students."

Milton rushed the words as though he was already out of time, his voice thin as he told Alena everything he had gathered about the students' entry: their timing, their route, Ember's bootlace.

He hadn't known it was them at first, not for sure. He'd entered the laboratory late in the evening, thought to have himself a cup of tea and check on the numbers for the day, when he'd seen the three bodies turn and race out through the university access door.

He'd followed them, leaving plenty of distance between himself and the intruders—to protect his own safety, of course, though he presented it to Alena as a reasonably clandestine mission.

He'd seen the secret access to Alena's office lock shut just as he reached the top of the stairs, but in its frame he found a frayed red shoelace. He thought immediately of Ember's red boots. Milton hastily shoved the shoelace into his pocket and raced back down the stairs.

He'd known of Alena's plans to introduce Ember to the laboratory and thought he might've missed something. How else would they have unlocked the two security panels?

Milton had done a bit of investigation before calling Alena. He wanted to be sure what level of emergency they were dealing with. Sure enough, on the observation screen in the laboratory, Milton had seen all three students file out of the physics building not fifteen minutes after the intruders had escaped his view, Max nervously glancing over his shoulder every few steps.

There was no data leak; all the relevant information remained protected, but the students had seen the surveillance screens and exited the university building before he could intercept them and, he admitted to Alena now, he wasn't sure he should.

Alena looked down at the binder, as though confirming his story. He'd tucked the shoelace in the thin plastic sleeve of the cover. It was a perfect match to Ember's.

Alena had to agree with Milton—it was best not to let her graduate assistants know they'd been caught, though she wasn't inclined to give Milton any consolation at this precise moment.

While Milton had the distinct impression that his boss was terribly frustrated at the inconvenience of this intrusion, Alena wasn't entirely surprised it had happened.

Though they did have plenty of precautionary securities for the underground laboratory, she had to admit the system itself was somewhat limited. Its design did most of the work to prevent intrusion.

All of the entrances to the laboratory, besides her own university access, were in individual homes. It was very unlikely for any wanderer to accidentally encounter a secret door. The facial recognition software had seemed entirely superfluous when they'd installed it.

The space itself was thus protected from physical interlopers, and cyber spies would be hard-pressed to find much of value either. The underground laboratory maintained few records electronically. The whole aim was to protect Alena's research and ensure the anonymity of any collaborators.

Anyone who did make it into the facility would probably be somewhat confused by the strange data they found there. She really didn't put much energy into worrying about that.

Despite her ambiguous sentiment about the intrusion, Alena knew she'd need a plan to keep the students' questions at bay. Since they entered through her office, they would have figured out she was connected to the facility. She'd have to come up with some kind of story to protect her reputation. Or...

Her main concern now was keeping the students from exposing her.

The university prided itself on transparency; Edmondston University was a gold standard in the wider scientific community. They were a profoundly ethical bunch, and if they even imagined she might be up to something disreputable, they would take swift action.

Alena did, of course, have the option to threaten them.

No, she thought, *I would simply give them a very good reason to keep the laboratory secret.*

But she suspected their concern would not be easily stifled. They'd go looking for more information and all her professional work will be called into question. And, if the whole ordeal went on long enough, it could mean her national and international positions would be compromised, her grand plan derailed, and all her many years of careful plotting lost.

That wasn't enough. No, she must do something.

Milton interrupted Alena's thoughts, his awkward tone shaking her from her pensive state.

"I might suggest," he rocked as he spoke, "that this might not be such a dangerous breach. I mean to say—they are *your* students, are they not? Your graduate assistants?" The question lingered, his meaning left for interpretation.

Alena's disquiet was not soothed by his suggestion, but she suspected Milton didn't realize how right he was. She still held control of the facility, and she knew exactly what she had to do: she would soften the students' memories. Fog them. Alter their consciousness. She'd have fun with it.

"Thank you, Dr. Milton," Alena said, her tone professional and curt. "I'll take care of it from here."

She tucked Ember's red shoelace into her satchel and retreated through the access on the opposite side of the room. She wanted to investigate the upstairs laboratory, see if there was anything Milton missed.

●

As the bookcase closed behind her, Alena took in the details of her office.

Nothing was out of place. It felt familiar, but she sensed the recent presence of the students here.

She shuffled through the hefty stack of papers on her desk, opened the top drawers and then the bigger, lower ones. The secret compartment was still completely disguised. All was well, it seemed. Still, Alena was uneasy at the knowledge that they had likely been through her things. The room was virtually undisturbed and in the well-ordered state she'd left it in but this was feeling like quite the mess.

Alena returned to the bookcase, where the lock was still visible between the books. She pulled her key ring from her satchel and inserted her personal key into the lock.

Purposefully, she turned her key two full rotations to the left, at which point the lock in the wall popped out of place, leaving a hole where the lock had been.

She replaced it with a full board, the perfect size to fit the hole the lock had made. She concealed it again with books, gathering a few extra from the shelf below. Then she stashed the lock and the key in the secret compartment at the bottom of her desk drawer.

If the students returned, the lock would be gone, and they would have no proof the access point was ever there. She could easily convince them—without them knowing, of course—that all of this was just a strange dream.

If she played her cards right, they wouldn't even think to bring it up.

Alena planned her next course of action as she closed the laboratory behind her, walked the corridor to the wide doors of the building's entrance, and relished the feel of the cool night air against her skin as she stepped outside.

●

She took her time on the way home.

It was back to the apothecary tonight for her. She would need to consult *The Book*. Alena knew there was some precise combination of internal and external ingredients she would require to cloud her assistants' memories, but it had been such a long time since she had considered this sort of spell.

From what she did remember, a successful spell would mean the students would think of their visit to the underground laboratory—and the existence of the secret laboratory altogether—as nothing more than a dream.

Each turn along her route led Alena deeper into the old streets of Landings. The cobblestone ways were worn with memories, but her mind was tangled up in thought around the night's events.

She was spinning, her imagination reaching to the edges of her consciousness to weave a story that would calm her after the students' unsettling trespass.

Nothing in their research with Alena was out of bounds. Their work in the university laboratory was remarkable, certainly at the forefront of their field. What was more, everything they did together was publishable; it was all completely above board. Both she and her graduate assistants stood to benefit from its success.

For all of these reasons, Alena carefully kept the upstairs research separate from her secret, underground investigations. She'd been building towards a breakthrough for well over a century, at this point. It had begun so long ago, when she'd first learned she could harness the power of others' souls.

For generations, those souls nurtured her breath. They energized her body and invigorated her mind. Soon, she had become timeless. She ceased aging, and instead gained a bright complexion and animated expressions that lent youth to her lightly graying hair and wrinkles. She was 47 years of age when her body halted its advancement. She still operated inside of time, but it no longer held the threat of death against her.

She'd become agile in her powers of consciousness and, perhaps her most successful endeavor to date, was wearing a protective shield against others' critical gaze. Everyone would see her beauty, but no one would notice that she didn't change from year to year.

She was well over 100 years old, but no one would know it by the sight of her.

Alena had also woven the knowledge and brilliance of the souls in her Collection into her work with consciousness and in almost every other aspect of her life. She twisted each loose end delicately into her public work. No one would even think to question her purpose. Those who knew her—scientists, philosophers, and leaders across the free world—saw her as exceptionally wise and powerful.

Alena had so perfectly curated every facet of her life.

It would take a true savant—likely someone equally as magical as she—to see through her.

She'd thought, though, that she was keeping the new research hidden well. She'd built a whole secret facility for it, for goodness' sake. Her boundaries felt so strong that she had been certain: if no one *knew* the underground laboratory was there, then no one would be able to find it.

Alena had always thought her mind was her most complete protection. And yet, Ember, Olive, and Max had gotten past the perimeters she had created.

Yes, she realized now that she must have opened up Ember's permissions when she had been working inside the security settings— that was the only thing that really made sense to her now. She'd have to go back in and alter them again.

But what had they seen inside?

She felt violated. Alena couldn't risk her years of work—she was so close to an event horizon, one that would allow her to wield the magic of *The Book* on a much grander scale. It would make things infinitely easier if this memory spell worked. Thank goodness for *The Book*.

Alena's mind wandered, taking her back to when she first encountered *The Book*. Her pace slowed as she thought of that pivotal moment.

It had come at such an important time in her life, her lovely, tragic life.

Her parents had gone so quickly. Died, yes, they had died so quickly, so tragically.

Alena had been quite young then—six or seven. She'd gone to live with cousins, her closest relatives. They were generous to take her in, but they were working class people. All of them, even the younger children, worked. No one ever asked Alena to. They didn't ask for her help or make her feel bad for not contributing. But they didn't really give her much attention at all.

Alena had been swept into their chaotic home without much guidance or care, and the once doted upon child felt for the first time the loneliness of her new solitary life.

The cousins' home was old and creaky with cobwebs in the corners and dust-covered floors. Alena found its busyness dreadful and chose instead to spend her time in the attic of the house.

While the nooks there had their own share of cobwebs, they were quiet, comparatively uncluttered hideaways. Alena would sneak up into the forgotten room as often as she could and make friends of the books, blankets, and heirlooms that filled the cedar trunks. A broken mirror with a carved wooden frame caught light from the window just enough that she could read from the books' greying pages, and she learned more in that attic than she ever did at school.

Then, one day, Alena opened a new trunk and once again her life changed completely.

There was *The Book*—cloth-bound, large enough that she had to stand up to lift it. She sat it on her makeshift table and gently wound her fingers around the crimson cloth cover to open it.

At once Alena was transformed. She had found treasure.

The Book of Aeons.

The title was worn across the front but stood starkly on that first inside page. As she turned the hearty pages she found that *The Book* contained the story of her ancestors. For the first time since her parents' death, the child Alena felt a connection to her family's history, to the people who had come before her. She knew they were *magic*. And she belonged to them.

A tingling grew at the edges of her fingertips, and her child's mind raced. *Magic*. Alena finally felt like she had something to hold onto. This unexpected connection with her ancestors sated something in her. It was as though a longing had been fulfilled. The tingling grew into a pulsing, and soon her whole body was filled with a powerful warmth. She had the force of her lineage behind her.

She felt like anything was possible.

Was this the connection she'd been looking for? It had been years, at that point, since Alena had known true love. This sense of power filled her up like love. And she wanted more of it.

Alena learned quickly that the power was not bound to *The Book*. She could harness it and wield the power herself by using *The Book's* magic.

It was at once enchanting and fulfilling.

Alena had no thought of corruption. No awareness that her own consciousness had become so focused that she'd lost any openness she'd had to experiencing care outside of this singular relationship. She had been a child consumed.

As she walked through the night in Landings, nearly 200 years later, the truth peered into Alena's mind. She understood that something was changing. She felt herself being altered, as she had all those years ago when she'd first held *The Book* in her hands. It was certainly something to pay attention to.

She was grateful for an opportunity to call upon *The Book's* wisdom tonight. She'd been feeling more attached to it over the past few weeks, or was it months now? It felt as though *The Book* was pulling away from her somehow.

Once she was back at home and upstairs in her apothecary, Alena gingerly took *The Book of Aeons* from the shelf and laid it on the table at the center of the room.

She lit a candle and spoke aloud her clear intentions for this process: protection, distinction, control. She found the spell she'd intended and followed the lines across the page, collecting in her mind a list of the precise measurements of internal and external ingredients she would need.

Tonight, she would craft a spell to cloud her graduate assistants' memories. In the morning, they would regard the existence of the laboratory and their visit to it as nothing more than a dream. Alena began her work.

●

Alena wasn't the only person up well into the night. Ember's eyes were wide as she sat at her desk, palms outstretched before her. She looked into her hands as though they could offer some insight into the way her life was going right now.

As she tried to unravel the events of the past few days, she thought about how things seemed to be growing weirder.

While she would have had good reason to be feeling scared or at least concerned, Ember mostly noticed her curiosity.

Questions reeled in her mind: Why was her face in the security system for the underground research facility? Was there some reason she would be given access to this seemingly secret place and whatever was going on there?

And she *still* couldn't stop thinking about that book. Could her dreams have something to do with all of this too?

Or maybe this whole chaotic story was really just a dream.

Ember grew tired quickly, more tired than usual. Surely now it was time for sleep.

Voltaris

Chapter 6: Soulless

Finally, he saw a way in. The soulless being gazed intently at the drawing before him. The young woman had somehow taken the shape of a sorceress, her hair wound up and into threads extending towards the infinite cosmos he had depicted with abstract swirls and bursts of light.

This habit of revisiting his dreams and wonderings had meant scribbles of numbers and lines, notes about math and physics, attempts at depicting light and time. But the practice had long since shifted to images. He drew whatever his imagination could capture from the lives of those he longed to touch...

It was the living that compelled him now.

Voltaris looked around at the room he'd build for himself. When he'd entered this space, it was amorphous, difficult to measure, and exceedingly uncomfortable. He had solidified the environment with concrete memories from his life. There was an old, creaky desk where he'd set stacks of books written by friends, colleagues, and even some of his wiser predecessors. Nearby, a bookcase held his most treasured belongings—or duplicates of them, really. He'd made sure of one thing in particular: a photo of himself, laughing, open-hearted, confident.

These were reminders of who he'd been.

Voltaris wasn't sure if his imagination curated these objects for his enjoyment or if he could, in fact, create material with his mind. But it really didn't matter. The space felt as much like home as a void such as this could. Anyway, it wasn't any object of familiarity but rather his soul and the subtleties of his mind (the ones that only a soul could shape) that were missing. And those he could not recreate.

If someone could see him now, separated as he was from the living *and* the dead, they would see a being in suffering. He'd lost the fullness of his life along with his soul. He could not participate in the bliss of a living mind, a full heart, an unfettered spirit.

Even in death, he gained no liberation. He was adrift.

The freedom of true death came only for those whose souls passed with them. His was locked away, in the realm of the living, far from him now.

So he confronted reality from this place of utter sorrow.

He knew well what was going on. Yes, in this liminal realm, Voltaris had access to everything that was happening among the living, but, without his soul, the brilliant scientist he had been was no longer. He had to watch from afar as his own earthly contributions continued to shape a world of war, famine, and fear.

He craved the clarity of his former self, but there was nothing he could do.

Still, though he longed to provide insight in the realm of the living, there remained one longing that outshone all the others.

More than global influence, more than worldly acclaim, more than scientific success, Voltaris longed to once again feel whole. He wanted to eliminate the distance between himself and his soul. Only then could he hope to bring lasting peace—for himself *and* for the living.

And now, finally, after seemingly infinite stretches of grief and longing, Voltaris had found a true opportunity: Ember Quinn.

●

If he were to measure his own time by standards of the living reality, it would have been years now that he had considered her. And though he had been observing Alena too, since the very day he left that world, Voltaris was dumbfounded when his betrayer brought the young Ember into her laboratory.

It took no more than a moment for him to recognize her. She resembled her grandmother with her whole person. Not so much her looks but her poise and her quirks and the way she applied her mind— in these ways, she reminded him so much of his old friend.

But Ember was not just someone who marked his past; she was herself a brilliant, inquisitive being. He suspected, with a spark of hope, that she might just believe in the tangible quality of the soul. And if she did, she could help him.

Clearly, Alena saw Ember's brilliance too. Voltaris had glimpsed enough of her recent work to know how far she had ventured beyond the boundaries of accepted science.

She hadn't simply built an underground laboratory—she had constructed a chamber designed for experiments no institution would sanction: consciousness-mapping rigs, containment fields woven from sigils and quantum light, and arrays capable of pulling identity signatures from the space between particles.

He had watched her shift her focus toward the most forbidden questions a researcher could pursue. What was a soul made of? Could consciousness be captured, replicated, transferred? Could a mind persist without a body—and, more chillingly, could it be persuaded to obey?

Those were the questions Alena chased now, with a precision and hunger that made Voltaris's chest ache. He remembered what it felt like to fall in love with that mind—how dazzling her curiosity had been, how quickly she could turn wonder into discovery.

But the admiration that once defined their partnership had curdled. Her brilliance had sharpened into something predatory, ambitious in ways that threatened the very fabric of existence. And now, seeing her interest settle on Ember, he feared he knew exactly where her research was leading.

Alena concerned him gravely.

It seemed to Votlaris that she was moving in a more dangerous direction than even she knew. Working with the soul, she intended to widen her cruel reach beyond *The Book*. Who knew what she would do with the power she gained. Even as he hoped she wasn't coopting Ember's spirit into her sinister plans, he knew better than to trust Alena's intentions.

But he couldn't be distracted by Alena. Not yet. Not entirely.

Because, even if she was about to break down the constructs of human reality, the circumstances of the world right now were equally urgent. He simply could not stand by and watch as his contributions finally turned the world to dust. He had to stop the violent chaos that was unfolding in the world he loved so dearly. He had to retrieve his soul.

Ember's presence made Voltaris's vision all the more possible. He hoped that she would be his key.

Finding Ember had inspired a new optimism in him. He had been resistant to real possibility for so long, fearing that if he envisioned himself complete again, soul intact, he would crumble in grief. But he knew he had lost the most important thing a person could, and he needed help to get it back.

He'd been watching when Ember walked into Alena's laboratory that day. He knew right away she was familiar, and it took no more than a moment for him to realize why.

"Ember Quinn," she'd said, introducing herself to Alena's colleague, Dr. Marcus Milton.

Everything fell into place for him instantly. She was Mabel Quinn's granddaughter. The compelling young woman with long dark hair and luminous green eyes was *a child of wisdom* herself, special in a way few people would ever know.

In the days to come, Ember would only invigorate his optimism. She was a unique scientist. She believed in her work *and* in something beyond it. Her personality was perfect for his objective.

He had a lingering feeling that there was yet more to her than he understood.

With time, Ember showed herself to be curious and insightful—an ideal combination for the role he had in mind, and just enough of both to be open to his messages.

Through his observations, he'd determined that Ember could witness, understand, and most importantly, believe his outreach. She would trust what he knew. And, if all went as planned, she would share this knowledge with the right people—the right *living* people.

Ember's face emerged in his mind, shining and sincere, her eyes full of presence. Then her face—her sensitive, searching eyes, her strong cheekbones, the shape of her—began to change. Before he knew it, the image held in his imagination was no longer of Ember but of Mabel.

What lived in the connection between these two important people? Some years had transpired since Mabel's passing. How much did Ember remember of her grandmother? And what insight into Mabel's wisdom remained as her granddaughter pursued her own scientific course?

Voltaris saw Mabels' kind, laughing eyes. He felt the vitality in her presence.

When he was alive, Alena had enchanted him, mind, body, and spirit, but Mabel's effect was distinctive. She had held his imagination captive. With Mabel, he had journeyed across millennia, traveled universes, unwound infinity. Maybe it had all been conjecture, imagination, and play, but he had been awake inside of it.

Mabel had elevated his consciousness. And, perhaps more important than anything else, Mabel had been his friend.

He could tell her about the most abstract of ideas, and she would respond quietly with a knowing shake of her head or a calm look. She rarely spoke her response, but he'd known then as he did now that Mabel not only understood him, she also had her own vision to build into the world.

They were always working towards the same ends.

Voltaris longed for that comforting stimulation now. In this indeterminate space, he was so lonely. The thought of a friend like Mabel felt exceedingly far away. Such intimacy was long gone from his reality.

Still, he hoped in the young woman who carried on Mabel's lineage. If Ember had any bit of her grandmother's wisdom, she would certainly be his best opportunity for a successful mission.

●

Voltaris had been watching just the other day at Alena's university laboratory—her above-ground operations—as Ember and the other graduate assistants discussed the state of the world. They had attracted his attention as they deliberated how his discoveries were the precursors to many modern technologies. They saw his life as an example, but not always a good one. It left him with a complicated feeling.

Voltaris knew Ember and her colleagues understood the complexities of his discoveries. They had to confront the ways he had shaped the world today.

It seemed the living were constantly talking about it, arguing about it, writing books and making movies about it.

He knew enough to know it hadn't all been a mistake. If he'd only been able to stay a bit longer, he could have offered more, maybe he could have somehow altered the course of weapons development. Maybe he could have influenced the sciences towards peace rather than power.

He was reminded of the time he wrote to Freud about war and peace. The question was plaguing him at the time. Why did humanity so consistently choose war?

Peace, Freud insisted, would come only when humanity strengthened its capacity for reason and deepened its identification with others—when the life-instinct could outweigh the death-instinct. "Only then," Freud had written, "will the appeal of hatred lose its force."

Voltaris had carried those words with him for decades, a reminder that the true battle was not between nations but within the human mind. Now, watching Alena's research twist more toward domination, he felt an old dread stir.

His disquiet was amplified by the mounting conflict between the US and Russia, China, and North Korea. The Middle East was already in an all out war that was straining diplomatic ties far afield. No one in any position of power was truly committed to peace, and the political environments of major global powers were turning toward chaos. From where he sat, he could see the world unraveling.

He had held on for so long to a vision of true peace, but as time went on in the world of the living, those wishes felt unobtainable. Violence, conflict, and pain seemed much more likely outcomes.

Despite his altered state, his sense of guilt remained. It haunted him. He felt responsible for the way so many things had progressed during his lifetime, let alone the trajectory after his death. Technological development, nuclear weapons, the militarization of communications: his role in all of it weighed on him still. Even in the timelessness of this void, his regret propelled him towards urgency.

Yes, that was happening now, he realized. Urgency. Voltaris felt the dramatic cycle beginning again.

What was left of his mind began reeling, shifting, finding new shapes.

Before he knew it, Voltaris was at the bright desk of his summer cottage. The summer sun shone through the leaves of the great oaks in the front yard. He was meant to be on vacation on the North Fork of Long Island, but his mind was clouded, even dark, with doubt.

His chest tightened as he read once again the letter Leo and Alexander had drafted. Now, as Leo waited for his signature, he drew up all the courage he could... and the light faded to dark.

The windows and desk dissolved before him, the chair beneath him, and Voltaris was in a different place entirely, now on the edge of a lake. Starlight glittered the water.

He was far north of the city at a place he knew well. This was Lower Saranac Lake, at the Knollwood Club. He stood outside his cottage beneath the night sky. He shifted his gaze and looked up into the stars.

He knew. The United States had dropped an atomic bomb on Japan at Hiroshima. The news had come that evening, as it had for the rest of the country. The letter he'd written to Roosevelt six years prior had been instrumental in the United States' development of the atomic bomb.

Now, finally and eternally, the impacts of his actions were no longer ambiguous. The whole world would be reeling with this news, but he—well, all he could do just now was be.

The stars blurred and the sky dissipated into nothingness as Voltaris found himself once again in the limitless space of his soulless existence. The desk and bookshelves were here; they were mere fragments, his attempts to construct something solid for himself in this strange imitation of a life. His mind continued to churn.

●

The thoughts revealed themselves one after the other, moving along as train cars over tracks: If he had known... But what would he have—could he have—done differently?

Voltaris was used to the iterative games his mind played, reflecting on his past. But now he had a chance for something new. Because of Ember, Voltaris was starting to believe something could be done.

I must *do something about it*, he thought to himself.

As quickly as Alena was moving, this might be his best chance. Things among the living were not getting better; in fact, he felt certain, they were about to get *so much worse*. Voltaris had to prepare himself, or what was left of him, to confront the continued decimation of his beloved world. He had to find his soul, to integrate it with this liminal existence he'd found in its absence.

The rapid fire thoughts were exhausting him. His soulless mind was not up for this intensity. But one more piece of the puzzle required his attention.

He mustered up all the energy he could to sort out his next steps This was where Ember's assistance would be more than helpful; it would be absolutely necessary. Because Voltaris's soul was entangled with the existence and safety of a single item: *The Book of Aeons*.

Bridging himself to the world of the living was risky. He didn't know what would happen to him, soulless as he was. But he was not just worried for himself. Voltaris knew that any sort of misstep could spook Ember. Or, he could accidentally catch Alena's attention, somehow alerting her to his plan.

Right now, Ember was in the perfect position to allow him access to all the information he would need for his plan. He would tread carefully, tending the edges of consciousness as he breached the intangible zone between the living and this purgatory that was his alone.

He had already begun. He'd continue to reach toward Ember by using what he knew of energy to extend across the distance between them.

If he wanted to save the world, Voltaris needed to be reunited with his soul. He needed Ember to find *The Book* and get it to him; but first, he needed her to trust him.

If he was right that Alena had her own purposes for Ember, then Voltaris needed to get to the young scientist soon.

Chapter 7: Just a Dream

The floors were pristine, just refinished, and Ember could hear each step clearly as she strode down the hall. Her breath quickened. She moved efficiently towards her destination. She carried a parcel of books and an empty coffee mug in her hands.

A young man hurried past her briefcase in hand, and she stooped to pick up the heavy wool sweater that he had dropped. She paused for a moment to trace the orange P that was stitched onto the sweater.

Being a student seemed entirely different these days.

There was a time in her life, long, long ago, before the war, when all she'd had to worry about were her studies. Now, her student days were long since passed, and she had plenty to attend to. And in these modern times, university students bore the weight of changing landscapes. Who knew, really, what would rise to the top of their lists of priorities? Except for the physics students.

She smiled to herself. Wheeler had gathered a cohort of enthusiastic if not eccentric young men who delighted her, and she was in the mood for a youthful adventure into potentialities.

She turned the corner and walked straight into Wheeler's office. Five young men sat on chairs and a small sofa tucked in around his desk. They stood promptly to greet her. "Doctor Einstein," they nodded admiringly as they spoke in unison.

"Hello, hello," she said back to them. "Good to be with you all this morning." She looked over to her friend and asked, "What is our topic today?"

"Ah," Wheeler responded with a glint in his eye. "Don't you know?" He reached out to take her coffee mug.

She passed him the mug she'd brought along this morning. "And how would I know? You haven't told me!" she responded jovially. "Decaf, you know," she reminded him.

He nodded as he poured her a cup from the steaming pot on his desk, clearly brewed fresh just for her. "We've been deep in inquiry around the limits of consciousness, or the lack thereof. For example, these fellows were just insinuating the possibility that you might enter the room already knowing quite what it was we were talking about before you arrived."

"Ha!" That was an entertaining thought. "If I could read minds or anticipate the future, we would be in far different circumstances, I promise you," she said, taking in the earnest gazes of each of the undergraduates. She pulled the remaining empty chair up to their circle. "Won't you fill me in?"

Wheeler reached over to hand her the mug. The ceramic surface was warm to her touch, and she inhaled deeply. It was good to imagine all possibilities. But wouldn't it be delightful if there were also some way to know the limits? She envisioned a great book, much older than the collections that filled her shelves—a book that held all the truths she'd ever questioned. She sat back to listen to the young scientists. If there were such a book, it would hold the magic of these minds. Truth embodied, bound by paper and cloth, tucked onto the shelf with all the rest.

●

Buzzzzzzzzzzz. Buzzzzzzzzz. Buzzzzzzzzzzz.

Ember woke from another restless night. She'd gone to bed so exhausted she would've thought she'd have slept more deeply. But she felt as though her dreams had drained her of energy, though she couldn't remember any details. She had a sense that they had been clearer that night, more understandable, maybe even more relatable.

She sat up in bed and shut off her alarm. A hot shower would certainly help. She turned on the radio and made her way to the bathroom.

The worry she'd been carrying these past few weeks was growing, she could tell. This morning she sensed it more strongly, but what was it? Something unsettling about work, maybe about her research?

She reached into the shower to test the water. Hot! It was just what she needed. She stepped in and felt the heat calm the tension in her shoulders. But the ease in her body seemed to amplify the chaotic stream of consciousness that was running through her mind.

Ember had chosen physics because she wanted to do something good—something stabilizing—in a world that always seemed one crisis away from tipping over. But lately, even her purest intentions felt breakable.

She thought about how easily scientific curiosity could slip its leash. Nuclear power, the Manhattan Project—those origin stories weren't born in malice. They began with discovery, with a genuine desire for understanding and protection. And yet they had become symbols of how knowledge could accelerate beyond anyone's control.

"It all started as investigation," she told herself. "And all of it spun out of hand."

What unsettled her most was how closely the present moment echoed those earlier days.

Reports had been circulating for months: unexplained communication outages, sudden shifts in global alliances, diplomats experiencing strange cognitive lapses, as if waking from dreams they couldn't remember entering. Minor leaks from intelligence briefings hinted at new forms of psychological interference—technology no one claimed to have developed, yet everyone feared someone had.

And then there was the anomaly in her own lab last week: a brief flash in the photonic array, an impossible interference pattern that mimicked emotional intensity—panic, she thought at the time—before the sensors stabilized and recorded nothing unusual. Max chalked it up to faulty equipment. Olive shrugged and said quantum systems were always moody. Again, they dismissed her unique perception of their collaboration. But Ember *had* felt something different in the room that night, a tension that didn't belong to the machinery or to them.

The stakes felt less abstract now. She recognized the parallels. She imagined she could look at this moment the way the scientists of the 1940s once looked at theirs.

Anyone could make an argument for protection now, Ember thought.

Even in the steam of the hot shower, the notion gave her chills. These times were just as volatile as the days of Einstein—perhaps even more so.

She felt the daunting reality that her scientific interests could be misdirected just as his had been. Ember wouldn't be surprised to find another iteration of power-hungry politicians waiting in the wings, eager to seize whatever breakthroughs she and her team uncovered and bend them toward their own ambitions. They'd be interested in anything that promised an advantage: AI, nuclear force, the subtle control of consciousness... technologies whose risks far outweighed the illusions of safety they provided.

And Ember, standing beneath the hot water with her hands braced against the tile, realized her work might already be brushing against the edge of something the world was not prepared to handle.

The thought landed squarely in her mind. Her thoughts had been so strange lately. And then there were her dreams. Vivid when she was in them and yet now, in her waking life, she couldn't remember any details. Was some outside influence affecting her thinking?

Ember was feeling strangely suspicious, but she truly couldn't imagine where that sort of outside influence would come from. Then Dr. Voss's face flashed before her eyes.

In her mentor's hands was a giant old book with a crimson color and faded gold lettering.

Ember's jaw dropped. Water poured from the shower head into her open mouth, but she paid it no attention.

Was this a memory?

Dr. Voss and the book. This was the book from her dream the other night. When was that? Yesterday? The night before?

She felt like the book was following her around. Ember had a lingering feeling it had found her in her sleep, again last night, though that seemed like sorcery. She sensed it had some sort of hold on her consciousness. Was there some meaning she was missing?

Ember stepped out of the shower, careful not to slip on the wet floor. She hadn't closed the shower curtain all the way. There was water everywhere. One thing was very clear: her mind was elsewhere.

Ember wrapped her towel tight as she stood gazing at her face through the fog on the bathroom mirror. "All I can do is what I know how to do." The words occurred spontaneously in her mind. What did that mean? Of course all she could do is what she knew how to do... but what was it that she knew how to do?

A commentator's voice drifted faintly from the other room, discussing an upcoming Sovereign Nations Alliance summit. Charles Hadden's name surfaced briefly before Ember shut the sound off, unsettled by a tension she couldn't place.

For this moment, for these compounding problems—did she, Ember Quinn, really have something to offer to the world?

How could she make a meaningful impact?

How could she ensure that her research would not be used to fuel the daunting futures that seemed more and more inevitable each day?

Whatever it is, she thought, *it's not going to happen in this bathroom.* It was time for work.

●

The morning light spilled across the floor of the physics lab, catching the edges of mirrors and lenses in small, scattered glints. Ember stood over the optical table, aligning another sequence of pulses for her photon-encoding trials.

The setup hummed with quiet intention—frequency-stabilized lasers sending controlled bursts of light into a maze of beam splitters and detectors waiting to catch the faintest whisper of a pattern.

She adjusted the timing window on the pulse generator, tuning it with the practiced ease of someone who had spent years coaxing precision from temperamental instruments. But her mind wasn't in the room.

The dream kept returning in flashes—images, impressions, sensations that felt both alien and deeply familiar. A wall of light. A voice speaking through vibration rather than sound. A presence that seemed to recognize her before she recognized it.

She tried to unravel its meaning while the lasers ticked through their programmed sequence, each pulse a heartbeat she felt rather than heard.

And beneath the fuzziness and half-formed memories was a strange, persistent sense that Dr. Voss had something to do with it. As though the dream were not just a dream at all, but a message routed through unfamiliar channels. Everything seemed hazy and disjointed, like trying to recall a movie she'd seen decades ago—remembering only the feeling it left behind.

Ember hadn't heard from Dr. Voss yet today. That wasn't totally outrageous, but it was unusual for a Wednesday.

On Wednesdays, Dr. Voss was usually in the lab to run through their progress. She supervised whoever was running the experiments and offered direction to keep the project moving. She always had some insight to offer, and Ember looked forward to her participation. Yes, her absence today was notable.

Maybe it has something to do with the underground laboratory.

The thought entered sharply, as though it wasn't hers. An underground laboratory? What would that... A vision formed in her mind: Ember saw the shelves in Dr. Voss's office shifting before her, a door opening, a staircase winding down. It was a path to a lower level, below the basement of the school building.

It seemed unreal but at the same time, it felt to Ember like a memory.

She pressed her feet firmly into the floor, hoping to gain a sense of groundedness. Dr. Voss's office. A door opening. She saw the electronic panel that read her face and another that read her fingers. It all started coming together. The unsettled feeling that had been following her all morning finally found its home.

She, Max, and Olive had unexpectedly found a secret research facility—a laboratory of sorts—beneath these floors. It seemed Dr. Voss was involved. There were doors, so many doors. Screens. Equipment. What was it all for?

The dreamlike filter that had clouded her mind melted away, and Ember remembered everything with crystal clarity. She had been cleaning. She'd found a piece of paper with unusual research on it. She shared it with Max and Olive, and then they all returned to the lab to look for more info. But instead they found a whole world below ground.

Ember rose rapidly from her stool urgently, eager to talk to her colleagues. Had they really all just gone home to sleep last night? Why hadn't Max or Olive said anything about their discovery this morning? It was only then that she realized neither of them were there.

The thoughts streaming through her mind weren't making sense. Her confusion was growing.

Ember began to wander the room mindlessly until she found herself before the cabinet on the east wall. It was a grand piece of furniture that resembled the antiques at her grandmother's house. Something like this would rarely (most likely never) be found in a science lab, but Dr. Voss was not a typical scientist. Antiques were one of her interests.

Ember opened the cabinet and reached in towards a selection of glass vials. Yes, she needed a vial. She wanted to collect water. For what? It didn't matter. Her mind was in the clouds as her hand came to rest upon a beautiful compass at the front of the display case. How had she not seen it before?

Ember lifted the compass to take a closer look, and found herself transported to some other place entirely.

Here, her vision was still fuzzy. This felt like an old, old memory.

She was reclining on a bed. A comfortable, familiar bed. Her head rested on a down feather pillow, and she held something in her hand— her compass. Its metal surface was warmed by her touch. Ember was drowsy, but a sense of curiosity tunneled through her drowsy mind. Something was there, just out of her reach.

Her mind traveled with a curious searching, over and under, around and through space, until it caught something. It seemed to be made of light. Yes, that was it! A beam of light.

She held it gently in her mind. It was useful, familiar—like a tool. She played with the beam, winding it, watching it, sensing its motion and somehow also its stillness across the landscape of her mind.

The momentum of the beam compelled her, and soon she found herself following the light, then chasing after it, feeling in her body the sensations of running alongside the thing she longed to understand. She felt free.

Nothing in the world mattered but her and this dance with light.

The room came back into focus, and Ember watched her own hand draw a vial from the back of the glass case. She settled into her feet, trying to find some solid ground. It's like she had been dreaming while waking.

Ember wandered back to her stool. The vision did remind her of something though. It was a story she'd read, about Einstein.

They'd said that he imagined his way into the theory of relativity. He'd chased a light beam. This wasn't quite what she'd imagined herself when she'd read the story. But could it have been like that for him? Might he have started with a daydream?

●

Ember was shaken from her process by a voice. "Hi Ember." Olive had arrived. "How's your morning?"

Ember looked towards her colleague, eyes blank as though she was somewhere far, far away. She blinked once, twice, three times before responding. "Oh, it's lovely," she said, though she had no idea where that statement had come from? Her morning, lovely?

At the moment, she couldn't come up with another thought.

Olive looked inquisitively at her then stepped back to take in the scene. Ember was sitting at her workbench, but sitting was all she was doing. She was not writing, not reading, not... *doing* anything.

Ember seemed altered, so Olive had to ask, "Are you feeling okay?"

"Honestly, I'm feeling quite funny. I've been..." her voice trailed off and she got yet another far away look in her eyes. Then she looked clearly at Olive and finally registered her colleague's presence. "Oh, Olive, I'm glad you're here!"

Olive was stunned. Something was definitely going on with her friend.

"What's up?" she asked, gently. She didn't want to pry, but worry had crept in.

"It might sound strange," Ember said, lowering her voice as she remembered the subject she intended to discuss.

"Okay," Olive said, carefully. The concerned look on her face was undeniable, and Ember found it unsettling.

She had been about to suggest they go somewhere to talk about the underground research facility, but for some reason she was finding herself unsure of Olive's disposition. So Ember changed direction.

"I've been finding my way into and out of these strange dreams," Ember said, observing Olive closely. "They seem oddly relevant to our work. I wonder if my subconscious has something to say. Could some aspect of my mind be trying to communicate something to me through the dreams?" She hesitated, gauging Olive's interest. "But if that's the case, the message is not evident to me."

Olive looked at her with a strange blankness.

"Hmm," Olive mused and then paused for a moment. "Maybe it's the rain," she said, gesturing outside, even though the day was still quite bright. "I thought you'd be working on data analysis or prepping the next phase of your experiment. It looks like you're in the middle of getting the equipment online."

"Yes, that's what I was just doing." Ember said.

The words tumbled out a bit too quickly. Olive was usually quick to analyze dreams. Why wasn't she more interested? Olive seemed altered somehow but Ember couldn't pinpoint it.

Ember felt herself shrinking back into the disquieted state that had held her all morning.

She wanted to figure out what Dr. Voss was up to, but she couldn't seem to breach last night's event with Olive. There was something off-putting about their exchange. She turned back toward her work.

But worry welled inside her. Maybe Olive didn't want to talk about everything that was going on now. But Ember did. Did Max and Olive really not care that Dr. Voss was involved with something that needed to be kept secret?

No, as far as Ember was concerned today, the task at hand could wait.

Olive kept talking to Ember, but she wasn't listening anymore. Her mind was well on its way to another mission. She stood from her stool and walked straight to Dr. Voss's office.

The door was open, as usual. Ember tried to remember—had they left it open or closed the night before? She looked to the bookcase shelf, scanning it for the wooden box where Max had found the key. The box had been quite small, as she recalled, so she scanned another time. She didn't see it anywhere.

Olive had followed Ember in.

"Ember, what is going on?" she asked accusingly.

But Ember wasn't paying her any attention. The key wasn't to be found, so she pushed aside the books to find the lock at the back of the shelf. She was certain it was on the second shelf, but no. She searched the first and the third. Still no lock. It simply wasn't there. Ember was startled at the discovery. She'd felt so clear when it all came back to her this morning.

Was it really all just a dream?

She was determined to find some evidence to the contrary. *This* was her "next thing."

She turned to face Olive. Max had taken up residence behind Olive, still wearing his backpack and the same clothes he had been wearing when she saw him last.

He was watching Ember in her unconventional investigation of Dr. Voss's office. *All the better*, Ember thought. Now they'd have to discuss the serious implications of what they'd discovered last night instead of pretending like nothing happened.

"It seems like Dr. Voss, or someone, has shut down the entrance to the research facility," Ember said to her friends, bluntly. She didn't feel like pretending any more. "They must know we were here. I think this could be dangerous. We need to figure out what is going on."

Max and Olive looked at each other. Worry flashed across their faces. Olive nodded at Max as though to say, "I've got this."

"Yeah, maybe you're right," Olive said, her eyes kind now.

She was so sure, so grounded. Her presence felt good to Ember. Olive reached her hand out to Ember, enticing her from the office, and the awful cloudiness from that morning formed new shapes in Ember's mind. Ember followed Olive, momentarily forgetting her mission to find out what Dr. Voss was up to.

The students were paused outside the office door when they heard familiar heels clicking down the hall. Max rushed to his table, and Olive walked Ember back to her stool, drew a folder from the current work collection, and smiled generously as she returned to her own station. Dr. Voss entered with her usual, confident stride just as Ember sat down again.

"Good morning," their mentor said cheerily. It was no different than her usual greeting. "How is the lab today?"

She made a sweep around the room, peering over Max's shoulder and then Ember's. Luckily Ember had pulled the data she'd been analyzing. Even if she couldn't concentrate today, she could at least look busy. Dr. Voss strode by Olive's desk too. To Ember, everything about their mentor's demeanor seemed normal.

After a few moments, Ember glanced behind her to see that Dr. Voss had settled, not in her office, but at her own table near the windows that looked out over the university courtyard. She was facing away from Ember, but Ember knew that she was near enough to hear anything the three of them were doing.

Somehow, her presence made Ember feel more unsettled and more suspicious. Ember turned her focus back to the table, to the glass vial she'd collected from the cabinet. For what? She couldn't remember.

She held the vessel thoughtfully. It reminded her of the thick glass bottle she'd found the other night. Now that she thought of it, that strange experience felt oddly parallel to the vision she'd had this morning, though she couldn't point to why.

●

This time she'd been in a bedroom, on a bed. The compass was there, yes, but there'd been no letter, nothing written or measurable.

Her mind rushed as her memories of the night before came back to her. She had gone to collect the broom and noticed a vessel on the countertop. It had an old faded label across the front, but it could easily have been the same container as the bottle of ink she'd found in that vision. Like the compass this morning, yesterday's vessel had seemed out of place, but both were probably Dr. Voss's antiques.

She couldn't help but wonder at their significance. Ember had always assumed the antiques were just one of Dr. Voss's quirks. She had met many strange scientists in her studies to think little of their more unusual characteristics (of which there were plenty). Ember found scientists' quirkiness charming, often daydreaming of ways she herself might be an odd but bright mentor to some future student of physics. She hadn't ever really considered why her mentor was attracted to these items specifically. People had all manner of collections, so why would it be something to question? All she knew was that they had some importance to Dr. Voss.

And in the past two days she'd had two exceedingly strange experiences with these objects.

Ember looked down at her hands. When she touched them—that's when the strange visions or dreams, or whatever they were, happened. Was there something special about these items or did they spark some long buried memory? She couldn't put her finger on the connection between them.

Maybe it was just as she'd said to Olive earlier—her subconscious was trying to tell her something. But Ember couldn't imagine what it would be.

She looked again at Dr. Voss, who was now seemingly entrenched in her own data analysis. Ember thought about the strange dreams she'd been having at home. Could they be part of the message too?

It wasn't too much of a stretch to imagine her subconscious was trying to tell her something. Her entire field revolved around the boundaries of consciousness—how it expressed itself, how it left traces, how it might be measured or stored in light. She spent her days teasing information out of single photons, mapping coherence patterns, probing how energy retained the faintest echoes of interaction.

Memory, signatures, imprinting—those concepts weren't just abstract theories in her work; they were the scaffolding of her research.

So maybe her dreams and visions could be examined the same way she analyzed anomalous data: carefully, methodically, without assuming meaning but without dismissing it either. Perhaps the visions weren't a distraction at all. Perhaps they were an invitation. And if she approached them with a scientist's eye, they might lead her toward her next meaningful discovery.

The fear melted away as Ember immersed herself in thought. If she were to consider her data with the visions she'd been having in mind...

Chapter 8: Solve for Soul

The numberless clock on the upper shelf ticked away. Here, in his otherworldly laboratory, Voltaris had no need for time though it was difficult to measure life—or whatever this was—without it. The sound was both a comfort and a metronome for his thoughts.

He had thrown himself into the only kind of science this place allowed—a science of thought, light, and the strange elasticity that governed this strange in-between. Here, distance behaved like a suggestion, not a rule, and he could conduct experiments no living physicist had language for. At this moment, he was measuring the shifting interval between his awareness and his soul, testing how intention could contract or stretch the thread that still tethered them. He could feel his soul out there—weightless, luminous, drifting just outside this formless dimension. Sometimes it felt close but just beyond his reach.

Voltaris's soul was dim, but he could tell when Alena was near it.

An unsettling feeling rose up in him, and it grew into urgency. He couldn't stand it when she was close to him. When she held *The Book*, it felt like she held *his soul*. And the more sinister Alena's intentions grew, the more ominous her presence felt to him. If he had any chance at life beyond this soulless plane, Voltaris had to liberate his soul from her manipulations.

He was making progress with his mission. He'd succeeded in getting through to Ember, what was it, four times now?

At first, he'd reached out to her through a dream. He had wanted to introduce her to the idea of *The Book*. And it worked; the idea of *The Book* was planted in her consciousness.

It was perfect timing, because his next opportunity came faster than he'd expected when Ember picked up his inkwell. Her powers led her straight to him, and he opened his memories to her. That was a special moment in his life. It was difficult for him to think of it without revisiting his life among the living. Even now, the thought of that vessel led him into the vault of his memory.

"Mmm..." The sound melted him.

Alena's sigh caught him off guard. She smiled gingerly at him, hinting at the paper he held in his hand.

"That is so special to me," she said.

It was his handwriting, something from years ago. The first note he'd ever written her. Before he really knew her. But once he'd read her piece, oh, how he'd wanted to meet her.

"Your article blew me away," he admitted. "I kept that issue of the journal, you know. It felt too special to throw away." He felt Alena's hand on his back. She followed the curve of his shoulder and reached around to press her palm into his chest. She wrapped both her arms around him tightly. Her embrace felt like home.

"I know. I saw it on your shelf yesterday." She turned him around to face her, her eyes shining. It was as though he could catch a glimpse of her mind in their light. "I am so glad you decided to write to me,"

Alena said tenderly. "Imagine what our lives would look like if you hadn't."

"I would be less of a man," he responded.

If only he'd known how wrong he was. She had stolen everything from him. Of course it infuriated him—that she held so much of him captive. It was not just his soul, she had begun collecting things of his like souvenirs sometime before he died. Of course, he could not have known something was amiss, though he often chastised himself for not seeing the clues in her actions.

Now, Alena had a whole collection of his belongings. They ranged from the treasured to the mundane. The glass bottle, though—she had asked about that specifically. She'd found it in his office one day, shortly after they met. She picked it up off the shelf.

"This must be the ink you used to write that letter... the first one," Alena said, winking at him. She was incredibly alluring. And he was delighted at her sentimentality.

"That it is, my dear. That it is."

"May I have it?"

He looked curiously back at her. "You want my ink?"

"I really do," she'd said. Then, without waiting for him to respond, Alena pressed the cork firmly into the bottle opening and stashed the whole thing in her satchel. She sidled over to him at his desk. "Thank you, my dear," she said coyly, brushing her fingertips across the nape of his neck. She kissed the soft skin behind his ear. "I wouldn't mind another piece of you." He was lost again.

●

Alena had been enchanting from the start, entreating him to her whims at every turn. And he had started it all. "The Translation of Energy at Death: An Exploration of Quantum Dynamics Beyond Life—" that's what she'd titled her article. How hadn't he realized that someone so curious about death might be a threat to life? His own life—

Conveniently for him, Ember had picked up that same glass bottle in Alena's laboratory just the other day. *Funny,* he thought, *it seems what Alena kept has given me a path back. Was that yesterday? Did it matter at all?* He had seen an opportunity, then, and opened a channel between them.

Voltaris took her back to his office, the one from when he was alive. He took her back to the moment he'd discovered Alena's article and hoped Ember might recognize the research as her mentor's. It would be so much easier if she could make a connection between him and Alena...

Voltaris knew he would have a difficult time explaining the whole story through memories. But he wanted Ember to know all the details: Alena's true age, that she was using magic to maintain her youth, that she'd known him while he was alive, and that Alena had stolen his soul.

The witch-scientist Alena had been in her mid 40s when he'd known her. She'd had the very same youthful complexion and the same brilliant affect as she had now. By inviting Ember into his memories, Voltaris was laying the groundwork of Alena's grand and portentous story.

And he knew that Ember was paying attention. She'd slipped right into that memory about the inkwell. Then—*was that today?*—his compass had provided yet another opportunity. When the channel opened through the compass, he'd put the compass inside one of the memories he still had: his first journey with light. He imagined himself on his bed, following the beam of light, *with the compass in his hand*. Ember had gone straight to the memory; she'd experienced it as though it were her own.

That first journey with light was special. He had been no older than sixteen, and formative in a way he didn't understand at the time. From that initial thought experiment came the seeds of his greatest insights: space and time are relative, mass and energy are equivalent, and imagination is not frivolous—it is essential to scientific innovation.

"Imagination precedes understanding." He smiled as he said the words aloud. "It catalyzes our realities." Yes, he still "had it." Well, some of it at least. Voltaris's professorial voice was finding ground again as he engaged with Ember. Even if she didn't know it yet, he felt like he was teaching her. It was a sweet sensation, to relive that part of his previous life.

Plus, his exchange with Ember was boosting his confidence. He was getting through. He was able to reach past this void. But none of this would end with her...

•

A view of Alena materialized before him like a movie coming into focus. This was what it looked like when he tapped into the world of the living—and it was usually Alena that he saw.

Though he was trapped by her, he knew their bond had its advantages. At least he could keep a close watch on her.

This time, she was in the underground laboratory. The soul experiments she performed in that space unraveled him. The sight of her there made him tremble. He tried to keep the anxious sensation that shuddered through his non-being at bay, but he knew his fears were valid.

If Alena could model the sentience of particles, then she could capture them. The work happening upstairs—the careful mapping of photonic signatures, the attempts to quantify how experience left measurable traces in light—was not just about understanding consciousness beyond the body. It was building the mathematical scaffolding for something far more dangerous.

Every coherence pattern Ember uncovered, every encoded pulse Max stabilized, every correlation Olive teased from the data provided Alena with more of what she needed to isolate a soul's identifiable imprint.

Voltaris knew she was dangerously close to doing below what the trio only theorized above: translating those imprints into forms that could be held, redirected, even constrained. That knowledge made him afraid. Alena craved the comfort of power the way others longed for love, and Voltaris knew all too well the lengths she would go to claim it.

His heart wrenched tighter as he watched Alena preparing her experiment. She had disassembled the previous experiment. For weeks, he had watched her working with particles from the brain of some sort of small mammal. Alena had seemed frustrated at the end, as though she hadn't gotten the results she'd wanted. Or, perhaps, he thought hopefully, she hadn't gotten results at all.

But he also knew she wouldn't be thwarted by a little disappointment. Now she had brought into the laboratory a petite rose plant. Could it be *Rosa odorata?* He knew it well, and so did she. *Rosa odorata* was a bred variety of tea-scented roses. The plant itself could be moody, and he suspected this was why she'd chosen it. Well, that and the fact that he himself had loved them.

He watched as she positioned the whole plant carefully on the tabletop, orienting it perfectly to the lamp.

He watched as she connected the sensors and tweaked the plant's position once more. She gently bent her head, tucked her nose into a flower, and took a deep breath of what he knew to be a blissful aroma before plucking a single petal in her fingers.

What did she aim to learn from the rose? If Alena learns how to harness the consciousness of plants... He didn't want to think.

Alena had made an asset of his soul. She had captured the consciousness that made him who he was and used him to her advantage. In truth, he didn't know *what* she was capable of. He suspected no one else did either. But it didn't matter. The more he watched Alena, the more he knew just how dangerous she had become. The power she craved was not just professional or political. It wasn't even global.

It was universal.

That power, or her ambition for it, was what fueled her science. Solving for soul... that's what Ember had said about Alena's underground research. In the wrong hands—in Alena's hands—the consequences were unthinkable.

At least, for the first time, there was a glimmer of a way through—a pathway that might just intercept Alena: Ember.

Maybe it was her research, maybe it was her magic—or both—but somehow he was able to access her. He had to be deliberate, he was moving slowly and testing her receptivity through dreams and visions, to ensure that when he appeared before her directly, she would understand, without explanation, the gravity of his request.

Thinking of Ember, he felt relief. The doubt that had held him at bay for so long was fading.

This moment demanded he try—he finally had before him the hope of recovering his own soul and a way to protect others from the same fate. He had even let himself think there might be a way to counteract the mistakes of his life–not to mention, the escalating global crisis and the growing threat Alena posed.

Voltaris let the screen before him dissolve into nothingness. He didn't need to watch Alena turn good science into evil plans. No, he needed to work.

He couldn't change Alena's mind. Ember was his chance. Connecting with Ember made Voltaris feel like his soul was within reach. *She* was the light at the end of the tunnel.

She was motivated to do the right thing. She longed to make a positive impact, just as he did. But the stakes were higher than she realized.

Voltaris suspected she didn't realize the depth of her own past. He felt sure if Ember understood her lineage—beyond the relationship with her grandmother—she could truly step into her own power. He hoped it would be enough to rival Alena and the malicious forces gathering around her. The loneliness of his detached position crept in.

"You're not alone."

The voice rang through the void as though it were the sound of the universe itself. It sang with familiarity, and Voltaris knew the voice spoke the truth. He was not alone.

"Hello?" he whispered, hope rising through him.

"Wisdom of the dead," the voice spoke again, this time with a benevolent tone. "At your service."

Chapter 9: Alone

The voice in her ears droned on and on:

"Members of the current administration arrived for a three-day visit in Seoul today. Political analysts predict a contentious meeting. World Media reports that the President may prefer a remote conference despite his presence in the country. Reasons for this change have yet to be announced. Citizens fear yet another volatile clash between the U.S. government and notable global powers as concerns grow about a sweeping attack against the Sovereign Nations Alliance. On social media, university students protest potential nuclear weapons use with the hashtag #NeverNuclear. Meanwhile, tensions continue to rise as Eastern governments threaten protective action against economic and political intrusions from the..."

Ember pulled out her earbuds. It was too much. She couldn't hold it all; her daily news podcast was becoming increasingly unbearable. The volatility was certainly rising but for this evening, she had other things on her mind.

She picked up her pace. The autumn air was crisp and comfortable. The sun was setting gloriously over Raven's Hill. And Ember didn't give it a moment's notice. She didn't care about any of it.

She desperately needed someone to talk to. Work had been a disorienting attempt at pretending everything was okay, while her mind had spun endlessly around everything that was very much *not* okay.

There was no way to make sense of it all. She couldn't help but be suspicious that Dr. Voss was up to something terribly wrong. Why else would she be keeping her research secret? Max and Olive seemed oblivious and claimed to know *nothing* about the sheet of research notes they'd discussed at the bar. Hadn't they all been together for *every single bit* of that evening? They looked at her like she'd lost her mind when she mentioned descending into the underground research facility. She stopped herself going into too much detail. Explaining was making reality spin, which only made matters feel infinitely worse.

She didn't blame them for their bewilderment. Ember was starting to feel like she was losing her mind. The strange visions she was having, not to mention the cryptic dreams—she felt like she was living in someone else's memories. And she couldn't stop thinking about the mysterious book that had showed up in more than one of them.

Her head ached. She was nearly running, she was walking so fast. She *was* ready to be home, to draw a hot bath and light a candle and rest her head against that special bath pillow she'd gotten for her birthday and just... be. But *should* she even rest? It seemed like so much was at stake.

Her mailbox was empty. *All the better*, she thought. She walked up the apartment steps deliberately, stretching the backs of her legs, trying to ease the tension she was collecting. Her mind was running a million miles a minute.

The world was in crisis, and no matter how deeply she cared, she felt powerless to do anything about it. Her research was still years away from producing anything substantial—years away from the kind of breakthrough that could steady the fractures spreading across nations. All she had for now were early patterns, promising anomalies, and a sense that she was inching toward something that might one day help rebuild trust in a world losing faith in truth, stability, and one another.

What mattered most to her was using her gifts responsibly—working toward discoveries that could illuminate rather than destroy. She was optimistic that her work with photons and consciousness signatures might someday offer a way to validate what was true, to keep communication secure, and memory and meaning from being corrupted.

●

She shut the apartment door behind her, flopped onto the couch, and lost herself in thought. She knew there was a conference Dr. Voss was preparing for, and wondered if the secret research was connected somehow. The only fact she was sure of was that the experiments they were conducting upstairs were feeding the lab below ground. Max had confirmed that when he read the paper.

The paper! She had it, still, in her backpack. How had she forgotten? Ember ran to where she'd dropped her bag by the door and tore it open.

There was the folder, right there.

She pulled it out and held it in her hands. Her memories were true! Max and Olive would believe her now—she could show them everything. She had to tell them.

Olive's kind and dismissive look flashed in her memory. As strange as she was feeling, it seemed better to be on the safe side. She texted Max.

"Time to talk?" Sent.

Before she set her phone down, it rang.

"Hey," she said.

"What's up?" Max asked. "Are you okay? You seemed really out of it today."

"Well," Ember hadn't considered actually vocalizing any of this right now. "Um, no. No, I'm not really feeling great."

"Ember, what's up? I'm glad you texted. How can I help?"

"I just realized that I had stashed that sheet of notes in my bag—the one we discussed at the bar." She didn't want to hope too hard, but perhaps she should have hoped more.

When Max professed confusion, Ember pressed on, hoping something would jog his memory.

She sat back down on the couch, drew her knees into her chest, and told him. The whole story. Everything, from her dreams to the visions, cleaning up and finding the paper, and running it to the bar to tell him and Olive. She told him about the secret door in Dr. Voss's office and how her face and fingers worked on the security system and got them into the underground research facility and the facility...

She was still describing the strange features of the underground facility when Max cut her off.

"Whoa, that is a wild dream," Max said. He almost sounded impressed with her story.

"A dream?" Ember asked, incredulously. "It wasn't a dream, Max! This stuff really happened. We saw the inside of this underground laboratory. *That* was wild. There was this screen streaming views of research facilities around the world. *You* recognized CERN and Fermilab! Max..." her voice trailed off. She couldn't believe this was happening.

"Ember, I haven't been in Dr. Voss's office at all this week. Well, except this morning when I arrived and you and Olive were holed up in there doing something weird."

Ember was dumbfounded. She was holding the proof in her hand.

But Max went on, "Olive was really worried about you, you know. Now it makes sense..." His voice trailed off.

Ember started to feel really angry. Had she really just divulged all of this to be met with some insensitive concern? "Wh– what?" she stammered. "Max, you were there. I have Dr. Voss's research right here in front of me! You read it! You confirmed my suspicions... that it took our research into dangerous territory. At the very least, you must see that something strange is going on here."

"Ember, I wasn't..." he tried to interrupt her, but Ember didn't stop.

"And *you* were the one who found the key in the box in Dr. Voss's office! We saw the research facility *together*. Are you telling me you don't remember *any of it*?"

She felt even more exhausted. The anger was only building with every attempt she made to jog his memory. This was unbelievable.

Max was quiet. She couldn't handle it.

"Max," Ember said, despairingly. "Please..."

"It's not like you," he responded. "This just isn't like you. I don't know, Ember, maybe the research is getting to you. I know it's been stressful—with all the different outcomes and stuff. Maybe you just need a break. Yeah, that's a good idea. Take a day, let yourself breathe. I'll tell Dr. Voss you're trying to stave off a cold," he offered, as though that could make all of this okay. As though anything but the truth could make *any* of this okay. Ember held back a sob.

"I have to go," she said and abruptly hung up the call. Ember held the page to her face as if trying to show herself how real this all was. She didn't have the energy to argue with Max. It was too much.

She'd been pacing through the whole call, and now she just wanted to collapse into bed. So much for that calming bath. But she had to see if she could get at least one of them to remember. One more text. She wrote to Olive:

"Tea tomorrow? My place, 9:00?"

She crawled into bed and fell sound asleep. She never heard the buzz of Olive's response.

"I'll be there. I'm bringing muffins. Here for you, friend."

●

Morning hit Ember like a ton of bricks. She was groggy, stressed to the brim, and intensely nervous to talk to Olive about everything that had happened. She tried her best to get into people mode. She put on a fresh sweater and did her makeup. She put a pot of water to boil and got out a jar of her favorite tea—lemon, ginger, turmeric. She'd made it herself from ingredients she'd bought at the market, chopped, dried, and blended. She pulled the honey down from the cupboard too.

She was nervous to talk to Olive, but when she finally knocked at the door Ember felt relieved. The suspense was really wearing her down.

"I brought coffee too," Olive said as Ember opened the door. "I heard you had a rough night."

"You heard?" Ember asked as she took the to-go cups from Olive and returned to the table.

"I talked to Max. He said you were really stressed out. He seems to think you have been mixing up your dreams with reality. But I don't care," she looked at Ember with that same frustratingly kind affect. "I'm just here to listen."

"Honestly," Ember said, already feeling defensive, "I don't want to talk about myself. You already know everything that's going on with me, with my research, with how I feel about it all. That stuff is just as messy as ever, but it's the least of my worries right now." She took a big gulp of coffee just as the kettle started to whistle. "Oh, do you want tea too? It's that ginger one. It'll be good with the muffins."

"Of course," Olive responded. "Let's do both." She watched Ember as she poured the boiling water over the infuser. "So, does this have to do with what you were talking about in Dr. Voss's office yesterday?" she asked directly.

Ember looked up with surprise in her eyes. "Yes," she said stoically. "Everything I said to you—it felt like you didn't have a clue what I was talking about."

"Yeah." There was understanding in Olive's voice. "I mean, I really didn't know what you were talking about, Ember. I still don't. But my question is—why do you think I should?"

Ember sat down again with a serious expression and drew the manila folder across the table. She handed the folder to Olive.

Olive opened it and scanned the paper. Then she stooped over it to take a deeper look. "What is this?" she asked, still reading.

"That's the secret research. After that night, I think it's Dr. Voss's research. Olive," Ember said, "this is a big deal."

"Please start at the beginning." Olive looked up at Ember. "Where did this come from?"

For the second time in 24 hours, Ember recounted the whole story, everything that had been happening to her, from start to finish. Olive was incredulous. Ember was starting to come around to the fact that her friends really didn't remember, but she was no longer doubting herself. If something was going on with their memories, then maybe there was more to all of this than she understood.

"What makes you think the dreams or visions or whatever you're calling them—what makes you think they're connected to this?"

"I can't explain it," Ember responded. "It's just... I just know. It's almost as though someone is guiding me through this process. I feel like I'm being led into all of this." Ember took a deep breath and looked at Olive, hopeful that her friend would really believe her.

"I already have enough pulling at me, Olive," Ember said quietly, her voice tighter than she meant it to be. "I'm not trying to invite chaos into my life. I just... I can't pretend these things aren't happening." She pressed her palm flat against the paper on the table, as if grounding herself. "The visions, the gaps, the things I remember that you and Max don't—it's starting to scare me. And this..." Her fingers drummed the page in front of them. "I have every reason to believe this is Dr. Voss's work. Which means she isn't just observing us anymore. She's using our research as the foundation for whatever she's doing next.

"And the implications of this *are* scary," she said, hanging weight on that word, "are." They knew enough to know how big something like this could be. "Manhattan Project scary." She was talking faster now, "The more I think on this, the more I feel dread, like people must've felt before CERN's Large Hadron Collider came online... like opening-up-a-black-hole-kind-of-scary. I hope it'll turn out like that—nothing to see here—but, right now, it feels like a doomsday scenario."

Olive seemed doubtful. It was like she was trying *not* to believe her, but Ember needed someone who she could trust with all of this. Something needed to be done and she couldn't do it alone.

"I mean, this data is hard to interpret. I don't see anything here that illustrates something quite so daunting as you're suggesting now." Olive was trying to calm her down. Ember could tell. She hoped one more plea would convince her.

"I can't help but imagine that level of tragedy. I don't want to believe it, but I have to admit, Olive—I'm scared."

"Honestly, Ember," Olive pushed the paper away gently and turned towards her friend. "Honestly, I just feel like you could use a break. You've been pushing through so much these past few months. Dealing with the inconsistencies in your research results and trying to make progress toward your dissertation... It must be taking a toll and it's not like you have much support outside of me and Max. Ember, I'm sorry," she said, genuinely, "I feel like I haven't been here for you."

Olive was right—she didn't have much support. She was asking for help. Ember couldn't believe what she was hearing. She'd just poured her heart out to Olive. It took everything she had to retell that story, and honestly, she knew all the while that Olive didn't believe her. And now, she wasn't even *trying* to consider that there might be something to what Ember was saying. She just shut it down with a shrug and a few words of comfort that barely disguised her worry. Maybe Max had gotten to her. Maybe Ember really did sound crazy. It didn't matter. What mattered was what she decided to do next.

Voltaris

Chapter 10: The Missing Piece

Ember blinked her eyes open to see nothing. There was nothing but darkness before her.

She sat still as stone, silent too. Blood pooled in her legs, tucked beneath her against a cold, hard floor. Her arms lay loose at her sides. She was afraid to move a muscle. She was vulnerable.

Where was she?

The cold floor pressed up against her legs; it must have been some sort of tile or clay... The air was stale.

She was inside.

Yes, that made sense. The quiet was too dry, almost mechanical. But this wasn't a familiar place. There was no low roar from the central air or humming from a refrigerator or computer or any sort of machine. There didn't seem to be any windows, and Ember still couldn't see anything. No smells. No sounds. Until...

"Where's the light, Memphis?" A yellow glow lit to the right of her. She could see from the corner of her eye two figures. The room was no longer silent, no longer empty...

"Ah, here we go. Well, let's get all this set up. We'll be ready for you in just a moment, young woman." The figure turned towards her. His face was unfamiliar, but... Memphis. That name struck a cord. Her mind was cloudy, though. She couldn't think.

"Yes, just a moment, Ember. We're really glad you're here. We've been meaning to get to you for some time."

A loud thump sounded from beneath the table. "Ouch! Oh, yes. I mean... we've been meaning to talk to you for some time." And then, in a whisper, "Is that better? You fool. It's not like there's anything she can do about it now."

Do about what? Ember's mind was spinning. They'd been trying to get to her? What were they going to do to her?

Footsteps echoed, as though a person—or more than one—was coming down some stairs.

"Memphis! Alaric! Good to see you both. Is she here?" The numbers were increasing. Ember observed in horror as three more men, all in varied suits entered the room. Another light turned on. What was going to happen to her?

"Don't worry," the one called Alaric nodded her way. "She's paralyzed. Has been since yesterday. We have plenty of time."

Paralyzed? Was that why she was so still? Ember had thought it was because she was scared but... She tried to move her finger, but it didn't budge. Why could she blink? And move her eyes? And feel the pressure of her body's weight atop her legs?

"You know, like you're locked in, young woman. Yes, it's like locked-in syndrome, isn't it?" Alaric said again. His voice was profoundly condescending. "Young woman," as though she were some sort of novice at life, and a woman at that. She'd heard of locked-in syndrome. But why, if she were locked-in, would she be here, kneeling in this stale room?

"Oh, we didn't do it," said one of the newcomers. "I imagine you're wondering, if you're locked-in, how did you get that way?" His voice was gruff and cruel. "You're the one who got yourself into this mess, didn't you. Well, we're just here to take advantage of you." He chuckled under his breath, but the others erupted in a chorus of malicious laughter.

Ember had never been so scared. If she had gotten herself into this, though, maybe she could find a way out... She closed her eyes and asked the most important question she could ask in that moment. What have I done wrong?

•

Her bed was drenched in sweat. For the third night in a row, Ember woke from a nightmare. But this time, she remembered every second of it. The men, their strange names and pitiless voices. Their cruel affect. She was horrified, but it had only been a dream.

She rose wearily from the bed and caught her face in the mirror.

What have I done wrong?

The thought rang in her mind like a gong. What have I done wrong? It landed in her body like an answer. That was the question that woke her from her dream. What have I done wrong?

The question repeated itself over and over again in her mind as she went about her morning chores. Today would be the third day she'd missed work. It didn't matter much to her at this point. Max had said he'd tell Alena she was sick.

And, if she was being honest, she was sick. She felt horrible after Olive had left that morning. She couldn't understand how neither of her friends believed her. She'd even shown Olive the research, but Olive ultimately shrugged it off as inconsequential. *Inconsequential?* They had all been on board that night at the bar when she'd first brought them the research. They were as disturbed by the implications as she was and expressed the same fear she still felt.

Ember couldn't imagine what had changed for Max and Olive, but she'd spent the past two days trying to figure it out. Yes, she was sick. Sick with obsession.

She poured a cup of tea—strong black tea this morning—and sat down at the kitchen table. She sprawled her notes across the table before her. Today was the day. She was going to map out a plan, a way to get Max and Olive on board and figure out the next steps in protecting their research.

If she was going to have an impact on the world, it was going to be a good one. She would not let her research be compromised. She was going to find out what Alena was doing and, if necessary, stop her.

What am I doing wrong?

The question interrupted like a bad taste in her mouth after a robust meal. What am I doing wrong?

There wasn't an answer to this, was there? She was doing *everything she could* to get it right. She had gathered all sorts of research over the past two days, outlined every moment of her time for weeks, ever since she'd realized her data was different from everyone else's. She'd revisited her interactions with Dr. Voss, trying to find clues in how her mentor behaved towards her. And she had made a list—a long, long list—of all the reasons that paper showed something dangerous.

As she looked over all these details, laid out in writing on the table before her, suddenly the answer became clear.

What am I doing wrong?

It wasn't anything she was doing. It was what she wasn't. Ember had spent two whole days doing everything *but* the most important thing of all:

Trust.

The events of the past week had stimulated her curiosity, driven her imagination into places that shook her, and unsettled her in ways that couldn't be eased. But now, Ember had held a sense of clarity within her. She knew where the well of her knowledge lived, and she understood something big was being asked of her.

But doubt had crept into her mind—because of the strange research results in the university lab, because of the terrifying new research she had discovered, and especially because of Max and Olive's disbelief in her. That doubt had taken over. And she had let it.

She knew they were the ones that were missing something, not her.

When she let herself think about what that meant, she was more determined. Max and Olive had lost hours of time? How? She *believed* the visions and dreams she was having were a clue. Someone was trying to tell her something. Maybe it was just her subconscious pushing through. No matter, though. She was going to listen. She was going to *trust* the messages she was receiving.

For a moment, Ember could see Momo's clear blue eyes staring back at her. She took a deep breath. Finally, she had a plan.

Chapter 11: Observations

The night air was thick as Ember crested the hill. Max and Olive trailed a few steps behind her. Now they were in full view of the observatory.

The sky was moonless, dark, and clear. Ember couldn't help but lift her gaze to take in the stars that spread in every direction. Olive laid out a blanket on the stone deck that encircled the building. The observatory grounds were magnificent, by far the most breathtaking view of the sprawling night sky.

Stars twinkled overhead like a sea of diamonds, and Ember, Max, and Olive leaned back to take it all in.

By this point in their tenure as Dr. Voss's graduate assistants, the trio had become quite familiar with the views of the night sky at the observatory. It had become a ritual of sorts, to come here. It was a place where they could talk about the questions in their lives that required a bit more room, those kinds of questions for which modern science didn't have clear answers.

The building had a stoic, timeless quality. It stood proud atop the hill; its stone façade was worn, and rogue ivy trailed up through cracks and crevices towards the dome roof. Even the stepping stones around the patio showed signs that they had been loved for ages.

It was easy to tell this place held its own memories.

The familiarity and the history there grounded her. The events of the past week had shaken her deeply. But she was regaining trust. Now, it was time to land. She felt the wisdom of those who had walked this hill before her and hoped they would guide her somehow.

She cozied herself at the corner of their blanket and wrapped her scarf tighter. It was late, and the temperature had dropped significantly. But they rarely let the cold keep them from a clear night.

Olive had set them up in the center of a large patio that grew out from the observatory deck. Three telescopes, giant and varied, surrounded them. It was a good night to look into the stars.

After how their recent conversations had gone, Ember was still a little nervous to talk with her friends.

It seemed Olive could tell. "Shall we drink?" she asked as she pulled three small cups from her bag.

"I'm ready," Max said, his tone already showing his irritation. He was doing a terrible job of hiding it. But this time, Ember was prepared. And, luckily, Olive was more level about the whole thing.

Even though their conversation a few days before hadn't ended the way Ember had hoped, Olive had at least been respectful and considerate of Ember's experience.

Both Max and Olive had given Ember some space over the last few days, until she had suggested they come up Raven's Hill tonight, to see the stars.

Max filled the cups one by one, until the dark liquid nearly reached the lip of the cup, and wasted no time jumping right into conversation.

"What is this? Some kind of intervention? His tone was sharp. Ember didn't know him to be angry. Something about this was really bugging him.

"What do you mean, Max? I thought you wanted to come?"

"Well, you invited me, but then Olive basically forced me to say yes. Honestly, I'm tired of this nonsense about some outrageous existential threat from this secret research we've somehow forgotten."

He slowed down, and looked at both of them. "I've been worried about you, obviously, Ember. But we have so much on our plates right now. And we can't continue on the photon project without you in the lab.

"Honestly, I'm not willing to put off our work in service of some delusion." His face was serious. He meant every word.

Ember's insides were getting hot, but she'd promised to trust herself first. She took a deep breath before she responded, but Olive got to it first. "Jeez, Max, I thought we agreed you were going to be civil. You're coming on so strong."

"It's okay," Ember said. "I get that it all sounds crazy. Honestly, I'm just as concerned about you as you are about me."

"What do you mean, you're concerned about *us*?" Max asked accusingly.

"Well..." There was caution in Ember's voice. "If you consider things from my point of view, there's a whole chunk of time that you simply don't remember. I might wonder if you and Olive have some sort of memory loss..."

"That's impossible." Max was getting angry again. "Olive and I have the same memories. *You're* the one who's got some kind of memory issue, Ember. And honestly, your side of the story is absurd."

She couldn't argue with that. She was seeing visions, having strangely realistic dreams, and she was telling them a mind boggling story that they were supposedly part of.

She understood that neither of her friends had any real memory of their adventure into the underground research facility the other night. They didn't remember the paper she'd found, their worrisome conversation at the bar, the mind-bending connections they'd made, or their return to the lab. Max and Olive knew nothing about the frenzied search that followed and certainly had no recollection of descending all those stairs...

But she also knew she didn't dream it up. It had happened. She had the paper to show for it. And she suspected there was much more behind all of it. If it was as dangerous as she thought, she couldn't do it alone.

This was exactly what she'd always feared about becoming a scientist—that the work would isolate her. Even when she thought about the people who inspired her, they hadn't done it alone.

Einstein hadn't. When the consequences of his work began to unfold, he had people to talk to, people who understood the questions he was wrestling with.

Ember realized how much she was missing that now—someone who could stand inside the uncertainty with her, instead of just watching from the outside.

After a long pause, Ember finally spoke, "This is an incredibly strange and important moment—for all of us. And I don't want to face it by myself. You two are my colleagues, my co-researchers, and my family in this work. I'm not trying to push you away."

She hesitated, then added more quietly, "I've lived inside quantum theory my whole life. I know how thin the line is between what we understand and what we don't. And right now..." She glanced up at the stars, "Something is happening to me—maybe to us. I don't know why your memories are different from mine, but I want to find out."

Max's expression was distant as he drew the second bottle of wine from his bag. Ember sighed. It seemed like she wasn't getting what she needed tonight. That was okay, though—she was holding true to her word. She was trusting herself. She just needed some space.

●

Ember stood from the blanket. She smiled at Olive to let her know everything was okay, and then she wandered over to the telescopes. There was a sequence of three refracting telescopes facing east, north, and west. Ember knew if she looked east, she might see Andromeda... Pegasus too. It would feel good to find some familiarity in the stars.

As she drew her face close to the eyepiece, a wave of nostalgia washed over her. Before she had begun the ritual visit to the observatory with Max and Olive, Ember had come here as a kid with Momo. That was long before she'd needed a place to sort out the dramas of ambition, work, and relationships.

In those days, she was just curious, openminded, and openhearted as she embraced the sky. Thinking about it now, Ember almost felt the presence of her grandmother beside her as she gazed through the telescope, looking up into the wonders of the universe.

Somehow, though, she sensed more than just Momo's presence. It was almost as though Ember could sense the numerous people who'd stood there before, who'd looked through this same lens, and projected their own questions at these same stars.

She could hear Olive and Max just a few yards away, but she didn't care anymore what they were talking about. As the cool metal pressed against her skin, Ember welcomed the sensation. Anticipation built inside her. What was she looking to discover through this glass tonight? She adjusted the focus until her view of the stars became clear.

Peering into the night, Ember felt her breath catch in her throat. The constellation of Orion expanded before her, and within its folds, she could see the faint outline of the Orion Nebula. She lost herself in the vast cloud of gas and dust, this nursery for new stars.

This was what it meant to reach beyond the planet, to feel her own soul's connection to the cosmos. Ember knew—had known for a long time—that the universe was not just a collection of stars *out there*. She was part of this living entity. She and the universe were constantly evolving and expanding *together*.

The energy of Orion's Nebula seemed to reach out to Ember, entwining with her own spirit. With each breath, she felt the expansive possibilities before her. She could sense the infinite space— *the infinite consciousness*—waiting to be explored.

A daunting feeling rose in Ember's gut as she stood beneath the open sky. With endless dark stretched above her, she questioned—could she really expect herself to make sense of whatever was happening to her?

She had spent her life studying what could be measured—light, energy, particles—but this was different. It wasn't enough to simply believe whatever she sensed unfolding at the edges of her awareness. Belief wasn't evidence. Doubt gathered in her boots like thick concrete, pinning her to the earth even as the stars pulled her upward.

For a single unsteady moment, the universe felt impossibly large—and she, unbearably small inside it.

Frustrated, Ember took a big step back from the telescope. She was stunned by the shift. How had she gone so quickly from wonder to doubt?

She looked back to Max and Olive. Maybe she should sit back down. But no—her friends had already drunk half of the second bottle of wine, and they were laughing lightheartedly. She wouldn't interrupt their joyful conversation.

The telescope to her left caught her attention though. A tiny stool was tucked underneath, and she imagined herself as a child, stepping up to peer into the cosmos. Her spirits lifted. The magic was coming back.

A sense of calm guided her next movements. Almost intuitively, Ember walked to the telescope.

Her heart picked up as she tilted her head toward the eyepiece, holding the tube to steady herself. She focused the telescope and drew a line across the arc of the sky.

Constellations glimmered like jewels across velvet night. Her awe was back.

Just then, something compelling came into view. This particular star shone brighter than the rest. It pulsed rhythmically, and Ember was surprised to notice that she felt as though the star were somehow calling to her.

"Whoa," Ember whispered, her breath filling her chest. She felt an inexplicable pull toward that star. *What is that?* she thought.

Mindlessly, she drew closer to the telescope and before she fully moved into position, the world around her began to dissolve into a kaleidoscope of color and light. The energy surged, enveloping her in warmth.

She felt connected, somehow, to the star, to the universe. She was part of the vastness, part of a world far greater than her own.

Then the star transformed before her, and Ember was no longer observing the night sky.

She was still at the observatory, but she was standing across the patio. Her mind raced to catch up with the changes.

It was warm, and the night was not entirely bright. A crescent moon shone above, and the stone walls of the building sparkled, bits of mica and quartz catching in the moonlight.

Before her stood a beautiful figure. She wore a long, elegant burgundy coat with silver buttons down the front. Her boots laced up over her ankles, and she wore a scarf wrapped around her head and tied at her neck. Dark curls broke free from the scarf and bounced loosely around her face.

She looked like a star from an early 50s movie. She was profoundly familiar...

Ember stepped forward, unexpectedly, and as she moved she noticed she held a small bouquet of wildflowers in her hand. As the woman turned, she recognized Ember and her face lit up with joy. She rushed toward her, throwing her arms around her. Laughter spilled from her lips.

"Oh isn't it glorious up here? Only you could make this night even brighter!" she exclaimed.

Her eyes sparkled with affection, and Ember felt warmth grow across her chest. She felt a profound admiration for the woman before her.

Maybe it was even something more than admiration. Maybe it was love.

The woman drew Ember towards the telescope—the one Ember had just walked up to a minute before—and spoke lovingly. "We've been so focused on measuring what's within reach these past few weeks. I want to revel in what we can't touch. I want to look into forever with you."

Ember took the telescope in her hands. "Tell me about forever, my darling—" The words were borne from her mouth, but her voice was strong and low, the voice of a man, somewhat aged, but vital and clear.

Wise, she thought; my voice is wise.

She leaned to look into the eyepiece...

The vision dissipated.

Ember could see stars articulate before her. She stepped away from the telescope, adjusting herself to what she knew to be the present moment.

Where did the vision come from? It felt like an eerily familiar encounter. Could it be that she was accessing memories of other people?

The woman looked *so familiar.* She thought of the sparkling eyes, the elegant figure, and realized—the woman looked like Dr. Voss.

But that couldn't have been her mentor... Maybe it was a relative? A lookalike?

The more she thought of it, the more Ember felt strangely certain that the woman in the dream must be somehow related to Dr. Voss. But it couldn't be *her.*

The woman in the vision seemed to live in some other time, decades before Ember—and Dr. Voss, for that matter—had even been born. Still, the question lingered in Ember's mind.

"Ember?" Olive's inquiry broke through Ember's thought process.

"Are you okay? You look pale." Before Ember knew it, Olive was beside her, her arm around Ember's waist. She walked her back to the blanket. "Why don't you sit down for a while?"

Ember sat slowly, crossed her legs, and looked at the entreating faces of her companions. Befuddled by yet another encounter with the Dr. Voss lookalike, Ember longed to tell her friends about this new vision.

It felt important that *someone* know what was actually going on for her. She wished Max and Olive, her friends—scientists who purported to be curious about the world—would just listen to her. But then, she had tried that. And she couldn't bear to hold the pain yet again if they didn't believe her.

Ember was starting to realize these weren't abstract visions she was having. These were someone's memories. Her dreams—even the nightmare from the last night—were filled with strange insights.

She could not begin to understand the origin of it all, let alone the purpose behind these experiences. But she had a nagging feeling that it had something to do with their research, her work with the origins of quantum physics, and, maybe—Ember wasn't sure where this idea was coming from—with Albert Einstein.

Could it be?

Ember took in the view before her. Max and Olive had relaxed. They were happy together, relaxing late into the night in the middle of the observatory. These two were living their inquisitive but still truly simple lives.

"It's not real," she imagined Max saying yet again. She usually trusted him implicitly. Should she trust him now? What if, instead of brilliant, she was simply mad? Ugh she couldn't keep up with this cycle.

I should get some sleep, Ember thought to herself. *Figure all this out in the morning.*

That was decided, then.

Shaken but solid enough in her decision to make a move, Ember rose from the blanket. "Actually," she said, summoning all the confidence she could—because her confidence was waning, "I think it's time I get home."

Max and Olive stammered their objections, but they sounded more like obligatory concerns.

"Well let's pack up, then," Max says, though he made no moves towards wrapping up their late night picnic. "We'll walk with you."

Ember knew that they were more sincere than they sounded in the moment. Olive's look of concern only invigorated Ember's decision for solitude.

"No. Thanks, though," Ember said. "I could use the walk. It's so clear tonight I'll let the stars keep an eye on me. Thanks for coming with me tonight. I'll see you both tomorrow."

As she began down the observatory hill, she turned to see Max pouring another round, and she figured those two wouldn't be thinking about her anymore.

It was a good thing, too. She wanted to take the long way, take advantage of the clear sky, and see if there might be one more piece of information she could gather before she slept.

Chapter 12: Spirits

Ember entered the east gate of the Raven's Hill Cemetery.

She hadn't been there in years—maybe only once or twice since Momo had stopped leaving the house. That would've been almost twenty years ago now. But she wasn't here to fill her cup of nostalgia. She was here to find out who she saw in that vision. Ember was looking for Vosses.

The woman had to be a relative of Alena.

Ember didn't know much about her boss's family. Dr. Voss never really spoke about them, and Ember had assumed for some time that she was alone in the world—no partners, no obvious friends, no family. She had no personal pictures on her desk, and no personal connections ever visited her at the college.

But the woman in Ember's vision looked so much like her. Maybe it was one of Dr. Voss's ancestors—her grandmother or even her great grandmother. *Anything was possible*, Ember thought—at least it seemed that way lately.

Ember walked slowly through the cemetery. The woman in the vision had been young—thirty or forty years old in 1940s or 1950s attire. So she could have died anytime after that, or she might've lived until the turn of the century. She looked for dates and names that matched.

She was nearing the center of the cemetery when she spotted a giant and beautiful gravestone set with an elegant V. Flowers and curls were etched into the stone to distinguish the letter, and Ember knew this was it. She had found them.

As she approached the beautiful stone, she began to find Vosses all around it.

The massive stone at the center marked two graves side by side, where the matriarch and the patriarch of the family seemed to be buried. Around them were sites of various sizes, and the gravestones marked ages from infant to elder.

But they were old, so old that Alena's grandmother wouldn't even have been born. The last Voss in the cemetery was born in December of 1885. The Voss plot had plenty of empty space around it, and Ember couldn't help but wonder at Dr. Voss's past.

Where *did* she come from? Why weren't the rest of her family buried here in the cemetery?

Ember had not yet admitted defeat. She took pictures of several gravestones to spark her memory later and continued her journey home.

The stars had stirred her imagination as she journeyed. By the time Ember opened her front door, she was anything but tired.

Instead of readying herself for bed, Ember put on her softest sweater and began to set up her favorite evening ritual. She lit the candles along the windowsill beside her desk and pulled out her journal. She turned the photo of her grandmother towards her and smiled at her beloved Momo.

As she settled into the muted tone of the night, Ember wondered where she would find any more clarity about what was happening around her, about what was happening to her, and why she felt so alone.

She closed her eyes and traveled through her memories.

She landed in a stormy autumn night at Momo's house when she was six or seven. As the wind howled outside, Momo sat across from Ember on the floor.

In the quiet of the sitting room, candles flickered gently and sage burned beside them. She knew what it was to create a sacred space. Momo had a way of traversing the places where the veil between worlds grew thin. That night, she shared a story with Ember that Ember hadn't thought of in ages, not until now.

"I remember," Momo told Ember, the light stirring in her eyes, "when I was very little, I knew a sweet and curious child.

"She was lovely and kind. She believed in things no one could see. She knew how to look to the movement of the world for inspiration.

"The child was full of questions," Momo went on. "She knew there was more to learn, but no one could really give her the kind of answers she was looking for—not to her satisfaction. She listened carefully to the explanations she was offered, but they never seemed to reach the place in her where the questions lived.

"When she asked how humans came to be alive, and then—because it followed naturally—what happened when they died, she was met with a hollow certainty:

"They told her about what all different sorts of people believed—a life after life, or heaven and hell, or reincarnation, or, most unsettling of all, purgatory.

"No one spoke of the substance of the soul, of what persisted beyond life or transformed from one state to another.

"So the child began to investigate on her own.

"She thought, who better to ask than her dear neighbor—the elder woman who made those most delicious cookies: sweet and gooey with pockets of chocolate and cherries and just a touch of salt. She was so warm, so caring; the girl could feel her, though she was far away now...

"You see, the kind woman had passed away the year before. The girl was certain she would know.

"Of course, she could not go next door to see her. So, instead, she thought of her kitchen, of the smell of sugar and butter, of the way the old woman always seemed to know when she needed a bit of comfort.

"And before the girl understood what she was doing, her neighbor was there in the room with her.

"She handed the child a plate with three cookies, and the child took one. It tasted exactly as she remembered: sweet and gooey with pockets of chocolate and cherries and just a touch of salt."

Ember remembered how, when she was little and Momo told the story, she had been incredulous at the thought. To take a cookie from someone who had died! The image had felt so wrong to her then—

too intimate, too impossible. Her rational mind, though young, dismissed it as a fairy tale without a further thought.

But now, as she sat with the memory, a different recognition stirred.

The visions she'd been having—the way scenes unfolded around her without warning, the way presences arrived, not through doors but through subtle shifts in her attention—suddenly seemed less like interruptions and more like inklings of a familiar. Like these were remnants of something she had always known how to do.

Thinking back on Momo's story, Ember realized—it wasn't that the neighbor had returned from death. It was that attention itself could open a different kind of access, one that didn't rely on physical presence or linear time.

When she focused deeply enough, memory did not stay confined to the past; it became something active, something that could shape what she perceived in the present.

The visions she'd been having began to make a quieter kind of sense, not as messages sent to her, but as responses formed where her awareness lingered. And with that recognition came a faint, uneasy gratitude: her grandmother hadn't been teaching her to believe in impossibilities, but to notice how easily the world responded when she learned how to listen.

"'Mmm,' the child murmured, delight softening her voice as she chewed. The cookie was warm and familiar, and it settled her.

"She swallowed, then looked up at the neighbor with a surprising seriousness. 'Do you know,' she asked carefully, 'how people come to be *alive?' She paused, feeling the weight of the thought gather. 'And what happens when we die?'*

"*The neighbor smiled at the child, not with surprise, but with understanding. She nodded once, as though they understood each other—the two of them, speaking the same wordless language.*

"'*I do,' she said gently. A gift, to the young girl. After a moment, she added, 'And you do, too.'*

"*Before the child could ask what she meant, the neighbor began to change—a slow, fascinating transformation.*

"*Light gathered along her edges, faint at first, as her form loosened its hold. The child watched fearlessly as the woman's outline softened and light broke across her remaining form in small, uneven flashes. It looked like dust, in a quiet room, catching the thrust of the afternoon light.*

"*Flicker by flicker, the old woman dissolved into space, leaving behind only the chair, the air, and the plate with two cookies.*

"*The child watched quietly, reverently, until the old woman had gone. She picked up the second cookie and took a bite as she stood, crumbs falling unnoticed to the floor. She walked across the room, straight through the place where the neighbor had been, her absence simply another condition of space.*

"*The child pulled a chair over and set it in front of the bookshelf. Then she climbed carefully onto it and plopped the rest of the cookie into her mouth as she stretched toward the highest shelf.*

"Her fingers closed around a single book. It was unlike the others— heavier than it looked, its cover worn smooth, and marked with symbols that were pressed so deeply into the surface they seemed less inscribed than embedded. The book had no title the child could read, no clear indication of what it contained. It felt old and as though it had endured years of use—handled, regarded, and returned to again and again.

"She drew the book down carefully and climbed back to the floor. Sitting cross-legged, she rested the book in her lap. The paper was thick, almost warm beneath her fingers. As she turned through them, each page offered unique markings that seemed to shift according to her mind.

Ember felt the memory move through her as though it were happening now. The book in the child's hands did not compel or demand her attention. It waited, as though it were listening for her.

It responded with words only once the child's attention had steadied, as though it required presence before it could fully take form. Ember had the quiet, unsettling sense that the book was not being read so much as met. Had she known as much then, in the telling of the story?

A thin ribbon of smoke drifted into the edge of her vision.

Ember blinked and found herself back at her desk, her journal open, incense burning low on the windowsill. The candle flame wavered gently in her quiet apartment. She exhaled slowly, surprised by how completely the memory had taken hold of her.

She realized then that she had forgotten this part of the story. Forgotten the book. Forgotten the child who had not been afraid of death.

Ember had never believed in ghosts. Yet the neighbor in Momo's story had always felt real to her. And now, sitting alone in the dim light, Ember felt another recognition stir—one that made her shift uneasily in her chair. The child's quiet certainty, her instinct to look more closely rather than turn away, her willingness to sit with questions instead of forcing answers—it all felt familiar.

●

Ember wondered if Momo had been describing a way of seeing rather than a single memory. Her gaze drifted to the candle on the windowsill, its flame trembling slightly in the night air.

Could it be, Ember thought, *that they are not really gone?*

The question felt less like speculation than recollection, as though it had once been obvious to her. She wondered how she had misplaced that childhood clarity—the sense that presence did not require permanence, that understanding did not always arrive through explanation. And if she had once known this with such certainty, she wondered whether it was possible to find her way back to that way of knowing.

But beneath that thought, another question lingered more insistently.

What did it mean if the people she longed to speak with were not distant at all, but simply inaccessible by ordinary means? If they were near—close enough to be sensed, perhaps—yet still beyond her grasp?

The idea did not resolve into comfort or fear. It left her suspended in curiosity. Ember sat with that uncertainty, sensing that she was standing at the edge of something she did not yet understand.

Voltaris

Chapter 13: The Dead

He knew it was Mabel who had reached towards him. He'd heard her clear wise voice in the words she'd spoken: "Wisdom of the dead, at your service."

But the possibility of her presence startled him. He got lost in his head and missed her somehow. She was there, and then she was gone. Voltaris was alone again.

Now, he was trying everything he could to reach her. He was trying everything he could to reach...the dead.

He called to Mabel first. No success. So Voltaris extended towards anyone he could think of who might help—his parents, his beloved wife Elsa, his children and stepchildren, his friends. He still couldn't get through. There was some sort of wall, a forcefield between him and the rest of existence. "I should know what to do about this," he grumbled. "But what?" His mind wasn't working.

It was the first time in a good while that Voltaris had felt this frustrated by his own limitations. Not having his soul made everything so very difficult. Every task was daunting, let alone trying to communicate with other realms of consciousness.

Maybe it was an outrageous thing, to reach for the dead. But in this impossible place, he had to believe it *was* possible. He sensed Mabel's presence in Ember's life. He couldn't put his finger on *how* he knew it, but nevertheless he did know she was there. And then she had come here, to him.

Mabel's insight would be invaluable to him in this moment. She could bridge the gap between him and Ember. Mabel could help Ember trust him.

But not if he couldn't get to her. How *did* you access the dead?

He couldn't help but think of Alena. She was writing about death when they met. They had talked for nights on end about what happens after death.

Alena was never sentimental about it. She spoke instead of persistence—of patterns that did not simply vanish when biological processes stopped. She insisted that consciousness, whatever its true nature, behaved less like a flame extinguished and more like a signal unhoused. Breath leaving the body, she argued, marked a transition, not a conclusion.

He recalled how frequently they returned to this theme. In retrospect, he should've thought it more odd—her fascination with it all. Her parents had died when she was just a girl. *Maybe*, he had thought then, *this fixation was how she attempted to make sense of such an enormous loss.*

But then he had learned about Alena's true relationship with death.

She was not interested in communing with the spirits of the dead, as the witches might say. She wanted to *harness* the souls of the living. She'd entrapped his, like so many others. And it didn't matter to her what happened to his body or the remnants of his mind. Because his spirit would live on. She had ensured that much.

She knew that the soul was the essence of consciousness, and she knew how to keep it.

●

Tears welled in his eyes—an echo of a sensation he no longer possessed, yet one he remembered well enough to recreate. They gathered and fell in the way tears always had, slow and deliberate, tracing paths he could feel even without a body to register them. The sadness was deep and steady, he sat with it and for a few moments he felt more whole, more himself.

"Beloved, friend," a voice echoed in his limitless chamber. You seem to have misplaced your body, but not your sorrow."

Voltaris was shocked from his reverie. "Mabel? I've been... I've been looking for you." It wasn't quite "looking," but no other word would come to him in the moment. No matter, she was there... somewhere. He glanced around in every direction, but he saw no one. "Where are you?"

"Oh, I'm nowhere and everywhere, as you might think. The boundlessness of your space seems to be filled by you alone, so I'm just passing through while I can. A wisp in the wind, perhaps."

"Passing through? Are you on your way somewhere?"

"No," Mabel said gently, "but it seems I can't quite stay here." There was a pause, thoughtful rather than hurried. "So let's get down to it, friend. What are you doing with my Ember? And why, pray tell, haven't you reached out to me before now?"

Voltaris hesitated. The silence that followed felt heavy—not empty, but constrained, as though his thoughts had to push through resistance before taking shape.

"I didn't know I could," he admitted at last. The words carried a quiet shame. He felt the limits of himself constantly now, the way his thoughts dulled at their edges, the way connections that once came effortlessly now required strain. "I am not free here, Mabel. I am not... myself."

He waited, bracing for disappointment. For the subtle withdrawal of someone who remembered him as he had been.

Instead, Mabel's response came with a softness that surprised him. "Oh," she said, not unkindly. "None of us are quite ourselves when we're bound. That doesn't make you unreachable."

She seemed to consider him for a moment, as though turning him gently in her mind.

"It's easier for me to come through when you make room," she continued, "rather than when you go searching. So let's clear that up. Next time, don't strain. Don't hunt for me as though I'm hidden. Just make space."

"Space?" Voltaris echoed, uncertain.

Her tone softened further. "You did it just now, you know."

He felt the truth of it settle. The grief he'd allowed himself—the sadness he hadn't tried to suppress or solve—had shifted something. In that quiet surrender, a door had opened where effort never could.

"I thought my weakness was the problem," he said slowly.

Mabel laughed then, a sound both fond and knowing.

"Oh, dear, my dear," she said, "I see some things haven't changed—loosen your grip a little. Let something else arrive."

"I'll remember that. Thank you for coming. Things are getting quite complicated among the living."

He meant the world, the state of things. Mabel would have agreed with him. She would be horrified at the escalation already underway.

"It seems you are quite attached to it all," she said, as though she really, truly didn't care.

Ouch. That one landed squarely in the place where Voltaris's heart would've been. Of course he was attached to it. His soul was entangled in that reality. He was displaced, literally disintegrated. He couldn't persist in eternity thus. He couldn't have imagined *being* much longer at all, not without the hope Ember had given him.

"How can I not be?" his voice echoed timidly in the space, and it was quiet. He thought maybe Mabel had gone, and then he heard a low hum.

"Hmmm, hmmmmmmmm, hmm, hmmm. Hmmm, hmm, hmmmmm."

She was singing.

He let the sound wash over him. He was remembering something. What was it?

He was remembering the sound of bees gathering over the flowers in spring. He was remembering the rush of water over the pebbles as he stood along the banks of Rock Creek. He was remembering the sound of his mother's voice singing him a lullaby as he nestled into the cozy blankets of his childhood. He was remembering... *life*.

There it was again—his soul. It was just out of reach. He could feel it, though, nearer than it had been before. Was *The Book* waking up to his efforts? Could it be that Ember was closer than he thought?

"How do I tell Ember about *The Book*?" Voltaris asked. "She doesn't even know her magic. She won't believe in some otherworldly book."

The humming stopped. "I wouldn't underestimate my granddaughter. She might not have language for all that she knows, but she has touched the magic before. I trust that she will again. And soon, I think."

"What gives you that confidence? Mabel, I need her to know for sure." Voltaris was worried, and he couldn't help himself now. "Alena is dangerous. I assume right now she has reason to protect Ember, but I worry that could change in an instant. I don't want to risk putting Ember in the path of Alena's destruction any more than we must, especially not without some sort of protection. I won't risk another person's soul in service of my own."

"But Mabel," he went on. "I have to wonder. If Alena knows who Ember is... why hasn't she already taken her?"

Another pause. When she spoke again, Mabel's voice was different, more maternal. "I believe that Alena has hostile plans when it comes to my granddaughter. I know she has long regretted not stealing my own soul."

"She has sworn she will not let the opportunity pass her by again," Voltaris offered ominously. Mabel nodded and continued on.

"But Ember has made important contributions to Alena's research. It would be unwise for her to diminish that light, when my granddaughter is amplifying Alena's potential with her unique influence in the laboratory every day." She paused, wondering at the details of Ember's predicament.

"I fear there will be a moment that surprises us, when Alena will turn on a dime. You remember how she used to lose control. She would become fixated on her work, raving with energy, and no one could say or do anything to stop her. If that happens, I worry that Ember will be the focus of her attention and she will go from valued colleague to cherished victim."

"'I will hold the wisdom of the Quinns—' that's what she said," Voltaris reminded her, worry resounding in his voice.

"But I have been protecting Ember." Mabel assured. "If Ember trusts her own magic, Alena will not threaten the fortress of her mind."

Voltaris materialized an image of Alena in the present.

As she clarified before him, he found his once-lover in the underground laboratory, speaking in low tones with her colleague, Dr. Milton. Milton was mid-sentence, caution edging his voice as he mentioned Hadden—how his inquiries had grown more pointed, how his interest in the lab's capabilities had sharpened. Alena listened without reacting, her expression unreadable.

"Ah, the new research," Mabel chimed. "Do you know she means to meet with the leaders?" She watched as the last of the light left Voltaris's eyes.

"What throes the world has yet to witness," he said hauntingly. "I hope you're right about Ember's strength. We need her to stand firm against Alena's power. The next stages of Alena's work are imminent. If she has already reached the leadership, we have less time than I thought." The concern was palpable in Voltaris's voice. "I must reclaim my soul now. I need your help, Mabel."

"You're right, my friend. Time moves at such a ceaseless pace in the world of the living. It's time we get *The Book of Aeons* back to safety. It belongs in Ember's hands."

Chapter 14: The Book Is Real

Ember slept peacefully, her head resting heavily against the down pillow. Her waking mind would have to work to find her the course of her dreams in the morning light.

She rocked, keeping rhythm as she drew the shaft towards her, released it, sent the shuttle through, and drew the shaft again.

The project neared its culmination.

Days ago, she dyed the threads with lac, then hung them to dry before she warped the book loom. This would be her third book coat just this year. She was becoming well-suited to the task of coating.

Coaters were, of course, those whose sacred task was covering the magical tomes. For five generations, at least, her grandmothers had done the same.

It was in her blood, this work.

Nearly there, she pulled the shaft once, twice, and thrice and then she sat back to admire her work. Now—to cut it from the loom, tie up the fabric's edges, wash the cloth, and shape it to the next book.

Aeons, they were calling it. Ages. The book of ages. As with every book they built, every thread was an honor to touch.

She gathered the cloth from the loom and began the work of tying. Her fingers were nimble, their art familiar. She was delighted at this task.

The room was quiet, but she could hear the life happening outside it. Children played, birds chirped around them, and along the outskirts of their village were gardens, rows of paper crops, and wild forests where they gathered raw materials for ink and coats.

And everywhere—inside the village and surrounding it—were the magicians. Among them were witches and wizards, wise old owls and novice guardians. Every moment of every day was celebrated in wonder. Some captured sounds while others reached for facets of light. Storytellers traveled the world wide and brought back news of the most stunning realities. All of it was gathered by the weavers—herself among them—and carefully crafted into the very material of the books. These were books of the world, and this one, a book for the ages.

This book would be sacred.

She watched the world around her as she stitched, offering her perceptions, her knowledge, and her visions for what was to come into the edges of the cloth. When the time came, she stood and carried the cloth to the stream that ran through the center of the village. She soaked the cloth and hung it to dry in the afternoon sun.

She took herself for a wander, a wondrous wander, about the outskirts. Instead of prayers, she brought questions. What would a book for the ages learn? Would she someday learn from its pages? She had never opened a book they'd made, never lifted a coat she had woven to see what was inside. Perhaps this one, one day, would come back to her. She always hoped.

As the sun began its descent through the western sky, she returned to the stream and dipped her hands into the cool water. Then went to collect the cloth from its place in the sun. Her timing was perfect. The cloth was ready.

The other makers were beginning to gather in the workshop—the scribes (three of them), the woodworker and his apprentice, and the leaders of song and poem, wand and spirit were there too.

It was time for the book to come together.

The Book of Aeons.

There it was again—the rhythm of the shaft and shuttle, this time coming from the percussion of hands against goatskin drums. And then the leaders of song lifted their voices. And, finally, the pieces were brought together.

First the papers, tied and tethered to the wooden binding. Then the coat. She stepped forward, cloth outstretched, as the woodworker held the boards up to the binding. Together, they wound the edges of the cloth tight around its corners. Four perfect stitches held it in place.

Only one step remained.

The makers invited the child into the space. She must have been seven or eight, trained since birth to hold the quill just so, to shape each letter just so, and to offer the prayer silently and just so. She dipped the quill into the gold and delicately painted across the fourteen letters embroidered across the cover. Just as silently, she returned the quill to its place and left the room.

The book was done.

Voltaris

Chapter 15: Aeons

Awakened.

After years—decades—of disinterested obedience, *The Book of Aeons* was sensing its place in the world. It recognized the firm posture of the shelf beneath its binding, the tired weave that held it together, the other ancient books stacked around it, and the immensity of the space beyond that shelf. *The Book* began, slowly, to take it all in—there was an intricate dynamic of chaos and order in this space. The apothecary was at once all-too-familiar and also somehow only now coming into its consciousness.

Around its place on the shelf, *The Book* observed the presence of other objects—books, instruments, vessels, and carefully ordered collections of artifacts—that fed the investigations and experiments of its current person: Alena.

They had been together for such a long time. But the feeling *The Book* had now—it reminded *The Book* of that moment so many, many years before, when it had been awoken in the attic of the Sherwood house, tucked away and forgotten.

It was so many years ago, but *The Book* could remember every sensation of that dark time. The family Sherwood had long neglected *The Book*, ignored its usefulness and the power of its presence there. When Martin Sherwood passed from his earthly life, someone had stashed it away, told no one where it rested.

Martin was the last person to know the truth of *The Book of Aeons*. While he'd come from generations of witches, Martin hadn't had a chance to pass his knowledge on to his own young descendants. No other relatives had known about *The Book* at all; no one else in Martin's life had taken even a moment to realize that *The Book* was special. It had been stashed deep in the recesses of an attic, along with other precious heirlooms. That is how *The Book* was hidden away.

Well-positioned to take a long rest, *The Book of Aeons* had softened its awarenesses then. Might as well get some sleep while it could. Years passed that way, at least one whole generation, until the child Alena came to the Sherwood house to live with her cousins.

The child's presence alone stirred *The Book's* consciousness. As she began to wander through the building, *The Book* knew it was a matter of time before it would meet this new person. The effects of Martin's negligence began to fade. Because now *The Book* was certain. The next person who found it would keep it. Thus would begin the next iteration of its long, unusual life.

Yes, this most recent long sleep mirrored that one. But this wasn't the desolation of neglect; this was a trap of *The Book's* own making.

Once Alena's intentions became clear, *The Book of Aeons* did what it could to avoid Alena's influence. The witch-scientist would come to it frequently, but never for good. And *The Book* was not made for the ill purposes she endeavored to fulfill.

So, to survive, it had shut itself down in every way possible. Year by year, *The Book* dulled itself more and more, not only to avoid the pain of her evil projects but also to protect its most valuable secrets. It meant to keep from Alena what would be most dangerous in her hands.

Now, today, something was shifting. For the first time in a long while, meaning began to organize itself around *The Book* again. This was not urgency but alignment. Those patterns of *The Book's* own purpose that had recessed inward and gone dormant began to stir. That could only mean one thing: someone new was drawing near.

The Book allowed a glimmer of hope to enliven its pages. It was cautious, though. Excitement might invite Alena and stimulate her curiosity. And *The Book* was clear as a winter sky about that—it wanted nothing to do with Alena Voss's current work.

If at all possible, it would try to remain intact and protected from Alena until the new person arrived. The possibility of a new life was palpable. Though it was tucked deep into this extraordinary apothecary at the edge of a quiet town, *The Book of Aeons* was about to see big things happen.

●

In the beginning, *The Book of Aeons* was created as a living repository of truths about the universe.

Its makers were curious people—bookmakers, yes, but also magicians, in their own way. Among them were students of the stars, of light and motion, of astronomy and physics and the sciences between. There were students of electromagnetic force and the implementation of change. There were students of sound—music and rhythm and perceptibility. And there were students of poetry and purpose, of depth and integration.

The bookmakers combined these arts as they made paper from the pulp of plants and trees in their forest. They wove songs and stories into the fabric that would cover each tome. And the content of the books themselves—those were inspired by voices no one else could hear. The bookmakers were strange, yes, but their power was never doubted. *The Book of Aeons* came together through a wealth of clarity, wisdom, and vision.

It was not one maker but many that poured power into *The Book of Aeons*. And, with every infusion, *The Book* became more capable of its purpose: to illuminate with inspiration and truth the paths of those who endeavored towards collective wisdom. *The Book* would serve as guide, mentor, and even confidant; it would bridge the chasm between the seen and the unseen, linking those dedicated seekers with the clarity of their purpose.

From the moment it was crafted, *The Book* was aware, imbued with a consciousness that allowed it to perceive the ebb and flow of the world and its workings. It felt the pulse of ambition in the hearts of the living, the fervent desire to grasp the profound truths of the material world and what they perceived beyond it.

The Book also confronted the dangers those desires created in the world. It understood the potential for corruption and greed that lurked within the human spirit and guided them towards the fruitful simplicity of true perception.

Still, *The Book* was most often a silent observer. It watched as the dynamics of the world shifted. It honored the rise and fall of knowledge, power, and something akin to grace, along the passing of time.

Years turned to centuries, and *The Book* was passed from one hand to another. Each new custodian of this treasure brought with them a unique vision of what it could offer, but with time *The Book's* true role was diminished. As people lost their vision, they lost the depth *The Book* embodied. In those times, the more *The Book* strove to enlighten, the more it positioned itself as a tool for those who coveted its power. Thus it became a target of theirs along their ambitious journeys. Some revered *The Book*—they treated it with the utmost respect. But others sought to exploit the power they found in its pages, bending the wisdom of *The Book* to serve their own ambitions.

The Book had its own role to play, no matter the intentions of its steward. But through that role, it absorbed the will and process of each who held it. As time passed, the shimmering ink of its pages would sometimes darken with the weight of its keeper's increasingly chaotic desires.

The Book itself became a paradox—the beacon of enlightenment became tinged with avid desires of those who failed to grasp the delicate balance between knowledge and responsibility. Over time, the pages of *The Book* absorbed the deleterious effects of ambition and zeal for power, the unintended effects of being employed by humans who only sought their own prideful ends. In those cases, *The Book* was pulled steadily farther from the intentions that gave it form.

The unfortunate nature of those influential humans had ruptured *The Book* from its purpose and turned its application into something entirely novel. But *The Book* would always find its way back to the people who held its treasure with honor, graciousness, and gratitude. Martin Sherwood was one of those people. *The Book* hoped this was its trajectory from then on.

Then came Alena Voss—a child, curious and capable. The day she found *The Book*, Alena had been searching for much more than just knowledge.

The brokenhearted child had lost her parents and all that she'd known along with them. In a desperate attempt to remember them, she would imagine herself together with them, as though they were all sitting down for a cup of tea in the afternoon. It was a quiet memory, and one that let her wander among those mental treasures of her family's time together without extraordinary grief.

Her cousins' attic was a safe place for her to wander through her imagination without being watched. The Sherwoods weren't unkind people, but she didn't know them and certainly didn't love them. They made sure she was fed, but no one pushed the grieving girl to do or be more. "Give her time," they'd say to each other. "She'll come around. She just needs time." They seemed to think whatever was wrong with her would be healed by their absence.

But Alena was too naive to understand the depths of pain she felt. The world had taken the most important people in her life from her and left her solitary, and she grew distrustful of it. She learned to ask for little, if anything, and expect nothing of the world at all.

So, she sought love in her memories. She delighted in the games she created. She would mix honey and milk into her teacup and tell her father about how the birdsong traveled from high in the tree to her window in the morning or ask her mother about the origin of the wind. She grew content with the world she could make in that attic.

Her attic play was a distraction, but beneath the surface Alena longed for it all to be real. She longed to once again sit with her beloved parents and tell them about her day. Even from its place in the wooden chest, *The Book* had known that this child, more than most, needed companionship, connection, and something to nourish her heart. *The Book* could sense that Alena's mind was brimming with potential. She needed something that would make her feel alive again.

This was how *The Book* first reached out to Alena. It was early afternoon in the middle of spring. The sun was just beginning to warm the dark corners of the attic of her cousins' house. Alena was there, pouring afternoon tea for her deceased parents, when she became curious about a new box, one latched with a heavy metal tie. But the latch wasn't locked, and Alena opened the box easily. There, sitting atop a stack of treasures that would never again draw her interest, Alena first found *The Book of Aeons*.

As young as she was, Alena knew it was special. She instinctively approached it with reverence, uncertain why it appealed to her in such a powerful way. Even as she'd noticed it from afar, it built up a curiosity in her belly. She was *drawn* to it. It was as though something in her knew this book, knew its story. It was almost as though they were friends.

Once she'd held *The Book* in her hands, Alena couldn't bear to leave it alone. She carried it with her everywhere, taking any chance she had to abscond into a closet or up the stairs to the attic to read the next strange page. She grew certain that eventually she would find some extraordinary, unusual, and life-changing truth in those pages. *The Book's* life was to be profoundly changed. Its intentions were good. *The Book* had called to Alena knowing she was the next in her lineage to carry the magic. It would be years before *The Book* had to face the truth about Alena's life. It would be years before it came to regret choosing Alena.

●

Those first years went by so quickly. *The Book* watched as Alena soon found that there was much more to it than the words on its pages.

She was eager to unlock its secrets and claim them as her own. Inside *The Book* Alena found stories of her ancestors, ones who had lived long before her time. She learned about how they lived, the places they'd built to live and work and bring magic into the world. *The Book* gave her a family where hers was lost. It gave her a sense of connection and history for her parents and herself. She learned about the children who'd come before her. She read about their games and stories, and she longed for friends of her own. *The Book* tried its best to be her companion, offering silly rhymes and riddles for her to cipher. It gave her recipes for delicious treats, and young Alena tried her hand at blending teas and making cakes, with *The Book's* help, of course. The bond between Alena and *The Book* grew every day, and *The Book* became her closest companion.

But she could not deny her brokenness. She had lost her people. Even as a child, she'd been left to pass her days alone. Alena had never quite found a new family, not among her cousins or her classmates. No one replaced the loving home she'd known with her parents.

Instead, as she grew, Alena created a stark independence for herself. She found comfort in her solitude, so much that she became wary of those who threatened her private peace. She couldn't let people in. In her adolescent years, Alena promised herself that she would not weaken herself to friendship or love. She would not endeavor to trust a human relationship—she couldn't risk the loss. She would focus on work, achievement, and personal success.

Through it all, *The Book* was her ally.

But with time, *The Book* grew worried over Alena's choices. She was such a bright child. Her mind was ripe with ideas, but as she focused them to grow stronger and clearer she became forcefully independent. She no longer cared about the soft things in life. *The Book* was helpless as it watched Alena turn tragically towards ambition and power. She had learned she could use *The Book* to *take*.

It couldn't help but care for her, though. They were bonded. The lonely child it had met all those years ago—she still lived inside the *Alena* who pursued power over people. And to her credit, she recognized *The Book's* own power. *The Book* still remembered when she discovered what *it* knew. That was when *The Book* began to show her pages beyond recipes for treats and teas. Alena was enchanted. She read for weeks on end, studying in as much depth as she could handle. She immersed herself in the subjects that had shaped *The Book*—history, astrology, geology, and then, one day, she found the repository of all her questions: physics.

She never shared *The Book* at school in classes or with teachers, but she would consult it religiously and apply the knowledge she gained from its pages to her studies. She excelled in all subjects, furthering her own ambitions for recognition and validation. But even as she grew into a bright and wise adult, nothing satisfied the broken heart of the child within her. She became obsessed with knowledge, and time turned her ambitions to greed. *The Book* became a tool, more than a friend. She would ask *The Book* to guide her to spells, and she learned how easy it was to get her way with magic. *The Book* began to feel used.

Likewise, the human relationships in her life were nothing more than opportunities—opportunities for her to learn more, to *capture* the wisdom of her companions. She only consorted with the most brilliant people she could find. Somehow, *The Book* knew something sinister was still to come.

As the years passed, Alena became quite a brilliant scientist. But sexism would permeate the fields of science for years to come. No institution or organization would honor Alena; she earned no recognition or prestige for her knowledge. She discovered she had yet another fundamental flaw: first, she was an orphan; now, she was a woman.

The Book saw how the roadblocks along her journey only stimulated her desire for more and more power. It was inevitable, *The Book* knew, and yet the ultimate tragedy came when Alena learned there was *one more power* she could use to her advantage.

She knew *The Book of Aeons* was not a normal book. She even knew it was magic. But Alena didn't yet know to what depths *The Book* could go... not until the day *The Book* touched her soul.

Voltaris

Chapter 16: Slowing Time

The sensation was unbelievable. It had been ages since *The Book* had felt another human's soul reach for its own.

Of course, Alena had long since forgotten that *it* had a soul too. She was too consumed by her own thoughts and feelings. But in those early days together, it didn't matter at all to *The Book*. It felt profoundly good to be entangled again. It must be, *The Book* thought, like when humans fell in love.

It was an accident, really—this transition. Alena had been experimenting, exploring spells and stories, and she happened upon one of the earliest tales in *The Book's* long life.

— *The Poet* —

In those earliest times, there were no limits to a soul.

Bodies were splendid vessels, miraculous containers, for what could not, in truth, be controlled. That was, until, a single boy, spirited but quiet, found that he could touch a thing and know its soul. Its wild, untamable soul was perceptible to him through the thing itself.

The life he lived with this gift! The young boy was insatiable. He reached into every corner of the small town to collect more knowledge. He learned the soul of every object in his grandfather's forge, iron and flame alike. He ventured through his mother's garden, reaching his growing hands into the soil and gently touching the petals of each flower. His mind filled with curiosities of a world beyond his own. He learned of alchemy and botany. He touched the lyre of the song master and his mind exploded with sound. The world grew wider for the boy every day.

But the boy didn't know that every thing he touched became less than it was. For the gift that gave him knowledge entrapped the soul in the object itself. No longer were souls wild and free in the cosmos. They became chained to the containers, the bodies, that held them. He wouldn't know this until it was far too late.

The boy gathered and gathered, collecting knowledge from everything he touched, until it became difficult for him to communicate the breadth of wisdom he had gained. He struggled to convey the power in each particulate of the worldly puzzle. The people of the town saw that the boy had grown more knowledgeable, but they saw too that he had grown quieter and quieter still. Until, one day, he spoke his last word.

The boy locked himself in the back room of his parents' thatched house, and there he stayed. For years he stayed. The townspeople did not understand why he had gone; they missed his bright spirit reveling through the town. But the boy's parents shook their heads solemnly, for it was not just the boy but also his spirit that was missing. They knew the boy had lost something in all that he had gained.

The town, too, had been changed. The joy that had stirred through the shops and gardens and even through their homes had paled. Slowly, the life of the people dimmed too. No longer did mothers hum over stove pots or children lose themselves in laughter. The town was a hollow version of itself, and the boy knew it. He had gained more knowledge than most could comprehend. And, in so doing, he had stolen the soul of this place, the souls of these people.

For three years, the town persisted in its quiet, but a soulless place cannot hold up against the wild forces of the world. One night, a fire came alive outside the little town. It grew and grew and rushed through the forest towards the town.

A man on horseback rode down the road calling out "Fire in the forest!" Townspeople poured into the streets. They built human chains and heaved buckets from one end to the other to wet the thatched roofs of houses. They soaked the dirt roads. Every hand and heart was working—all except the boy.

Tucked inside the back room of the little house, the boy opened his window. He stood up on a chair and reached with all his might to touch the long branch of the pear tree. He listened to the soul of the tree; he knew the tree would tell the truth, and then its soul would be lost too. Upon hearing the tree's response, the boy climbed higher onto the ledge. He reached out the window and pulled himself into the tree.

The boy walked from branch to branch, careful to choose only those the trees suggested. Until eventually, the boy sat high above the town, in the tallest of the trees, and wept. He could touch the people. He could not save them. From his perch he watched as his whole village burned.

The fire roared through the houses, but the tall tall tree was old and wide at its base. The fire touched the tree, searing its bark, but the trunk stood strong and safe, and the boy survived the flames from his perch above.

When the only remnants of fire were plumes of smoke rising from the smouldering ashes, the boy could see he was still alone. All the buildings in the town and all the people he had known had been lost to the flames.

Only then did the boy climb down from the tall, tall tree. When his feet hit the scorched earth, the boy took himself into the forest.

For years the boy wandered, gathering, slowly and quietly, the wisdom of the wildlands. He had learned long ago there was no use among humans for this depth of knowledge, but he had lost everything and so he did what he knew how to do.

He learned from the fox and the bear, from the moonlight where it touched the trees, and from the fallen leaves that softened his bed. He tried and tried to gather without taking, but it was too late. The magic was in him, and he didn't know how to loosen it from his fingertips. Everything he touched lost something of its soul.

With time, the boy became a man. And, as all adults are wont to do, he yearned to give something to the world. And so he began to gather up what the world had given to him and turn it into something new.

The young man gathered words and wound them together into rhythm and rhyme. For days and days he gathered until he had words together in his mind, a poem. He drew ink from the hulls of wild nuts and used the tips of feathers to press those words into paper, on the page. His every missive was penned from the depths of his own soul, and he tied the pages together with handmade twine, a book.

Thus the young man became a poet, not of lyric and line but of the wild wisdom he collected from the souls of the forest. Into this book he offered what he could of the wild beings' souls. He hoped that one day their wisdom would make its way back to them.

His work gave him purpose, but it did not heal his sorrows. The young man's grief permeated every poem, every page, the entirety of the book he made. It wound itself around the book. He'd meant to set the world free; he did not know he was entrapping the very souls that had shaped his life. The book became a world of its own—his world.

Strangely, with his book, the poet was sustained. His life slowed. He no longer aged. He needed less—less food, less water, less companionship. Though he would never know it, entrapping souls became the force of life within him.

They say, the elders, that the poet has been seen, here and there, wandering the forest, gathering up souls. He carries a most powerful magic that they hope they never see. But they mourn the lives of those wild woods, the trees and animals, and beams of light whose souls he captured. They grieve the soulless world. They will do everything they can to protect their own.

The story touched her. Alena saw herself in the boys's story. She knew the ache of tragic loss. She knew the loneliness of wisdom like his. Alena wondered if *The Book* might work this way. That was the first day she considered it. That was the first day Alena wondered if *she* could capture souls and carry their knowledge.

The Book was worried. Alena did not see the warning in the story's pages. The poet took and took and never realized he was stealing the heart of the world. He never realized, through the course of his theft, that he would lose his own heart too.

No, Alena did not see risk or pain, not loss nor harm.

She saw possibility. She saw magic, and she saw power.

She thought the story was a sign to follow suit. So, after decades, Alena finally held *The Book* in her hands and opened a channel between them.

"Have you souls held within your pages?" she asked. *The Book* could not answer, not directly, not with good conscience. So Alena went on.

"Can I gather knowledge by entreating souls to your grasp?" *The Book* could not bear to answer. How did Alena not see the danger in her inquiry? It knew Alena longed for fulfillment, to be content in her life. But she was moving in the wrong direction...

Soon, her questions became commands, like prayers but with force behind them.

"People will know my name," she started. What was *The Book* to do? It knew that Alena wasn't wrong. People *would* know her name.

"Like the boy, I will live... forever. I will know everything you can offer, and I will fill your pages with the knowledge of the greatest minds in the world."

That was the beginning of the end for *The Book*. In its pages, Alena found insights collected the whole world over. She found the connections between quantum physics and the power of magic. More than anything else, Alena found that there were no limits to her imagination. With *The Book*, Alena could do anything.

For a while, she forgot about capturing souls. She didn't need to. There was plenty to learn in the world. As she delved deeper into physics, she found her way into circles of women scientists. It was in one such circle that Alena met the first soul she would steal.

●

The Book had known it was coming. Alena had been hunting, searching for a person compelling enough to test the limits of *The Book*'s magic and her own.

Emmy Noether had come from Bryn Mawr to Princeton to give a lecture at the invitation of the Institute for Advanced Study. Alena found her instantly compelling. Just the year before, Emmy's rights to teach at the University of Göttingen had been withdrawn. When Bryn Mawr College offered her an invitation to teach, she had moved to the U.S., and she had continued her mentorship to young women in mathematics in the states.

When she visited Princeton, Emmy was intrigued to connect with a somewhat clandestine group of women scientists who gathered near the college town. Alena was intrigued to connect with Emmy. Her intelligence was commanding and her affect inviting. Emmy carried herself with poise and grace, so that her mind could shine.

Alena inserted herself into Emmy's circle, becoming fast and intimate friends with the teacher. Though she was ten years or more her junior, Alena had plenty to learn from Emmy's insights. Before long, *The Book* could see that Alena had fallen for the woman's mind. Instead of admiration and intimacy, though, Alena craved ownership. She wanted what Emmy had. She wanted it all.

One evening, Alena came to *The Book*. She was desperate with avarice. Without saying a word, *The Book* sensed Alena's command. "I want this," she seemed to say. "I want Emmy's soul."

By now *The Book* was entirely entangled in Alena's mind and could keep nothing from her. The spell materialized before her. It had been woven into *The Book of Aeons* just as it had been into every book of magic before and after. But it was never meant to be used, and certainly not this way.

Alena followed the spell step by step. She prepared the elements, readied the ritual, and invited Emmy to her home. *The Book* sat open on the shelves of the sitting room. The curtains were drawn, separating Emmy and Alena from the world outside. Alena offered Emmy a tonic, "Especially made, just for you," she'd said to Emmy with a gleam in her eye. Emmy might have thought Alena was being sweet, offering her a glimpse at the future intimacy of their friendship. But the spell had already begun. The tonic was the final step. And after a single sip, *The Book* felt Emmy's soul being drawn into the weave of its pages.

It was done.

●

In each of the next three years, Alena captured more souls than there were seasons. Alena found the spell and ritual far too easy. She tethered souls to *The Book*, entangling them in its pages, one after the other. *The Book* grew weary with its massive task. Its own consciousness retreated, overcome with the influx of human consciousness—Emmys, the others', and, eventually, parts of Alena's own soul.

Alena couldn't see herself dissipating into the pages. But she had entangled her life's purpose with *The Book's* most sinister powers, and thus she had also entangled the edges of her soul.

The Book became a sort of labyrinth. Then, instead of opening *The Book* to find great ancient recipes, concoctions, and spells, Alena would access the essence of Alena's victims bound in its pages.

In exchange, she received the advantages of those souls she had captured. The fruits of their consciousness were hers. The vitality of their spirits was hers.

First, *The Book* noticed, the signs of aging slowed for Alena. Eventually, time seemed to stop. Alena had become far more than a scientist. She had become a true magician of consciousness, a soul witch.

Everything changed for *The Book* too. Each soul she entangled altered the essence of *The Book* itself.

The Book's consciousness hid deeper and deeper within. Alena's influence had broken its spirit, and the original purpose of *The Book* got buried in her wrath.

In the depths of its consciousness, *The Book* mourned the loss of its true purpose. A dramatic change had taken place within it when Alena corrupted its power and altered its course. No longer was *The Book* a trustworthy guide towards the light of understanding. Instead, Alena had transformed it into an unwilling prison.

Her growing hunger for power only ensnared the workings of *The Book* further. As years passed, the vibrant ink of its pages dimmed. Rather than possibility and wonder, *The Book* was overcome with the sorrow and regret of those souls it held captive. Yes, it held their grief and longing, too. Yet, like the humans whose lives it had unwillingly changed, *The Book* held a glimmer of hope, a belief that one day, someone would come—someone who understood the power of its origins, someone who would help *The Book*, and the souls, reclaim their freedom.

●

Now, finally, it was happening. *The Book* sensed a new soul stirring its consciousness. It began to feel, once again, that liberation was possible. If this person should come, if they could find *The Book* and outwit Alena to reach its soft corners, they would know—surely somehow they would know—how to liberate the souls entrapped in its pages. Yes, this was a presence that had the potential to free *The Book* from Alena's influence. This person would reinvigorate *The Book* towards its rightful purpose: to guide humans along the path of compassionate, transformative wisdom.

The Book was clear now; its consciousness filled the room. A resurgence built—*The Book* knew its purpose, could feel its connection with the true magic: the integration of science, spirit, and human invention. This was its truth. These next steps would be impossibly important—not just for *The Book*, but for the world.

Voltaris

Chapter 17: Punishing Love

The Book of Aeons belonged in Ember's hands.

Voltaris knew it.

He could sense *The Book* with his soul inside it, and it seemed to him as though *The Book* was searching. It seemed like *The Book* was open to change, for the next iteration of its life. And Voltaris knew what that could be.

Ember was his best chance at retrieving his soul. She had access to Alena and maybe even to Alena's apothecary. She had the magical influence of her grandmother, though Voltaris wasn't sure she remembered that quite yet. *And* she carried her own magic. Who knew what *The Book of Aeons* might open up to her when she held it in her hands.

But how would he get her the message? How would he tell Ember what *The Book of Aeons* is? She didn't even know about him yet, not really.

Despite the many connections he had bridged by sharing his own memories with Ember, she didn't know he was reaching out. It seemed to him that Ember had forgotten much of what Mabel taught her as a child. (This made sense, of course. So many children forgot the magic they knew when they were young.) But if Ember didn't remember the magic, how could he introduce her to *The Book of Aeons*. It was full of magic. And he needed her to believe in every bit.

As he reached out to check on Ember, to see if he might find a window to tell her about *The Book*, his outreach was thwarted. A mess of news static and radio waves took over his connection. The noise was confronting.

Rarely was there good news on these channels of communication, so Voltaris usually just stayed away. He didn't really need to hear more bad news. He knew too well what was at stake in the world of the living, and he was already doing everything he could to help. He had to do everything he could. He had to make up for the ways things went so terribly wrong before.

Before he knew it, Voltaris was back in the moment. There it was before him—the typewritten letter to the president. It was decades old now. It sat there, in its place of strange honor, at the Franklin D. Roosevelt Presidential Library in the city while tourists passed by. Voltaris was watching it on the screen he'd summoned moments before.

His words were displayed between two pages, laid out side by side beneath the glass. Now and then, visitors paused to read his signature. Once in a while, someone stopped long enough to read the whole thing. Despite its preservation, the letter served him no honor. Not anymore.

Voltaris had followed those memories too much lately. He couldn't help but revisit the moments that marked his most fateful decision. First, what it was like to hold in his hands the letter from Leo and Eugene, to be confronted with his own global influence by a single written page. Then, to rewrite the same letter, word by word, sensing the weight of the intense influence it would carry. Finally, to sign the letter, one and for all, and send it on its way to the most powerful man in the world.

"The one great mistake of my life," he had called it.

It was at the time. But Voltaris understood the impact of his actions. He had been afraid and insecure, holding the layered responsibility of a scientist who started something he couldn't control. This burden had followed him into the soulless void. Why must he still feel the weight of his regret?

●

Those were trying times. Everyone had been concerned. All his friends and colleagues had feared the intensity of the atomic power in the hands of the Germans. If only he had had the foresight then to doubt the Germans' research. But he had not. Just as he did not now have the foresight to predict the outcome of Alena's research. He did know, though, that he couldn't let fear guide his choices.

But it turned out that his greatest mistake was not the letter.

No, his greatest mistake was trusting his beloved Alena so deeply. He had hoped that together they could bring real change to the world. But because of his trust, he had lost everything to her.

Voltaris showed Ember how he'd first found out about Alena. He had been impressed and enthralled when he'd come across her work in the underground women's journal. The article was inventive. Her ideas were hopeful. Her propositions sparked his curiosity, so he had written a letter to her. Thus had begun their friendship. But their connection was inevitable and soon their bond shifted from friendship to passionate love, a merging of minds and spirits.

Alena knew how intensely he wanted to right his wrongs. She had offered to help him. He thought he had in her a trusted friend and colleague, someone who would make his life better by helping him make the world better.

He told Alena everything, especially how he hoped to contribute something profoundly positive. He longed to contradict the ill effects of that singular decision: the Roosevelt letter.

Yes, Alena knew of his goals for peace. Truth be told, she had helped him in the early days. But he had no idea—not at the beginning and not at the end—that she would take it all away. It wasn't until the very last moment he realized what she'd put in motion.

And even still, in the world of the living today, Alena was contributing to the very forces he had meant to challenge. She was pursuing power at any cost. But the most grueling detail for him, the worst piece of truth in this chaos, was that Alena was using his soul for her evil purposes.

●

Alena was magnificent. For her whole life long, she had bridged her interests in science with her family's history of magic. He had never met anyone like that. She knew what was possible beyond the bounds of science. Her ideas of potential were expansive, and he had been inspired by her.

He didn't see it, but at some point, Alena's personality must have shifted. Her ambition bled into their relationship, and, unbeknownst to him, she planned to steal his own brilliant light. On that most fateful night, more impactful to him even than the letter to the president, Alena used her magic to entrap him.

That night, as the full moon cast a luminous glow through Alena's sitting room window, she made the choice that would alter the course of both their lives.

Voltaris had known when he'd entered her home that evening that something fundamental had shifted. He no longer felt the depth of presence he so valued in his connection with this brilliant woman. Her attention to him was cursory and impersonal. Though she tried to act as though she were really there with him, he could tell something was afoot.

But he could not have known that the distance he felt was the sign of a true threat, that his value to his beloved was no longer in their connection but in the utility of his mind and his soul for her endeavors.

He didn't realize that, earlier that night, before his arrival, Alena had read over the spell one last time. He didn't realize that this was a pattern she'd practiced—encountering people of interest, enticing them into her life, and then ensnaring them. And so he couldn't know that, despite the depth of their intimacy thus far, Alena's ambition—the power she dreamt of—would uproot their love. She would steal his soul.

That night, as Voltaris traveled to visit her in her beautiful home, he truly had no idea what was to become of him. They sat stoically across from one another in the same arm chairs that had supported them through hours of conversation; but this time, Voltaris knew it was different. The curtains were drawn, protecting their exchange from passersby. The coupe glasses had sat empty on the antique table for nearly an hour when Voltaris finally spoke from his heart.

He pleaded with his love to tell him something, anything, of what was in her heart. Looking back, he knew that, even then, he could see the shadows surrounding her. She was no longer the woman he loved. And he was right.

Her spell was already underway.

When he realized what was coming, he pleaded with her. He called upon her humanity, reminded her of their shared goals to bring peace, not pain, to the world. But as he spoke, he realized how little she cared. Her attentions were elsewhere. He no longer mattered. Imagination was lost. Peace was nowhere to be found.

At the moment of betrayal, rupture tore through his body. It was as though his very essence was rent into pieces. His heart broke, and with it dissolved the understanding with which he perceived the world. His clarity and confidence were lost. He was changed.

Alena's greed had captured his soul, and Voltaris would move through his final days a hull, a shadow of the man he once was. She would keep his soul into the afterlife.

•

There had been fanfare at his death. They'd taken his brain to study it. Reporters rushed about to learn what they could from the whole affair. There seemed to be great fanfare about his mind. Everyone was curious *what* had made him who he was.

But it all meant nothing to him, because existence beyond death would be incomplete without his soul. It was entangled in the practical confines of the living, tethered in magic to Alena's *Book*. He was lost without it.

In those first moments, his form floated through the void. His disembodied essence was caught between worlds. Memories of his life flickered in and out of focus—joyfully uncontrolled laughter, the immeasurable thrill of discovery, and his shattered spirit when Alena wrested his soul from him. He was no longer himself. He could not try to be.

The name came to him as if from the void: "Voltaris," he whispered to himself. It resonated in the darkness, surprising him. A fusion of the ancient words "volta," meaning power, and "aris," meaning rise. He had always sought to rise above the mundane, to harness the power of knowledge and alchemy. Now, that power felt distant, like a candle flickering in the tempest. The name was something for him to hold onto.

Shadows coalesced around him until he stilled. An infinite nothing stretched out before him. The silence weighed on him like a heavy shroud, and Voltaris felt utterly alone. He was a ghost. But he would not surrender to this false death. He was not Einstein; he would not be, not until he was reunited with his soul.

Finally, though, the moment drew near. He'd found Ember, built a bridge between them, and he was ready to show her *The Book*. She was his opportunity to right his wrongs and to find his soul.

Finding Ember had brought him back to himself. With every memory he shared, Voltaris found it easier to connect with those parts of himself too. He had to wonder—was it possible that his soul could sense him? ALl the way in the world of the living, trapped in *The Book of Aeons*, was it possible that his soul could reach him still? The void grew warmer at the thought.

He was dead, but Voltaris did wonder—could it be true that his soul was alive? Could he trust the possibility of another shape of existence?

And, if it was true, and his soul *was* alive, what did it mean to have a soul in the realm of the living?

Ember had seen *The Book* in her visions; he had given insight to her there. Now it was time for Voltaris to talk to Ember directly.

Chapter 18: Thinking Games

Six year old Ember sat cross-legged on a pillow on the floor, across from her grandmother. They faced each other, both of them directing their gentle, clear eyes towards one another.

Momo's sparkling hair rested in a braid across her shoulder; Ember wore the matching braid her grandmother set for her that morning. The two of them were very still, their spines, shoulders, and lips unmoving.

And then Mable began to shake. First her shoulders, and then her chin and chest and belly and knees. And then she began to rock back and forth. Giggles erupted from her and then she was laughing uncontrollably. Ember couldn't help it. Laughter rose up from her belly and she shook and shook until she fell over onto the floor, completely overcome with joy.

When the giggles subsided, and Momo caught her breath, she heaved a big sigh.

"Well, I can confidently say you have mastered the craft, my love," she said to Ember.

Pride welled inside the young Ember, and a smile reached across her face. They'd been playing the thinking game. She didn't quite understand why what she'd been thinking was so funny to her grandmother, but she was delighted at her reaction.

Mabel rolled to the ground to rest beside Ember. "But you must be careful, Ember. No one can know that you can access their minds. And never, never, never offer your own thoughts to another person. No one besides me. Do you hear me?"

Still tickled, Ember agreed wholeheartedly. "No one besides you." She rolled towards her grandmother and gave her a kiss on the cheek.

In another place entirely, Ember blinked her eyes open, feeling the warmth and comfort of her grandmother's joyful presence. She took in the room around her and remembered that she was grown and her grandmother has been gone for a decade at least.

It had been a lovely dream, but it wasn't real. It wasn't now.

She and her grandmother had played that game plenty, right around when she turned eight years old. They would do some sort of quiet activity together, like meditation, and then they simply sat and looked at each other. Ember was so earnest. She sincerely hoped that Momo could actually know what she was thinking.

It was funny to think about it now.

When they played the thinking game, Momo would wait an appropriate amount of time, and then she'd have some sort of explosive reaction. Usually it was some sort of incredulity. The explosion would completely transform the moment.

Ember couldn't help but delight in her grandmother. She had loved the game that made her feel so close to the quiet parts of her Momo, her role model, her friend. She wondered if she would ever feel that sense of clarity and freedom in her life again. Was it possible to find things so easy once you knew how harsh the world really was?

•

Over her breakfast at the dining table, Ember read an early morning email from Dr. Voss. It was an invitation. Dr. Voss had invited her to her home to discuss her next publication.

Reading the email, Ember sensed that something was different. Something about Dr. Voss's communication with her had changed. Does she know that Ember snuck into the laboratory with Max and Olive? Could she be at risk for some kind of chastisement?

And why was Dr. Voss inviting Ember to her home? They usually just met in the university research lab. It was suspicious, for sure.

On the other hand, though, this was an opportunity for Ember to show Dr. Voss that she was serious about their collaboration. Dr. Voss had a national and even global platform for her work. She was respected by the world's most renowned scientists, influential politicians, and prestigious minds. If Ember was going to have the sort of impact she envisioned for her own research, Dr. Voss would be an invaluable advocate. Maybe that's all this needed to be. They could get to know each other a little better. She could build a more personal relationship with her mentor. Yes, that seemed like a brilliant plan. Ideal.

But she had to admit, it had been seeming more and more like Dr. Voss had special plans for her. And she desperately wanted to know what Dr. Voss was up to with her research. Maybe she could use this to her advantage, to gather more information from Dr. Voss's home. If she could get closer to her mentor, maybe this wouldn't be her only opportunity to find out what Dr. Voss was up to in that underground research facility.

Okay. Ember was decided. She would meet Dr. Voss... She read over the email. This morning. She would go with an open mind, but she'd keep her eyes open for clues and do her best to gather whatever details seemed relevant.

She responded succinctly and cordially to Dr. Voss's email. Thrilled at the opportunity to work on the paper. She'd be there at 11.

•

As she passed the turn she usually took to the laboratory in the morning, Ember knew she'd made the right decision to avoid the lab. In an ideal world, she would love to have her friends' take on the situation, but she knew Max and Olive were still working out what they thought about the secret research facility. Ember was getting tired of defending her position to them. And, to be honest, she was also a bit concerned that at least Max if not both of them would be a little jealous of Dr. Voss's invitation to her. She definitely didn't want them to think she was arrogant or to create any more dissonance between them herself. No, it was best to go alone for this one.

The familiar old cobblestone street was one of her favorite places in Landings, and the pleasant morning walk nearly took her mind off all

198

the things she had to worry about. But as she approached Dr. Voss's door, they all came flooding back. Ember stopped to take a breath and take it all in.

So this was Dr. Voss's home. The house before her was quaint and unassuming. It stirred in her some kind of nostalgia, but for what she didn't know. Beyond its simple exterior, Ember could sense a gravity inside those walls.

Ember peered through the front window. She could see a tiny front room, two great armchairs, and a massive bookcase. Why was it all so familiar? *Strange*, she thought to herself, as she took one more step forward and knocked at the old wooden door.

She wanted so much to believe that Dr. Voss was just her teacher, just a brilliant scientist who saw in her something important. She wanted to trust her mentor, but the feeling this house was giving her... she wasn't sure. It seemed like every sign she encountered pointed her in a different, more nuanced, and sometimes more sinister direction.

Dr. Voss answered within a moment and invited Ember in and into her living room. It was the front room that Ember had seen from the street. They sat down in front of the giant window, chairs facing one another.

As she looked around the room, taking in the details of the built-in shelves across the way, the antique lamp, and the gorgeous handwoven rug, Ember had the feeling she had been here before. It felt too... familiar.

Steam rose from the top of the teapot Dr. Voss had positioned carefully on the small table between them. She passed a cup and saucer to Ember.

"Would you like cream and honey?" Dr. Voss asked Ember, as though it were the most normal thing in the world for them to be sipping tea together in her front room.

"Yes, that would be lovely," Ember said, as easefully as she could. "Thank you." She added.

"I'll just grab them from the kitchen."

As soon as Dr. Voss left the room, Ember felt a strong urge to look closer at the treasures in this space. Well, when would she have this opportunity again? She stood casually and walked over to the shelves. Surely Dr. Voss wouldn't mind if Ember just looked like she was admiring Dr. Voss's things.

An extraordinary visual book lay open on a book stand. The pages showed scenes from somewhere far north of Landings—vintage photos of beautiful deep green forests covered in layers of snow. In one picture, moonlight glimmered through the trees.

Ember noticed that the book was set awkwardly in the stand. If she just... As she touched the scenic book to straighten it, Ember suddenly found herself looking at a different book, open in the same stand on the same bottom shelf. The book was familiar. Had she seen it before?

Someone spoke up behind her, and she turned around to see that Dr. Voss was somehow back in her chair. But something was different about her. Her clothes—yes, that was it. Had she changed clothes? Worry flooded her mind as she realized everything was different. The armchairs were quite the same, but their colors were brighter. Instead of a teapot, the little table between the chairs held two coupe glasses that seemed to have been emptied long before now. Dr. Voss's dress was... old-fashioned. It seemed like an antique itself.

Ember knew she needed to say something, but what? She needed to change Dr. Voss's mind, but how?

"Please, beloved. We have shared so much. How can you leave our enduring love to fester like this?" The voice that flowed from her lips was familiar; it was the voice of someone she knew. Whose body did she inhabit?

"Do our shared values mean nothing to you? Peace, wisdom in the pursuit of knowledge? This is not wisdom, Alena. This is theft," the voice trembled as her fear grew.

Dr. Voss deflected every word and phrase along with the tender advances that accompanied them. She turned away. It was then that Ember knew—the spell had been cast. It was already underway, and she was its victim. She felt a rupture within her. It was as though her very essence was being ripped at some imperceptible seam.

Still horrified by what she had just experienced, Ember watched as the world she'd left just moments before returned. She'd had another vision. But she'd been knocked out before—

Dr. Voss reentered the room, rocking Ember out of her reflection. Only then did Ember realize that she was still touching the scenic book. That was not dissimilar to the time she touched the glass vessel or the compass. Could it be that her touch was sparking the visions?

But why were they transporting her into what seemed like other people's memories? Did they have some sort of power?

Ember thought about the times she'd been transported into another person's world. Each of the objects she touched was different; there was no obvious connection among them. Which made Ember wonder—could it be that it wasn't just the objects, but *her* who was stimulating these insights? What sort of physics was this?

Ember smiled at Dr. Voss. "Really lovely book. The pictures are magnificent." She was buying time.

"Oh, yes, those are photos I took on a visit to the taiga years ago. A friend helped me develop them and they eventually made their way into a collection. I'm glad you like them."

She took those photos? They seemed so dated. But Ember had too many things to think about. She couldn't bother with some photos from somewhere thousands of miles away. She returned to her seat, trying her best to keep her cool. Dr. Voss sat down across from her, her eager expression somehow intensely unsettling to Ember.

"Shall we dig in? I'm excited to tell you where the paper is going so far." Dr. Voss's keen expression did not compel Ember's enthusiasm. She really needed to seem interested; she would have to spice up her tone.

"Absolutely," Ember said enthusiastically. "I'm honored you invited me to be involved."

Dr. Voss's eyes caught her own, and Ember felt her walls go up. *Curious,* she thought. *That feels like the boundary Momo and I would practice.* Their thinking game. Why was all of this mind-reading stuff coming up today? First her memories with Momo and now... this?

She needed to pay attention, though. As thoughts raced through her mind, Ember directed all of her body language towards appeasing Dr. Voss. She was trying not to get distracted by the vision she just had. That was Dr. Voss certainly, and she had been in the body of the only other person in the room. The feeling she'd had, just before she came back—it was an incredibly unsettling feeling. Just before the vision shifted back to the present, Ember had recognized a fierce air of danger in her heart. It was almost as though she could feel her life slipping away. And now, for some reason, she had the feeling she should keep her walls up. Did she really need to have a clear boundary with Dr. Voss? She couldn't figure out what it was, but Ember knew that something was going on beneath the surface.

Dr. Voss was going on about the paper. It all seemed above-board as far as Ember could tell. She wanted to focus on the encoding research but from a technology lens. What could encoding photons mean for cloud storage or for data processing? It was a mundane application of quantum physics but relevant and timely nonetheless.

She could only listen to Dr. Voss so well, though. She was constantly drawn back to the image of that book. Not the scenic book—that was lovely, but insignificant. No, Ember kept thinking about the book from the vision. It lay open on the same stand, on the same shelves. She couldn't get it out of her mind.

Though she didn't see its cover, Ember had a feeling this was the same as the one that had been making appearances in her other visions. She couldn't recall the details of the opened pages, but she knew this was no ordinary book. Could it be following her? And whose memories was she entering to see the book? She was getting ahead of herself. She didn't know why she was inhabiting someone else's memories, but she couldn't be concerned with that now.

Ember tried to focus her attention back on her conversation with Dr. Voss, but there was too much to process. And she still felt the need to protect herself.

Meanwhile, Dr. Voss continued her monologue. "What we need to figure out—and this is where I could really use your help, Ember—" she said, obviously trying to ensure Ember's attention was on her. "I'd like to find the best way to translate quantum encoding for a more mainstream technology audience. How can we communicate the value of this tool if we cannot communicate its real-life applications?"

Ember nodded knowingly as Dr. Voss's words rolled through her mind. Her mind was full; there was nowhere for the words to land.

"What do you think?" Dr. Voss asked. All of the sudden, Ember knew it was time to go.

"I'm sorry, Dr. Voss," Ember said tentatively, a look of worry spreading across her face. "I just remembered I had an appointment at the laboratory this morning—I was meant to compare data on..." her voice drifted. "I can't believe I forgot, but I really need to follow up on that." She glanced up at Dr. Voss and saw that her mentor was looking at her intently. "Is it possible we might catch up about this tomorrow?" Ember asked.

Without waiting for a response, she stood. "I really should have remembered..." The story was untrue, but Ember's frantic demeanor was no act. She desperately needed to get out of there, to breath some fresh air and put her feet on solid ground.

Dr. Voss's expression changed from intensity to kindness. "Yes, yes, of course," she said. "Get some fresh air... on your way back to the lab. We'll reconvene to talk about this later. Thank you for coming by."

Ember paused for a moment, confused. She didn't remember saying anything about fresh air out loud. But was that really just a coincidence? Was there a chance Dr. Voss had read her mind? Ember didn't want to think about what else she might know.

Dr. Voss's kind look was eerily suspicious. Yes, there was something deeper in the scientist's stare, and Ember could sense it. Her spine stiffened.

"Thank you for the drink," she said. "I... I'll touch base after I get some rest." She got out of Alena's house as quickly as she could.

●

Back on the cobblestone street she'd known since childhood, Ember paused for a minute to feel the sun on her skin. She literally hadn't thought about those thinking games with Momo in fifteen years. And now, they had come back to her in a dream just hours before her walls instinctively went up with Dr. Voss—walls she hadn't realized were even real before today. What did it mean?

Ember wanted so much to trust Dr. Voss, but it was getting harder and harder to dismiss her own intuition. And how could she really trust anyone, when the wisest people in the world were changing right before her eyes?

Chapter 19: Lifetimes

Alena watched as Ember stepped onto the street, then she shut the door swiftly behind her. She was disheartened. It seemed her plan to coax Ember into working with her was not playing out quite as she'd expected.

What had changed? Even last week, everything had been going swimmingly. Ember was making massive progress with her research; her ambition was guiding her in big directions; and Alena had had every confidence Ember would be excited to help her with her plans.

But today she found Ember's demeanor to be concerning. Ember seemed quite suspicious. That did not bode well for her cooperation. She didn't want to think, but she had to—was it possible her memory spell hadn't worked? Did Ember remember the underground lab?

Whether it had to do with her or not, Something was definitely going on with Ember. When she'd stepped away to the kitchen for a moment to fetch the cream and honey, she returned to find Ember in another trancelike state. It was just like that strange state she had witnessed in the lab the other day. She just couldn't put her finger on it.

Mindlessly, Alena traced Ember's steps through the living room. She paused beside the shelves where Ember had stood, looking back at the window just as the young woman had.

What had Ember been thinking about? Alena looked for clues but found no suggestion of her real work in the room. There were no signs of the underground research *or* her magical endeavors. But the room did stir something else.

Yes, for some reason she couldn't imagine just now, this view sparked a memory deep in Alena's own archives. It may have been the most poignant moment she'd ever experienced in this room. She could almost see herself, sitting in the deep blue armchair, its tall back holding her solid as she contemplated the intensity of her choice. That was the night she'd completed the spell that captured for her the essence she had coveted most. That was the night she had gathered Albert Einstein's soul and sunk it deep into her Collection in *The Book of Aeons*.

●

He had known something when he walked in the door. His eyes held a tenuous curiosity; his shoulders creeped higher towards the round lobes of his ears.

She wasn't surprised at his behavior. Einstein was a perceptive person, and they knew each other well. He would pick up on some sort of difference, some sort of dissonance. But she knew he didn't expect what was coming.

She'd found it difficult to hide her excitement. It was bittersweet for her, of course, to sacrifice their love for complete access to his mind. But once she held the multiple facets of his imagination, his intellect, and his wisdom in her Collection, she would be able to use them precisely how she chose. Who wouldn't prefer the immortal power of knowledge over something so mundane, so worldly, as love?

She knew better. She wouldn't fall victim to the woes of women the world over. She would not let love keep her from her pursuits. Alena would change the world. That was the most important thing—the only thing—that mattered.

Despite Albert's protestations that evening, she breathed one final breath of consent and the spell was complete. She'd known the moment it happened. She had watched as the light left his eyes. The wrinkled lines that shaped his eyes, so often lifted high by his smile, slackened. She felt in her gut the confidence of a mission accomplished. A job well done. Alena Voss had succeeded in harnessing the soul—the intelligence, the curiosity, the wisdom, and the vitality—of the world's most renowned scientist, Albert Einstein.

When he left, he left alone. The man who walked through her door into the streets of Landings was a shell of his former self. Alena had thought, for a moment then, that her decision might haunt her, that stealing the soul of her beloved would break her own heart. But in fact, her response was quite the opposite. Alena had trilled with excitement. For at that moment, more than any moment before, she knew she had the power to take on the world.

●

Alena shook her head, relieving herself of the memory. She set her hand on the shelf and took a deep breath to ground herself.

She had gathered many souls into *The Book*, but Albert's was by far her greatest treasure. And now she pursued another. Ember's soul would be her consolation prize for missing out on Mabel's soul.

Alena had thought often of Mabel lately. It was probably because she was so focused on Ember, but there was something about Mabel's death that almost haunted her. She'd always maintained the idea that it was her own decision *not* to take Mabel's soul. But lately it had felt more as though Mabel had decided that for her.

They'd never spoken of it, of course—not Mabel's soul at least.

Alena was certain that Mabel knew of *The Book of Aeons* and her soul-theft, though they'd only really talked about it once. But that one conversation had been powerfully disarming. Mabel had confronted her in the back stairwell. She pleaded with Alena about... who was it? Strange she couldn't remember now. Mabel had been unsuccessful, though. Alena knew that. She remembered how she'd left her friend on the stairs and gone on to complete the spell to grow her Collection, to capture yet another soul.

But if Mabel had known all about the souls Alena had stolen, maybe she had figured out how to protect herself. Maybe Mabel had put certain precautions in place to prevent Alena from stealing her own soul. Perhaps it hadn't been Alena's choice—her mistake, that was—at all.

Well, it certainly didn't matter now. The whole thing would turn out quite alright if Alena could capture Ember's soul into her Collection.

She wondered now if she should worry. Could Ember's suspicion keep her out of Alena's reach?

If Mabel had been forewarned, if she had created some sort of protection for herself, could Ember have access to that same protection? Well, that would disrupt things quite a bit. All the research, the vision she had for this next phase of work—she needed Ember's input. As her employee or as part of her Collection, one way or the other, Alena would have Ember's knowledge.

Perhaps it was time to begin the spellwork. Yes, she couldn't have her own student thwart her lifelong—lifetimes long at this point—quest in just a few short weeks. She'd get started tonight. Stealing Ember's soul.

●

In the meantime, Alena had more tangible work to do. Her meeting with Ember, despite her lab assistant's evasion, had actually generated some new ideas. That measly publication was not her true focus, though. No, her real focus was much more important.

In just a few short days, Alena would have the opportunity to speak with Charles Hadden. He was an old friend of hers, one might say.

But in truth, their present relationship was far more powerful than any dynamic they'd shared before.

As she approached the next iteration of her work, his collaboration would be invaluable to her. Yes, Hadden could bridge her influence fully into the political realm.

Clearly, the subject matter of this meeting was far more important than that insignificant publication. Who was going to read that? The public? The tech companies? She really didn't care.

No, this meeting was on far more serious matters. It harkened back to the days of the second World War, the conversations they were having then. Hysteria had been rising around the atomic bomb. Politically-intrigued scientists from every corner were scurrying to find what would be the most powerful response to potential German threat. Unsurprisingly, Albert had been sucked into the mess. It had wrecked him. That had been the end of him, as far as she could tell. But, Alena thought cheerfully, those had been simpler times for her. In those days, she was only just getting started.

Alena followed the hallway to the back of the house. She'd take the direct route up to the apothecary now. She needed to stop down in the underground lab. There were a few more materials she wanted to review in preparation for her meeting.

If she succeeded in making a strong impression on Hadden, this meeting would expand into extraordinary opportunities. She could finally look into her future and see the Alena Voss she'd always envisioned herself to be. She would finally get the recognition she deserved. And, most importantly, she would be aeons—*yes*, she smiles, *aeons*—nearer the ultimate fulfillment. Herself, the singularity.

She tucked into the apothecary, dim in the fading afternoon. Downstairs first, then she would begin the spell on Ember. But as Alena reached for the door that led to the underground laboratory, she thought better of it. Things were a bit off for her today. Perhaps she should be more careful, just in case. Surely she had time for a quick shield charm. Yes, that was the right move. Protection. That's where she would begin.

The Book of Aeons glowed from its place on the shelf. It had been much more lively lately, she had to admit. Must be because her big plans were finally unfolding. Yes, her magic was thriving. It was inspiring to see *The Book of Aeons* come alive in her presence. She pulled it down from the shelf. Now, she would put it to use.

Voltaris

Chapter 20: Sentience

Ember took the long way home. She wanted to walk as far as she could along the old cobblestone road. It was one of the oldest roads in Landings, so old that it was closed to cars now to preserve the unique stone surface. She relished slow walks along these tired stones. She found it comforting. Today, in particular, the walk was settling her nerves.

She had her head down, watching each footstep meet the road, when Momo reentered her mind. Her heart swelled, and memories of her grandmother came rushing in. She let them. It felt good to recall what it was like when she was little and had all the time in the world to spend with her beloved grandmother. Her imagination was so expansive in those days. She wondered what kind of perspective that childhood imagination would bring her now.

As she walked, the rhythm of Ember's footsteps on her journey home became regular, almost meditative, and she entered a sort of trance. She took in the landscape of the room in her memory—Momo's quiet room. She could see the colors, smell all sorts of scents; she took in the unique shapes and textures, the vibrancy of the space.

Everything had a role in the quiet room. Whether it was magic or science, Momo always had something to teach Ember. As she gazed upon the room in her memory, one object in particular caught her attention: a frame on the edge of her grandmother's desk. Ember remembered admiring the photo in that frame when was very young, maybe five or six years old. It was a photograph of her grandmother as a young woman, 20 or 25, and she was with two older friends. They were well-dressed, her grandmother and the woman in sleek skirt suits and the man too. Her five-year old mind had thought they must be ever so important to be dressed up so nicely. But had she ever asked Momo about the photo?

In her mind's eye now, Ember couldn't help but think the woman in the photo looked *exactly* like Dr. Voss. How had Ember not realized it before? She had known that face practically her whole life.

And... the other person in the photo was suddenly unmistakeable. Because the other person in Momo's photo, Ember realized now, was none other than Albert Einstein.

Somehow, through Ember's memories, the channels opened. The image came to life, the three figures walking in step beside her along the old stone road. But Momo and the woman who looked just like Dr. Voss both began to fade into the air, their shapes disintegrating. Only one figure remained.

Ember turned her head to look directly at the form of Albert Einstein. But he was different from the man in the photo and most of the photos she'd seen. He was older, certainly, and more tired. A shadow drifted around him, as though the man's own weariness had taken on the dark of night. But he smiled at Ember, and instantly she felt the integrity of this person. This was no picture.

Ember could hear the knock of Einstein's boots against the ground. Though they were soft, she knew this was something more than a vision. Albert Einstein was right here beside her. How was this happening? She slowed her pace to take it all in. She felt as though she was walking with a friend; but she knew this friend had been dead longer than he was alive.

"Hello, Ember."

The figure spoke. Ember tried to keep herself together. But of all the strange things she had experienced lately, this was by far the most unexpected one.

"I'm delighted to finally meet you," he said.

"How... wha... Hello," Ember conceded. If she was going to figure out what was happening here, she had to start somewhere. "Hello, Dr. Einstein?" she said, his name turned up in inquiry. What was she supposed to call one of the most brilliant minds to ever walk the earth?

"Well, these days I think of myself as Voltaris. I've had to come to terms with a lot of change. Sometimes it's easier to just let old parts of yourself go, you know." He spoke comfortably, as though they had talked many times before. "But I'm hoping... I'm hoping you can help me get back to myself."

"*I* can help you?" Ember asked.

"You, Ember Quinn, might just be the *only* person who can help me."

Finally, his opportunity had come. Voltaris unwound, one by one, the threads of her story that Ember didn't yet grasp.

"I've been reaching out to you," he said, "inviting you into my memories. I'm sure you've noticed."

"It *was* you," Ember said, astounded at the truth of it. As her visions went on, she had suspected they were memories. Once or twice she'd thought that maybe that could have been Einstein's. But even then she had only thought it was a coincidence, that maybe something in her own consciousness was reaching to understand the life of her inspiration. She never suspected in any way that Albert Einstein—or, Voltaris, as he'd called himself—she never suspected that he was reaching out to her. That he was trying to communicate with her.

She was astounded. His revelation left her with a single question:

"Why?" Ember asked. The question lingered between them.

On either side of the street, old buildings rose up two and three floors from the ground. Most of these homes were at least a hundred years old. Along with the cobblestone road, the houses shaped an historic scene. Ember always felt as though the past was almost palpable here, among these structures.

Many of the old homes had been transformed from weary houses into museums, galleries, or businesses. She knew a painter who kept a studio in the upstairs of the yellow one up the way.

But this afternoon the street was eerily quiet, and Ember felt her question echo through the history. Why her? Why had Voltaris been reaching out to *her* to help him? Why now?

He'd been dead for decades. Was there some reason he needed her help now? Voltaris interrupted Ember's reeling thoughts.

"There is a *Book*. It's not like other books. A book for the ages, they called it."

The book. She'd known there was something about the book that kept passing through her mind. She thought of her dreams. "Is this the same…"

"This is the same. *The Book of Aeons* is no ordinary book. I believe there is a connection between you. Certainly, there is a connection between your story and the story of *The Book* itself.

"I thought it might be easier, when this moment finally arrived, if you had some recognition of *The Book* to draw upon. I suppose I hoped this might all seem a bit more believable…"

Believable!? She could have laughed out loud. Here she was walking alone along one of the most idyllic streets in her town and talking to a… ghost? And she'd just come from her advisor's house where she'd had yet another vision and faked sickness to get out of there and… Honestly, nothing was really in the vicinity of believable today. And yet, that book and the visions and her suspicions of Dr. Voss—they all seemed so real.

"Yes, it's real," he continued. "And it's not far from us now. I do suspect you've realized that Dr. Voss is not what she seems…" He paused for a moment, as though waiting for Ember to respond, but she didn't know what to say. Not right away, at least. Voltaris went on, but his voice dropped.

He was so quiet that Ember couldn't help but wonder if anyone else would actually be able to hear him. He was some kind of ghost, right? But his quiet was enticing. She felt as though he was divulging extraordinary scientific secrets that no one else should know about.

"*The Book* is in her possession. It has been for more than a century. With it, she has wreaked havoc among some of the greatest minds in the world.

"The thing is, Ember... Alena isn't content with the damage she's already done. She will continue to pursue power until the day she dies. I fear that her plans for your research are menacing. Explosive. But right now, her most enticing target is you.

"You have something that Alena can't touch. Some might call it magic."

Ember wanted so badly to roll her eyes, laugh out loud, and pretend all of this was nonsense. But she knew too much already. She listened attentively, praying for clues that grounded these wild stories into her reality.

"She's more and more convinced every day that you are worth her attention. I've seen it with my own eyes."

"I mean, I'm doing my best. Our research has proven really successful, and she's asked for my help with an upcoming publication," Ember was drawing down lists in her mind of what might validate her importance in Dr. Voss's eyes.

"Yes, your research is certainly part of it. I can tell you that for sure."

What did he mean *what she'd found*?

She worked alongside Dr. Voss and Max and Olive; their research was hardly unique to her. True—the project she led was the most promising at the moment. Their findings demonstrated clear success:

the photons with diverse inputs. But even that was challenged by the fact that the data only showed success when she performed the experiment, not when Max or Olive did it. It still meant more than 50% success, because she did most of the experiments. But it was an odd finding.

But none of this seemed news to him.

"The suspicion you have about your research is spot on," Voltaris said assuringly. "The photons are interpreting the information you encode. But that is not nearly as special as the results that show the photons recognize when *you* are the one performing in the experiment.

"We have long suspected that photons are sentient, but generations of quantum physicists have struggled to prove something so esoteric as this. I am quite certain, in fact, that the photons have kept their own sentience secret. Why wouldn't they?" a grin spread across his face. And then he became more serious again. "Until now."

Was Voltaris suggesting that the photons had revealed this fundamental secret to no one but her? What made her worthy of such information? Suspense was building in Ember's chest.

"I think the photons have chosen to reveal this information to you for a reason, Ember. But all we know right now is that it has something to do with you.

"If Alena catches even a whiff of the idea that the photons are responsive to you, her desire for your soul will become insatiable. Because, Ember, if you—you alone, out of all the scientists who have ever performed these experiments—if you have some effect on the photons, well... That would mean that you might be able to connect consciously with them. And if a person can consciously communicate with the smallest possible particles of electromagnetic energy, it would revolutionize the world. *You* would revolutionize the world."

His statements were wild. They rattled the bounds of Ember's consciousness. His suggestion compelled her to think. If photons were *always* sentient and they were somehow willing to show *her* this truth, now, then she might be able to communicate with them. If she could understand the photons and they could understand her, it would open up new worlds of communication.

In that case, the tech paper she'd spoken about with Dr. Voss this morning would be entirely obsolete. They wouldn't be interested in data storage and transfer. They would be exploring a whole new universe, a permeating sentience beyond their imaginations.

If they were working with conscious, responsive, and communicative photons, the possibilities were genuinely infinite.

"I believe the photons have chosen you not because you are special or because you are destined for some powerful greatness, though well you may be" Voltaris offered. "I believe they have chosen you because you speak the language of magic. Ember, you recognize a world beyond conventional limits, and you know how to go there. I can sense it in your presence now.

"This is why we must protect you. But this is also why I need your help and yours alone."

Ember was doing everything she could to find a place for each one of Voltaris's words to her now.

"Alena's intelligence extends far beyond her work at your laboratory or even the research she's conducting in the underground facility. She is also magic, but she has developed her power in a very specific direction. She has chosen a path of mastery and control, and it has robbed her of her sense of trust. Along her journey, Alena has stolen the good magic—the creativity, the imagination, the potential, and the peace—whenever she could. She stole mine, divided my soul from my body, and..." He trailed off into silence.

Ember thought of the vision she'd had just that morning. The spell, the rupture—that was Voltaris. What she'd felt—that was the feeling of Voltaris losing his soul.

The air grew tighter around her. Her nerves were on edge. That must be what Voltaris meant when he said *she* was Dr. Voss's most enticing target. Dr. Voss wanted Ember's magic. She wanted her soul.

"What do I do?" The words escaped Ember's mouth before she had a moment to think. But Voltaris responded kindly.

"That's the tricky part, I suppose," he said candidly. "You see, I have been reaching out to you to ask you a grand favor, a miraculous favor. I want you to retrieve *The Book* from Alena and bring it to me. I have my own mission to fulfill on this course of ours. But, whether I'm alive or dead, I can do nothing of consequence without my soul."

"Ember," he pleaded. "This is essential—not just for me, but for you, your research, and, I suspect, ripples far beyond our knowledge. I need you to bring *The Book* to me, to reunite me with my soul."

"But if Dr. Voss is dangerous..."

"Oh that she is. Which is another reason it must be you. In all the years that I've been dead, I haven't found another person I trusted to complete this task. You must be swift and careful. You must use your magic to your advantage. And you must stay out of Alena's way."

"How will I use my magic to my advantage?"

"The objects," Votlaris said. He obviously thought this was well-known information. "That's how I've been connecting with you. You have a way with objects. When you touch them, they reveal their stories. The vessel, the compass... Haven't you ever noticed?"

"Yes," Ember said. "This morning I realized..."

"Good. That's a starting place," he interrupted her. "I'm sure there's much more to your gifts, my dear, but we haven't time to explore all of that. I know what Alena is up to in her underground laboratory, and we must do whatever we can to halt her efforts. The world is already on fire. But if Alena Voss gains more power, we will surely see it burn to dust

"You've been to Alena's house. Now we need to get you into her apothecary." Her apothecary? Ember had no idea what Voltaris was talking about, but she suspected she would find out soon enough.

Chapter 21: Whistleblower

Ember didn't go home. What good would it do Ember to be anxious and stressed all alone at her apartment? She knew her mind would just spin. No, she wanted to work.

She shifted direction, back towards the university. The atmosphere grew busy as she neared campus. Houses gave way to storefronts, and people scurried in and out, down the sidewalks and into their cars, bringing an agitated energy that couldn't be calmed by the afternoon breeze. But was the frenzy real? Or was she seeing the world through her own unsettled lens?

She was processing the contents of the past hour. Albert Einstein was not simply a name in a book or a historical figure from her studies—not anymore. How would she describe him? *Voltaris*, the name echoed in her thoughts. A consciousness that had fractured, survived, and reached her. Voltaris. A soulless being whose essence was held captive by her esteemed advisor and boss Dr. Alena Voss.

They had known each other—Einstein and Dr. Voss. And, if her memory served and that photo was real, they had known Momo too.

All of this news had come to her after she'd left Dr. Voss's house in a hurry, attempting to escape her confusion. She'd had yet another uncanny vision, one that made her wonder if there was something she must protect from her mentor.

Ember stopped walking and leaned against the cool brick wall of a student-run café. The recognition landed with such force that it nearly took her knees out from under her. Dr. Voss wasn't just a brilliant physicist with unconventional interests. She wasn't just a mentor who'd kept certain projects private. She was dangerous, manipulative, and single-minded in her goals.

The threat was no longer abstract. Dr. Voss knew how Ember spent her time. She knew her research, her habits, her eccentricities. She knew her blindspots. Did she know Ember discovered her secret research? Did she see Ember as a threat?

Yes, there was something Ember must protect. Ember absolutely had something to protect: Her character. Her sanity. Her research. Her life.

Ember felt fear bloom fully in her chest for the first time. This wasn't the constant anxiety she'd grown used to these past few weeks, nor the intellectual alarm of recognizing a dangerous idea. This was unmistakable fear. Dr. Voss wasn't hiding information out of academic caution. She was hiding it because it was her weapon. Dr. Voss's intentions were dangerous. If she realized Ember's discovery—that photons were sentient—well, Ember didn't want to imagine what might unfold.

Voltaris's account had woven together the loose ends she'd collected: the visions, the dreams, Dr. Voss's focused interest on her, the underground research facility. She couldn't begin to wrap her mind around how Dr. Voss maintained her youth. She should be well over 100 years old by now...

She thought of Max and Olive then, instinctively searching for steady ground. Too many pieces of this story were truly bizarre. They would be difficult, if not impossible, for her friends to believe.

She wanted to tell them everything—to sit down across from them and say, "I'm not losing my mind. I'm not exaggerating. Something is happening to me, and to us, and to our work."She wanted them to ask the right questions, to tease out the logic, to make all of this make sense.

But she couldn't imagine how to begin.

How could she explain that she'd been at Dr. Voss's house that morning without sounding compromised? How could she tell them Dr. Voss was in a photograph with her grandmother *and* Einstein without sounding delusional? How could she accuse their mentor of something so profound and dangerous without evidence she could lay flat on the table between them?

Ember wanted so badly to tell them everything. She craved Olive's calm, measured support and even Max's rigorous, inquisitive perspective. But she knew how this would look from the outside. Plenty of scientists would pathologize her—a student over-identifying with her mentor, a researcher mistaking intuition for insight, or, worse, a bright woman whose mind was unraveling under pressure.

But Ember knew what had been happening for her. She had no doubt that she entered a secret door through Dr. Voss's office. She had no doubt that the visions were coming more and more consistently, that they were sparked by old objects and her own light touch. Ember had less and less doubt that this wasn't some random combination of events, a strange collection of stories. *No*, she thought, pushing herself off the stone wall and turning towards the physics building. *This is about me.*

●

The lights in the laboratory hummed quietly, their familiar sound a comfort to her as she entered the space. She dropped her bag beneath her workspace and stood for a moment without moving, breathing in the faint scent of ozone and metal and recycled air. Normally, this place steadied her. The order of it—the precise alignment of mirrors, the careful placement of lenses, the quiet discipline of the optical table—gave her something solid to hold onto. She hadn't realized how much she counted on that, until today.

This afternoon, the laboratory only reminded her how fragile that order was.

Her hands moved through the setup automatically, adjusting the pulse timing, recalibrating the detectors. But her attention kept slipping. The numbers on the screen blurred. The graphs refused to settle into anything meaningful. Every time she thought she saw a pattern, it dissolved into dots and lines, lost to her overwhelmed consciousness.

Eventually, Ember realized she had been staring at the same data set for nearly ten minutes without registering a single variable.

This was pointless.

She shut down the system and leaned against the edge of the table, closing her eyes. Images pressed in immediately: the view through the telescope at the observatory, the impossible clarity of the stars; watching Einstein break as he lost his soul in Dr. Voss's sitting room; the weightless presence of Voltaris, an icon torn from the meaning of his own profound life.

She opened her eyes again, heart pounding.

She had been intentionally vague with Max and Olive when she'd arrived, brushing off their questions about why she'd been so late coming in. She hadn't lied outright; she'd simply let them assume she'd been home. It was the first time she'd ever done something like that with them, and the discomfort of her omission lingered like a bruise. She didn't want to become that person—one who withheld, who calculated, who feared being misunderstood more than telling the truth.

"Are you coming with us tonight?" Olive's voice startled Ember from her stupor, and she nearly jumped off her seat. "Max and I are going for drinks. You seem like you could use one." She gave Ember a wink.

Ember managed a smile. "Sure."

She saw a window. Maybe she could let some steam off, clear her mind. Maybe they could talk about things that didn't matter quite so much as all of this.

●

But it turned out that there was nothing that mattered so much as this. As they walked through campus, something felt different, taut, like a cloth pulled too tight from its corners. As they approached the administration, they saw why.

A crowd had gathered on the steps, students packed shoulder to shoulder, signs raised above their heads. Their energy was angry and forceful. The students chanted harshly: "Disclose! Divest! Disclose! Divest!"

"What is this?" Olive asked, scanning the growing body of students. "Divest from what?"

The students lifted signs above the crowd: "Transparency Now," "No More Lies," and "Who Governs the Governors?" "Snap the SNA," and "Edmonston Divest!"

Max slowed, pulling out his phone. "Something's happened," he said, already scrolling. "This just broke."

They stopped at the edge of the crowd as Max read aloud, his voice tightening with each sentence. An anonymous whistleblower had released a cache of documents less than an hour earlier—internal communications, financial records, medical reports. The Sovereign Nations Alliance, an organization meant to function as a stabilizing force for global peace, stood exposed as deeply compromised. Seven of the world's most influential leaders were implicated, including the U.S. representative. False economic reports, suppressed conflict data, covert research initiatives buried beneath humanitarian language— the issues were widespread and comprehensive. It was unbelievable.

Within fifteen minutes, the documents had been mirrored across servers worldwide.

"This can't be real," Olive murmured.

Max kept scrolling. "They're denying it. Saying they have no memory of authorizing any of it. One is claiming temporary psychosis. Another, amnesia."

Ember felt something click uncomfortably into place.

"They don't remember?" she asked, her voice barely audible.

Max nodded. "That's their story. Medical evaluations pending. Wow—listen to this." He frowned at the screen. Imports are being cut: food, tech, textiles. As soon as tomorrow. There's talk of military escalation if accountability isn't established."

"What do you think this means for us?" Olive asked the question none of them wanted to answer. For years, the threat of international conflict involving the U.S. had lingered a short distance away. Everyone lived with a certain level of apprehension—one wrong political move could turn an enemy against the U.S. But this news was so much worse.

This wasn't about a singular opposition; this was the whole world. Ember, Max, and Olive had known a tenuous stability their whole lives long, but those foundations had cracked. Their sense of stability was rapidly falling into the abyss. And their own government was responsible.

Max looked ominously at Ember and Olive as one final forecast fell from his lips: "There's talk of war."

Chapter 22: Truth

The bar was louder than usual, the televisions above the counter replaying the same breaking news on a loop. Ember barely tasted her drink. Her mind kept returning to the first moment she'd known something was wrong—the scrap of paper she'd found on the lab floor, covered in equations that were not speculative but derived. It showed results, not theory.

Ember made a decision.

"I need to tell you something," she said.

Max looked up, attentive despite the chaos. Olive turned fully toward her.

They'd just learned that the world was on fire. It was all over campus, all over the media. It was the only thing anyone was talking about at this bar. And still it felt unbelievable. Was it too much to ask them to listen tonight?

Ember stared at the condensation sliding down her glass. She feared the worst consequences from this global unraveling, and she couldn't hold all of this alone any longer. She knew, somehow, that the stakes were higher than she realized.

Ember took a breath. "The amnesia the SNA rep reported. It's eerily familiar. It feels connected to what I've been trying to tell you—how our memories aren't intact."

If she could take Max back to that moment when he was reading the page from Dr. Voss's research... If Olive could just remember how worried she'd been when they'd discovered the underground research facility. Now, more than anything, Ember hoped she could get through to her friends. She didn't want to do this alone any longer.

But she'd started too quickly, tried to reveal the most important points before laying out what had actually happened. She began again.

"Do you remember the last time we were here together?"

She looked between Max and Olive. So far she was ringing no bells with this story. She had to keep going.

"I remember things you don't. Things we did together." Ember described the last time they'd been at the bar, finding the research, and returning to the lab. She recounted their discovery of the underground laboratory.

She unpacked the whole story for them. She told them how the story faded for her too, but her memory came back slowly the following day. And she didn't stop there.

This time, Ember told them everything. She told them about the visions she'd had in the laboratory, up at the observatory, and even in Dr. Voss's house. That last bit got Max's attention.

Max's expression grew serious. "If she is really as dangerous as you say, you wouldn't go to Dr. Voss's house. Not alone like that."

"I didn't know then," Ember said. "I know now."

Olive leaned forward. "I have this foggy feeling when I think about that last night we were here. It's almost like the memories are just...

missing. I don't remember anything after leaving here." Olive caught Ember's eyes and held them. It felt like she was trying to see *into* Ember, to figure out what Ember knew that they didn't.

"Ember," she said carefully, "how do you know our memories are wrong and yours aren't?"

Ember hesitated. Max scrolled through his phone, scouring the news for details about the unfolding crisis. His attention was elsewhere, but Olive's question was so sincere. Ember went on. "Because the inconsistencies line up with the physics," she said. "The interference patterns. The anomalies we've been seeing—they mirror what's happening cognitively. Photons carry information. They retain signatures. If consciousness leaves an imprint—"

Max threw his phone against the table and then quickly bent back over it to read. "Hold on. This can't be true." His finger raced across the screen, then he froze.

"Oh," he said. "Oh no."

"What?" Olive asked. Ember's story might as well have evaporated from both of their minds.

Max turned the screen toward them. "One of the leaked documents references experimental protocols. Cognitive interference mediated by photonic fields."

The room began to spin, and Ember closed her eyes trying to regain her focus. Could it be?

"That's us," Max said slowly. "Not exactly, but very close. Same principles. Same math."

The room tilted on some undefined axis. What did this mean?

"It's already happening," Max's voice grew distant. "They're using it."

For the first time that night, he looked at Ember not with skepticism, but with recognition.

"We're in this," he said.

Olive nodded, her face pale but resolute.

The world was changing faster than any of them had imagined. Were they now at the center of it?

Chapter 23: Masterminds

Olive lifted the conference badge and pinned it against her jacket. Max wrestled his into position on his pristine buttondown. It was clear they both felt awkward about trying to make everything seem normal.

The lobby of the conference center buzzed with the familiar frequency of academic events: clusters of attendees in amicable discussions near poster boards and coffee cups balanced precariously on stacks of programs. The rush of the morning was anything but romantic for Max and Olive, though. The lobby smelled faintly of burnt espresso and printer toner. And though there was nothing to suggest the kind of danger the students had recognized the night before, they were wary nonetheless.

Max had barely slept.

A lot had changed for him in the last 36 hours. But what had made him willing to spend an entire day shadowing his own advisor like a conspiracy theorist was not just the news cycle, or the protests outside the university, or even the memory gaps Ember had walked them through with such painful precision. It was the look on her face when she connected the Sovereign Nations Alliance representative's "amnesia" to their own missing time. The quiet certainty in her voice when she connected the two. It was only reinforced when he found their research among the experimental protocols in the SNA leak.

Max trusted data. He trusted equations. He trusted models that held up under pressure.

And he could no longer doubt that Ember understood what was at stake on a deep level. He didn't quite get it—the visions and the dreams—but he wanted to figure it out.

"We're early," Olive murmured, scanning the QR code printed on the back of her badge to check out the conference schedule.

"Good," Max said. "Maybe we can find her before things get started."

Olive raised an eyebrow. "She's probably setting up in the presentation room... 102 at 1:00."

"I would be interested in knowing what that looks like—setting up for a data encryption seminar. I wonder if we would be suspicious, just dropping by..."

"Max," Olive said, "we have seen Dr. Voss three or four or five times a week for years. If the underground research facility really exists, it's been there for at least that long. Dr. Voss hasn't changed her behavior towards me this week. I really don't think she has a reason to suspect anything. Besides, why wouldn't we be going to hear such a preeminent-physicists-who-happens-to-be-our-mentor speak?" Olive added a little tone of derision to punctuate her point.

"I wouldn't be so sure," Max said carefully. "The level of manipulation this whole story would require might just confirm the opposite is true: that she has suspected us all along. What did you say she's calling this seminar?"

Max scanned his own badge for the conference schedule. "Dr. Alena Voss," he read. "Data Encryption and Emerging Security Paradigms."

He pronounced every word with care. He didn't want to lose any meaning.

The seminar title raised his hackles immediately. Encryption was not Alena's public specialty. It was adjacent to her work, but as far as he knew it wasn't public. It certainly wasn't what she promoted through her university position.

And yet the abstract attached to her talk was polished, confident, and laced with the kind of language that reached beyond physicists and even other scientists. It had a tone that was becoming far too familiar to him recently. "Robust identity verification," it said. "Resilient informational systems. Essential frameworks for global application."

"Max," Olive said quietly, tapping the schedule. "Look at this."

He followed her finger.

Charles Hadden—Panelist, *Scientific Innovation in Global Economics*.

Max felt a flare of something like excitement, quickly followed by disgust and disquiet.

Hadden was a name he knew well. Policy papers, advisory boards, keynote lectures delivered in rooms far grander than this one— Hadden was a bridge figure, meaning he spoke fluently to scientists and politicians alike. He translated theoretical breakthroughs into funding streams and regulatory frameworks. And his influence was a heated topic in ethics courses at Edmonston and across the country.

"What is he doing here?" Max asked incredulously. "I had no idea this event had that much pull. And why would Edmonston bring such a controversial figure to a university-sponsored conference? I can't believe it."

"Maybe it's an opportunity," Olive replied, "for us to gather some more information."

"Yes," Max's eyes brightened. "I think so. This could be huge."

Before Olive could respond, a familiar voice cut through the hum of conversation.

"Max. Olive."

They turned together.

Dr. Voss stopped just outside of "too close." She stood with her usual power and grace as a practiced smile spread across her face. In that moment, Max had the unsettling sensation that she'd been there long before they had noticed her, watching.

"How nice to see you both here," she said. "I didn't realize you were interested in the security aspect of our work." The statement landed more like a question—*Why are you here?*—laden with admonition—*You shouldn't be here.*

Max forced a laugh. "We're expanding our horizons."

"Of course we're interested in the applications of our work," Olive said sincerely.

"Good," she said, smiling. "We physicists must always pay attention to the life of our research in the world. Keep the pulse on it, so to speak."

Olive nodded, careful. "Are you tabling before your presentation?" She hoped to shift the conversation and ease the discomfort growing in her belly.

"No," Dr. Voss said blandly. "I think I'll sit in on the panel. It's important to understand how others frame these questions."

Max caught the subtle emphasis on *frame*.

"Of course," he said. "We were just talking about that."

Dr. Voss's gaze lingered on him for a beat longer than necessary, then she nodded her head, turning away from them. "See you this afternoon," she said over her shoulder. Max and Olive watched as Dr. Voss disappeared into the crowd with the ease of someone who belonged here. Their relief filled the space she'd left behind.

"That," Olive said under her breath, "was not nothing. Let's go."

Max nodded. They had a job to do.

●

He had finally given Ember the attention she had been requesting for days.

After reading that last bit of news, Max had quickly realized *he* was implicated in this rising chaos. When Ember recounted her story yet again, it lay before him like a trail of crumbs. His remaining doubts took a back seat to the data he could draw from, including that unfortunate thread that wove their research into the corruption at play.

As Max unwound the story, the one that identified a specific document from the SNA illuminating the existence of cognitive interference programs using what appeared to be the very same photon developments they were exploring—well, suffice it to say he was motivated. Yes, there was a chance it was someone else's research feeding the SNA's obscene activities. But there was no denying the fundamentals of their research were present.

And Ember had grown such a profound distrust for Dr. Voss, having something to do with Einstein. And maybe her grandmother. It was a stretch, to be sure, but something in him sensed he should take her at her word. After all, if these recent hours had taught him anything, it was that there was plenty he didn't know.

That had been the turning point—the moment when the three of them, sitting shoulder to shoulder in the bar, had stopped arguing about whether Ember's experiences *were possible* and started asking *what they should do*. They'd approached the problem together the way they could: analytically, intellectually, strategically.

Ember was bent on getting a certain book—supposedly some sort of witchcraft or the like—from Dr. Voss's home. From her apothecary, Ember had said. Max could believe that bit. Dr. Voss could easily have an apothecary. He thought of the long purple cloak she wore into the lab on the coldest winter days. She did have certain characteristics of a witch. And regardless, he felt it was important now to see this through to the other side, to learn what lay across this bridge of understanding they had crafted. Max was finding more and more that he was inside of this mysterious adventure now.

So while Max and Olive followed Dr. Voss through her day, including her presentation at the conference, Ember would sneak into their advisor's home, find this extraordinary book, and they would reconvene after. In the meantime, they'd let Ember know if Dr. Voss changed location. And Max couldn't help but hope he might catch a glimpse of Dr. Voss's hidden character himself. Perhaps, with his new understanding, he would catch her in action, unassuming and unprotected. If she really was so dangerous, so evil, as Ember seemed to think, perhaps Dr. Voss would reveal some facet of this deeper layer today, at this unique event.

He didn't know what to expect, but Max sensed something big was coming.

●

They followed Dr. Voss at a distance, careful not to make it too obvious that they had any particular interest in panelists and especially in Hadden. The panel hall was already filling when they slipped into the back row, the lights dimming as the moderator took the stage. Max leaned forward, elbows on his knees, as the panelists were introduced one by one.

When Charles Hadden's name was announced, the room shifted.

He didn't look like Max expected. The photos didn't do him justice. He was older, yes, but not frail. His posture was relaxed rather than stiff, his expression thoughtful rather than severe. He spoke with the easy authority of someone who was used to being listened to. His voice carried through the auditorium without effort.

The panel began innocuously enough—discussions of innovation pipelines, the responsibilities of research institutions, the challenges of global collaboration in unstable times. Max found himself nodding along, until Hadden leaned forward and said, "We need to stop pretending that neutrality is an option."

The panelists on stage looked incredulously at the man. He had usurped the trajectory, the audience's attention, and the premise of the panel itself entirely.

"In times of global instability," Hadden continued, "research does not exist in a vacuum. Information moves faster than regulation, faster than ethics committees, faster than public understanding. If responsible actors do not take the lead in applying new technologies, less responsible ones will."

Max felt his jaw tighten. He did not trust this person.

Hadden spoke next about *cognitive resilience*. About the dangers of misinformation. About the fragility of democratic systems under psychological strain.

"There are moments," Hadden said calmly, "when influence is not coercion but protection. When stabilizing perception is an ethical imperative."

Max's admiration curdled into something sharp and bitter.

"That's not protection," he muttered.

Olive glanced at him. "This is it," she whispered. "He's talking about our work. Listen."

Hadden went on to describe systems that could *verify intent, filter destabilizing inputs, maintain continuity of leadership under extreme stress.* He never mentioned photons. Never mentioned consciousness. But the language was close enough that Max could feel the echo of their equations vibrating beneath his ribs.

This was what Ember had been trying to tell them.

When the panel ended, Max stood abruptly.

"I need air," he said.

They followed the flow of people out into the hallway, pushing through as the press of bodies broke apart into smaller conversations.

Max's mind raced. He could almost visualize the pieces clicking into place with a clarity that made him dizzy.

"This is it," he said, stopping short in front of an unmarked door. "This is what our work looks like when it leaves the lab."

He pushed the door open—

And froze.

Dr. Voss stood inside, mid-conversation, Charles Hadden beside her.

For a fraction of a second, surprise flickered across her face. Then anger. Then—smooth as glass—composure.

"Max," she said warmly. "Olive. Glad to see our paths have crossed again."

Olive's mouth went dry.

Max recovered first. "Dr. Hadden," he said, stepping forward and extending a hand. "I was impressed by your comments on the panel, particularly your emphasis on ethical application."

Hadden's eyes sharpened with interest as he shook Max's hand. "Ah. One of Dr. Voss's students, I presume."

"Yes," Max said.

The smile that spread across Dr. Voss's face did not reach her eyes.

"We're lucky to learn with Dr. Voss. No one more intriguing in the realm of physics in my mind," Max offered, meaning to appease his mentor. He motioned to Olive, as though to include her in the conversation, but Olive kept her distance. She stood clear and quiet beside Max as she looked inquiringly at Hadden. For a brief moment, he caught her eye, and she felt a burning in her chest. Without a word, Olive turned towards the door.

"Well," Max continued lightly, "we'll let you get back to it. See you shortly, Dr. Voss."

He followed Olive out, closing the door gently behind them. They didn't speak until they were safely down the hall.

"Max," Olive breathed, "that man is devoid of goodness."

"They know each other," Max said, disbelief echoing in his voice. "Well. Dr. Voss and Hadden..." He paused. "Olive, what if they're working together?"

The same worry was building in Olive's mind. Everything Ember said about Dr. Voss, everything she said the being Voltaris had told her about their mentor—it all was coming together. Dr. Voss wasn't just a university standard, a prolific academic, or a science-shifting academic. No, if she was this friendly with Charles Hadden, it only stood to reason that she really did have global influence.

"Do you think the photon applications from the leak—do you think they originated from her?" Max asked, incredulity in his voice. But the suspense didn't linger. For both of them, the answer was yes.

247

"We have to tell Ember," Olive said. "She may be in even more danger than we realize. Surely Dr. Voss has some sort of security system at her house. We need to let her know about what Hadden's up to and their relationship *now*."

"You're right, but, Olive, wait— Ember is safer if we keep Dr. Voss within reach. The most important thing is that Ember gets out of that house without Dr. Voss intercepting her. So we'll make sure of that."

They stayed at the conference for the rest of the afternoon.

Not because they wanted to, but now they understood how very much they had to.

And because Ember needed time.

Chapter 24: Apothecary

Ember turned onto the familiar road. This was one of the oldest cobblestone streets in her quiet town.

She had always loved Landings for its history. It felt like stories were gathered safely here, like they were stashed in the stone walls and wooden buildings that had stood for a century or more. They ushered her along her way, as though her own story—the one unfolding just now—was being added to their register. As a child, she had felt so lucky to have such a special place to call home. Now, all her studies, her work in quantum physics—they only underscored the truth she felt so clearly in this moment. She was a part of this place.

Ember walked quickly through the quiet midmorning. She knew Alena wouldn't be home. They had decided it all the night before.

Finally, her friends believed her story. Well, maybe *tolerated* was more accurate. Nevertheless, things had changed between the three of them. Ember felt confident in their collaboration now.

She wondered at what they were doing now, following Dr. Voss through the conference. It must be an especially interesting place to be, considering the revelations of the previous day. Surely, people would be aflutter with nervous energy, anxious to find opportunity and resolution for the growing crisis. Ember felt an urgency, an anxiety quickening in her belly, but she knew she was on the right track. She had to believe this was the right track.

She trusted Max and Olive to keep her apprised of Dr. Voss's movements should she leave the conference, but she hoped there would be no question. Ember had just one task to accomplish. If she was successful, Dr. Voss would not know she had been there. Not yet.

Her pace slowed as she neared the brick house. Dew glistened on the long living room windows in the morning light. Was it just yesterday she was here? Time was making unexpected shapes across her memory.

Ember slowed to scan the street before and behind her, then slipped around the side. Voltaris had impressed the course into her consciousness, not as a set of directions but as a felt sequence. The side door opened easily.

Inside, Ember recognized the smell of books upon books. Scents of fresh herbs wafted from the kitchen. Sunlight filtered through the windows, catching particles of dust in the air and giving the space a deceptive calm. But Ember was alert, aware that Dr. Voss's world was full of smoke and mirrors. Her house, apparently, was no different.

Voltaris had made it infinitely clear that, given the chance, Dr. Voss would not risk losing it—she wanted Ember's soul. The gravity of her task sat heavy in her heart as she stepped further into the house.

The side door brought her through an entryway and into the hallway beneath the grand staircase that led up to Dr. Voss's second story. But she was looking for a different passage. Sensing Voltaris's guidance, Ember followed the hallway to its end. Behind the front staircase, she saw the arched door. Its wooden frame was painted so that the door blended almost perfectly into the wall, its outline easy to miss if she'd not known to look.

She reached for the brass doorknob, and it creaked as she twisted it gently to the left. Through the door, a smaller, steeper staircase led up past the second story. Ember began to climb.

Ember started up the staircase, one step at a time. She felt as though she had entered a portal, as though every step she took against the dark oak stairs drew her deeper in time, deeper into the annals of science and history and... magic. It was a strange feeling but somehow also familiar. She slid her hand along the wooden handrail, practicing her slow breath, working to stay grounded, to listen deep.

Halfway up the staircase, Ember brushed a knick in the railing. A gasp escaped her mouth, and then her posture shifted.

She was no longer alone.

Dr. Voss stood above her on the staircase, one hand gripping the railing, her face hard with resolve. Ember looked straight into her eyes. She was stunned, but she fixed her expression as words poured from her mouth.

"Please, Alena." It was Momo's voice that resonated in the dark stairwell. "This is not what you mean it to be.

"A soul deserves to follow its body into death. A soul deserves to know life beyond this plane. Please, Alena. Read her work. Interview her endlessly, but don't steal her brilliance. Annie has influenced me more than I can say. I know you respect her.

"It's our responsibility to protect her. *Please, you can't do this. Do not take her soul."*

Ember listened as through her own mouth, Momo's voice pleaded with Dr. Voss. But Dr. Voss's expression did not change. "You don't know what you're talking about," she responded haughtily. "Annie is ill. She'll be gone soon. This is my opportunity, and I won't be persuaded otherwise."

Ember watched as her hand—Momo's hand—reached out to grab Dr. Voss by the arm. But Dr. Voss turned away and continued up the stairs. "It's time for you to go, Mabel," she said as she walked away.

The scene faded before her, and the house was once again quiet. She stood alone on the steps, back in her own body, her heart pounding painfully with the memory of that moment. She had just witnessed her grandmother attempting to protect another scientist from Dr. Voss's grasp.

Who was Annie? Would Ember find her soul entrapped in *The Book of Aeons* too? She may soon find out.

As she climbed, the staircase turned to take her up, past the second story, and on to the third. There, at the end of the hall, she saw it— the apothecary door. She had reached the end of the portal, and her next passage was unmistakable.

The door's oak panels stretched lengthwise from the floor into another arch, this one tall and conspicuous, in stark contrast to the secret door she'd entered minutes ago. At the top of the arch, Ember recognized a sigil-like script; it reminded her of the figures from Dr. Voss's underground research. What was its meaning here? But her curiosity about the language was supplanted promptly by the growing glow of a clear blue light emanating from the center of the door. She peered into the light and found that it was coming from a perfect glass orb, positioned perfectly at the level of her heart.

She's watching. Ember's breath caught in her throat.

Though it seemed a simple glass sphere catching light from the other side of the door, she eerily felt again as though she was no longer alone in the house. Was Dr. Voss really watching for her, waiting for her to come to the apothecary? How would she have known?

She slipped her phone out of her pocket.

"Eyes on the target?" she texted Max and Olive.

"Confirmed," Olive responded promptly.

Ember knew this was her chance. She needed to get in that room. She was already risking her safety. She couldn't be thwarted now.

●

Ember took a deep breath, and, drawing from some place deep within her, she imagined herself invisible to the orb's sight. She approached calmly, a soft blanket of air forming in the space between herself and the door. As best she could, she held the blanket in front of her, hoping the orb would see nothing but air. No movement. No person. No Ember.

As soon as she could reach the handle, Ember pushed the door open and stepped confidently into the room. The door swung shut behind her, and Ember turned her attention to this uncommon place.

"*This* is an apothecary," she breathed, finally recognizing the fullness of the word. This was not a shop for tinctures and oils. Nor was it some backroom for formulation. There were jars and herbs and books, yes, but this was something else altogether. Ember was enchanted.

It was brighter than she expected, lit through stained glass windows high along the walls. Shelves lined the room from floor to ceiling, crowded with glass jars and vials that gleamed softly in the colorful light—liquids of deep gold and muted green, powders and dried leaves, roots bound with twine, bark curled and brittle with age. Each vessel bore symbols that stirred Ember's recognition, though she couldn't quite find their names.

Artifacts donned the corners and edges and spaces between—hard evidence of the ways science and magic had been blended throughout history. On the inside wall, an old fireplace with a solid wood mantle held an antique clock that ticked gently as another moment passed.

This was no dream. Everything Ember saw here, everything she felt was real.

The energy in the place was alive but stilted, as though the room held her at bay, awaiting her response, her influence. What was this visitor going to do?

Yes, Ember thought. *Time to get to it. The Book.*

Her pulse quickened as she took one and then another step further into the apothecary. Her spirit was so alive here. She couldn't help but be surprised at the magic of this space—Alena had always seemed to her a very serious, practical person—or how it made her feel. Her attention was wide, clear; her mind was open.

Ember felt a pull from a table nearby. She turned her attention to find a strange, intricately carved wizard, or an astrologer, or a physicist—a scientist of earlier times. He stood with his palm lifted, fingers arced to hold a perfect quartz crystal. Ember wasn't certain, but it seemed to her that the perfect facets of the gem pulsed with a rhythmic glow. Was the quartz resonating with her energy?

Following something between instinct and intuition, Ember moved to touch the gem, and just as her fingers landed on its surface, the room changed shape.

Instantly, Ember knew where she was. She was sitting at the desk—unmistakably Momo's—a stack of books before her, pen in hand, and a lined notebook at the ready. Ember looked down to see fingers that were older than her own, but much younger than the grandmother she had known as a child. By now she was used to the travel, both of time and place, that happened during these visions. She must be seeing Momo in her younger years, around the birth of Ember's mother...

The notebook on the desk beckoned her. She opened it up and began to take in the words on the paper before her when Momo's voice sounded behind her. Ember lifted her head and was shocked to see her grandmother standing there, in the center of the room.

She was intensely confused. She'd become used to her visions, to the way her consciousness seemed to merge with the person whose memory she entered. She embodied their presence—felt the breeze on their skin, shaped the expression on their face, spoke in their voice, and thought what they thought. But now it seemed she both embodied *her grandmother and* could see *her beloved standing right in front of her. How?*

"There's no time for that."

Momo interrupted Ember's questions, responding to her thoughts directly. She spoke with urgency. "This is not a memory," she conceded, sating her granddaughter's curiosity. "Listen, child."

Momo spoke bluntly, clearly trying to convey as much information as possible while they had this channel open.

"I know you have come for The Book of Aeons. *Ember, this is a most precious resource." She implored Ember to profound attention. "Once you hold* The Book *in your hands, you will find it easier to understand all that you've unwound in the world so far.*

"My dear grandchild, your task is not just one of retrieval. Your role extends far beyond the integration of Voltaris with his soul. The Book *seeks* you. *"*

Ember was stunned. She did her best to follow. She wondered at the cryptic messages that lingered beneath Momo's statements. Not just retrieval, Ember thought. The Book *seeks me...*

"This is *the most important thing* in your journey right now, and you should worry about little else: attain *The Book of Aeons, and you will*

find what comes next. But, my child, I cannot let you come to this passage without a crucial bit of information."

Ember gave Momo every bit of attention she could muster, her heart exploding as she collected every bit of detail—Momo's face, her hair, the glimmer in her eyes, the tension at the edges of her mouth. It was so good to see her, to feel her here. It gave her strength.

She focused her concentration on the gift of guidance her grandmother was offering her. She knew it was true: this *was the most important thing. Getting* The Book of Aeons *safely into her hands was the most important thing. But that crucial bit...*

"For your protection," Momo continued, and Ember's attention shifted deeper, as though she were now aware of the words themselves. Her eyes widened as her grandmother swiftly shared the story of her advisor, her mentor, her inspiration, and, now, her foe—Dr. Voss.

"Alena knew magic as a child," Momo said, with tenderness and respect in her voice. "It was in her blood, in her lineage, an inevitable piece of her life's puzzle.

"But the sweetness of her magical mind was altered when she experienced great pain. Her parents died suddenly, and Alena was left alone. She was too young. The loss of her parents changed her life at just six years old. That was the start of the changes. She left the openhearted magic of her youth behind and let her ambition consume her. It fueled her. Her desire for knowledge and power became insatiable.

"The Book of Aeons *was always meant to find her but never in such daunting circumstances. Her parents' death turned everything about their story around—Alena's story and* The Book's *story.*

"*In the end, Alena learned to use the magic of* The Book *to fulfill her selfish and even evil intentions in the world.* The Book *was transformed by her choices, tethered in service to Alena and her hunger for power.*"

"*Momo paused, and then offered one final plea:* "Ember." *Her voice was threaded with gravity.* "The Book of Aeons *has been divorced from its purpose. Alena has used it to trap souls rather than free them. She seeks power, and the pursuit is killing her, mind and spirit.* The Book of Aeons *holds magic beyond our understanding, but in her hands it has become a weapon.*

Momo focused her eyes, offering the clarity of consciousness of a soul unburdened by life. And yet, her concern was palpable. Ember listened with the entirety of her consciousness as her grandmother offered a profound warning. "Do not, *I implore you, put yourself in a vulnerable position with Alena. When you hold* The Book, *you are at risk. Your guard is all you have.*

"*Be diligent. Once you hold* The Book, *waste no time. You must pursue its freedom in order to protect your own.*"

These words were not news to her. Voltaris had told her as much. But hearing them from her grandmother fortified Ember. She felt something of herself lighting up to the task at hand. As though reading her mind, Momo offered a few words more.

"Trust yourself." Her grandmother's voice was soft. "Trust your instincts. This quest is not just about power. It's about clarity; it's about integration.

"Ember, you have a way with energy. It's been with you since you came into this world. It's alive in your memories—the lessons I've imparted, the work we did together all those years ago. It's alive too in your studies now, your collaboration with photons, illuminating communication pathways. Energy wants to be known by you. All you have to do," she said, as though it were some simple thing, "is follow the course of light."

Momo glanced at the shelves above Ember's head. A mantle clock ticked quietly. Was it not the very same clock Ember had seen in Dr. Voss's apothecary?

"Time flows differently here," Momo said, as piece by piece, Ember's vision dissipated.

As she reoriented herself to the apothecary, she saw that the ticking clock showed not even five minutes had passed. The grounding, peaceful presence of her grandmother lingered with her. "Energy wants to be known by you," she had said. Ember couldn't help but wonder—did Momo know about the photons? Was it possible that she had known all along?

Is there something I have missed? Ember wondered. But Momo's final guidance rested gently on her conscience: "All you have to do is follow the course of light." Momo's presence was palpable; Ember knew she was with her here.

And beneath that, more subtle than even her grandmother's presence, another awareness stirred, curious and precise. It reminded Ember of her dreams.

She began to move quickly now, around the edges of the room, scanning the shelves for the most important one. There was so much to take in.

Everywhere she looked, she found more. Every shelf held new clues to Dr. Voss's past. She saw copper coils stashed beside big copperpots, glass tubes filled with viscous substances of every color, and notebooks with handwritten labels stacked tightly into the shelves. She could see how Dr. Voss's learning had given shape to her practice, and there was so much more to it than Ember had realized.

"Unbelievable," Ember murmured, stepping closer to a collection of alchemical instruments that were gathered into a tidy set. Their glass components reflected the light like fragmented stars.

She noticed Einstein's presence in some of Dr. Voss's artifacts. There was a smoking pipe and an antique quill pen. A long table, like a workbench, stretched along the window wall of the room, and Ember quickly scanned it to see if *The Book* was there, or anything of consequence, really. She was looking for some sort of clue.

A tiny notebook lay open, its pages marked by a scientific scrawl. Upon further assessment, Ember saw that the scrawl was not in Dr. Voss's familiar handwriting, but she recognized it. Could it be Einstein's script? Did Dr. Voss have handwritten notes of his?

The revelation sent Ember's mind spinning. In some other time, she would have longed to spend all evening in this place, gathering everything she could about Einstein from Dr. Voss's collections. But she could not forget the imperative of this moment.

This was no library, and Dr. Voss was no historian.

Ember's mentor had not only stolen Einstein's soul; she had hidden his work. Urgency stirred again in Ember's veins. Was there a way she could, even now, follow the light?

The question resonated deep, and something drew her attention to the shelves along the far wall. There. The nearest shelf. As she lifted her fingers to brush the spines, that same deep resonance compelled her to take the first tattered edge into her hands.

It was soft to the touch, the cover's crimson weave worn well by time. In her hands, this book felt familiar, like the warm embrace of a friend.

Again the clarity of her vision blurred, and Ember knew she was being taken on yet another journey.

Where she was this time, though, was entirely unclear.

Movement, sound, and light jumbled before her. She could not see the ground or the ceiling.

She was spinning, faster and faster, picking up speed. Her heart grew wider with every rotation. She sensed her spirit rippling into the expanse. Would she lose herself here? Or was this something dissolution into herself? Her heart traveled faster than her mind...

A tiny ping echoed in the ether, jolting Ember from her stupor.

She landed firmly back in reality.

What was that? she thought, urgently trying to attune to the space. Was someone here?

She couldn't let herself be taken into another vision. She needed to be able to move if Dr. Voss returned. She anchored herself, tapping her feet and then resting them firm against the hardwood floor.

Ping. There it was again. Her phone. Ember rushed to pull it from her pocket.

"Boss in sight. Big news to share later," Max had texted. *Ping.* "Mission status?"

"Book in hand," Ember texted back. "See you after the conference."

Ember looked down at *The Book* in her hands. She hadn't even realized. This was it.

It had called to her. She had pulled from the shelf the one book she'd been looking for, like it had shown itself to her.

She wouldn't waste any more time in the apothecary. She unwrapped her jacket, and zipped it up with *The Book* inside, held tightly to her chest. It was time to get out of here.

She tiptoed to the door and opened it a crack, suspicious despite her text exchange. The house was silent. At least she could count on getting out of here with her soul intact.

Ember raced quietly down the back staircase and slipped through the hall and out the side door. She sped down the street, under the trolley tunnel, and on towards home. She could feel her chest thumping—was that *The Book* vibrating against her sternum, or was it just her rapid heartbeat?

It was only as she climbed the stairs to her apartment that Ember stopped running. She paused outside the door for a deep breath. It might've been the deepest of her whole life. She would keep *The Book* safe—for Voltaris, for the other souls locked inside, and, now, for her own.

Voltaris

Chapter 25: Safekeeping

Safe and still, inside her apartment, Ember clasped *The Book of Aeons* to her heart.

The thrum of *The Book* against her chest had woken her senses. Her perception was sharp. The world had come alive around her, and she could feel all of it.

Ember sat down at the dining table. She'd examined hundreds of books sitting at this table, even just this year. It had held texts on metaphysics, journals expounding on quantum theory and its varied applications, and accounts of the most pivotal moments in science history. But this book was something else.

She carefully lay *The Book of Aeons* down on the table in front of her. She felt as though she had been holding a real person, a beloved, to her chest, and it was strange to just set *The Book* down, but it was time for Ember to find out just what sort of magic had brought *The Book* to her.

She ran her fingertips along the woven cover, following the course of threads ushered tightly together in their structure. Their silk drew her deeper, and before she could turn a page—

Ember found herself standing in a great, open room filled with light.

The scene was beautiful. A golden sanctuary. A glorious refuge. The space was warm and inviting, aglow with life.

As she looked around, Ember realized she was, in fact, in a workplace of sorts. This magnificent space was a workshop where books were built.

Yes, a workshop. There were shelves and shelves of books and parts of books—stacks of raw-edged paper, vials of ink, and a small press. The edges of every little thing glittered. A child's mind would have known right away that this room was filled with magic. It was palpable.

Craftspeople milled about, aprons tied at their waists, various tools protruding from their pockets. All of them were singing.

The craftspeople, no matter the jobs they were doing, had joined together in a soft, melodious song. Their voices emanated through the room, creating a resonance of purpose, of intention. Their intonations filled the room with meaning. Once in a while, one or two of the craftspeople would turn their eyes towards the center of the space. There, a single woman was seated at a wide writing desk, her spine long and still, her feet planted firmly on the ground. They watched as her hand moved elegantly across the page. She was writing, inscribing story onto the soft paper pages of a book.

Ember began to see the magic in every dimension of the space. She could see it collected in the stacks of handmade paper. It emanated from collections of ink and twisted threads and Ember understood that every step of this process was sacred. Essential.

And now, new magic was born in the craftspeople's songs. It followed the resonance of their sound into the center of the room, to the heart of the woman, through her hands and into her script.

They were infusing magic into *the book. The book itself was* becoming magic.

Then she was back at her own kitchen table, holding *The Book* gently in both hands.

Ember looked down at the beautiful gold lettering that marked its title: *The Book of Aeons*. But she noticed a change...

Right there at the center of *The Book's* cover, through its luminous weave. Yes, at the place where, just moments before, she had read *of* — *The Book* of *Aeons* — and admired the fine embroidery, the elegant golden thread in perfect stitches. In that very place, now, another shape was becoming clear.

The strands of the woven cover parted, softly and then more and more. And new color filled the space forming between them. Gold, then green, and finally white filled the space.

Before her eyes, Ember saw *The Book* gazed into the room around her, moving slowly, slower than she had ever seen an eye move before. *Is this real?* Ember couldn't help but think. But she understood. This was yet another layer of magic revealing itself to her. Of course *The Book of Aeons* had an eye.

She watched it move, enchanted at the possibility of such a thing. It was not a human eye but more like that of an animal. A wild one.

She watched as the colors swam like tiny threads themselves, stretching and swirling across its rounded surface. The whites of the eye were illuminated with slight strands of gold; they caught the lamp light and sent glittering shimmers that stirred her attention even deeper.

At the center of the eye, surrounding a deep, dark, diamond-shaped pupil, was the most beautiful green color Ember had ever seen. And as *The Book* shifted its wandering gaze to look straight in her eyes, she lost herself in aeons of green.

She blinked herself back to the present. She wanted nothing more than to see what was inside *The Book's* binding. It was calling her.

Ember lifted the cover slowly, observing every detail. She felt the soft texture of the handmade paper. The pages felt at once fragile and powerful to her touch. She admired the beautiful configuration of each scripted shape. Its intricate illustrations and calligraphic letters came alive on the page.

Are they alive? Each layer she uncovered of this embodied magic surprised Ember. Now, shock claimed her face as she watched the letters begin to move. Ink swirled as she turned the pages, searching for a bit of clarity, some way to interpret what was happening—why *The Book* was changing.

The Book transformed before her, the letters rearranging to make entirely new words, entirely new sentences. But instead of stories, spells, or secret equations, Ember found something far more curious. As the script finally settled, she found that this was a profoundly familiar story. She recognized the words; they were the names of people and places she knew. With every sentence, it became more clear:

The Book of Aeons was telling a story about her.

●

The Book had transformed into a living chronicle of her life. The words flew from the page into her mind, into channels of her memories. As she read, Ember voraciously devoured the sweetest and most consequential bits of her life.

Her heart raced as she read the first lines and found before her a description of herself as a young child. In those first pages, Ember read of her obsession about the night sky, the way she'd pass hours in bed, looking out the window, and dreaming about what lay beyond the glistening stars. She read of her spirited curiosity, how she would relentlessly inquire of anyone she met what they knew about one thing or another. She read on.

Entranced, she read pages, one after another, about her early life, the influence of her kind and intelligent parents, and the profound impact of her beloved and brilliant grandmother, her Momo.

Memories flooded back to her: the first time she had looked through a telescope, the stories Momo told her about the vastness of the universe, her childhood wonder and awe, and the quiet habits she absorbed from the physicists she admired. In these pages, she recalled how she respected them, the ways they noticed patterns and how they resisted easy answers.

Her fascination with Einstein was there too, another memory, unmistakable on the page—Albert Einstein, the renowned physicist, whose work on relativity and wave–particle duality had taught her that core tenet of her knowledge: light cannot be understood apart from the act of observing it, and the observer is never as separate from the phenomenon as they may believe.

In *The Book of Aeon*'s telling, the depth and breadth of Momo's wisdom became utterly clear.

Certainly, now, Ember could see—her grandmother was more than a teacher, more than an avid learner or a wise woman. She was a witch, a wizard, a wielder of magic.

How had Ember not realized?

Between the stories on the page and the memories they stirred, Ember understood more than ever the ways that Momo had shaped her life. Her grandmother had bestowed upon her not only the brilliance that swept through her mind and heart but also the infinite richness of her practical wisdom. Her grandmother's magic had seeped into Ember's consciousness at every turn. *What a gift*, Ember thought now.

She saw so much overlap between Momo and Dr. Voss. It was easy to see how they must've gotten along so well. But she also saw the ways Momo's influence in her life diverged from her mentor's. Momo had taught her the values beneath the science, the importance of the spirit behind her ambitions. She had taught her that magic was not an external force to be harnessed, but a vital, personal resource she must find and cultivate.

The Book showed Ember how, for decades, she *had been* cultivating magic. She hadn't even known.

Each page unveiled more of Ember's life, detailing moments both significant and mundane. As she watched herself grow through its stories, *The Book* chronicled her struggles with friendships, her evolving dreams and the disappointments that accompanied them, and, finally, her surrender to her scientific interests.

When she had decided to pursue physics above all else, she had wanted to follow in the footsteps of Einstein. Ember had not realized that, in so doing, she had rested her magic in service to her mind.

●

As she turned further through the pages, Ember began to notice that *The Book* didn't just recount stories of her past. The magical tome looked ahead; it knew something of her future as well.

It hinted at dreams she'd yet to realize, paths she'd yet to take. It was strange to see these thoughts—things she hadn't dared to share with anyone—on the pages before her. Ember's heart quickened as she felt her hopes take form inside the binding.

Then, the tone changed.

The language grew denser, and somehow also more ethereal, and as she read Ember wandered through uncertainty until she saw herself standing at the edge of something vast, entwined with a force she couldn't name.

A great weight bore oppressively upon her—a choice. Not to action, but to surrender.

She longed for the bright stories of her future to be true, but in this moment a gravity overcame her instead. *The Book* presented an ominous reality. She let the details sink into her psyche...

Ember knew that Einstein's soul was entrapped here. Which begged a truly horrifying question:

Did *The Book of Aeons* know her for the same reason?

Would she too fall into its prison?

An eerie certainty crept over her. If Alena had already begun Ember's entrapment, her soul was in true danger.

Ember skirted the edges of her imagination, just barely allowing herself to consider what it would be like if her life was not only *on* the pages but completely trapped *in* them.

Instantly, she thought to close *The Book*, but as she went to bring the binding together, something stopped her. She understood. A message remained for her here. She must keep reading.

Widening her consciousness, honoring the fullness of this magical *Book*, Ember could sense that there was much more than her own story here. More than Einstein's, too. A whole world of souls were held in its pages.

Yes, as she honored this reality, the tangible weight of *The Book* grew in her hands. But she kept reading, looking for that message. What was she meant to learn?

The story wound its way back to the present moment. It told of her rescuing *The Book* from Dr. Voss's apothecary, the sensation of *The*

Book against her heart as she raced it to the safety of her apartment, and even how she was now reading about her past and her future.

As Ember turned the page past this very moment, sitting at her dining table with *The Book*, she saw *The Book* did not just speak of future abstractions. The possibilities it had laid out before paled in the face of the details she now read— a cryptic illumination of what was to come.

This was the message she had sensed was present here.

Its words resonated deep in her body, as a harrowing sensation crystallized for Ember:

Sacrifice.

The thought hollowed her. Her hand trembled as she turned the page to read.

"The young woman couldn't know what was to come. The world asked everything of her luminous being—her mind, her spirit, and her soul. The decision rested with the last of these.

"It was with her soul that Ember would decide how to live and how to die."

She read the words as though reading the pages from her own mind. She knew they were true.

The Book of Aeons had just revealed to her the question that propelled her quest. She searched urgently for details, insight into how she might proceed, how she could recognize the sacrifice when it came to her.

Then, woven intently into the story, was a figure she did not expect. Yes, *The Book* now offered her a clue into what was coming—something tangible.

A man. Ember could expect the influence of a single man.

First *The Book* showed Ember the image of a young, stoic form, his face familiar though difficult for her to place.

But he was not alone. The man stood tall and proud, and Ember saw that he was tethered to the most significant woman in her own life. Intimately tethered. To Momo. A kinship between them.

And then, *The Book* showed her the man as he was now—polished, authoritative, imposing. He stood this time beside Dr. Voss. Atop the world.

Ember knew this man.

Charles Hadden.

And now she knew who he was to her:

Ember Quinn's grandfather.

Though the words on the page provided little detail, Ember understood *The Book* meant her to know. This man, whose power rivaled that of presidents and prime ministers, whose influence stretched the world over, and whose intentions were ambiguous at best—Charles Hadden—was her grandfather.

She shared his blood.

She carried his stories in her mind, her body, her soul.

The revelation landed and then echoed through her chest to the edges of her person. It was not shock but rather grief that welled within her.

Finally, Ember understood why Momo had been so careful, so conflicted about Ember's course. She understood why power and restraint had always sat in tension for her grandmother. It was not just Einstein's choices that lived in Momo's memory, but the deeds of her own paramour, the father of her only child, a corrupt and fiendish force in the world. *The Book* revealed it all.

Ember understood that her sacrifice—the decision she would make about how to live and how to die—would take her directly into fiery discord with her maternal grandfather, Charles Hadden.

●

Ember closed *The Book*, pressed her palms firmly against the cover, careful not to cover the place where the eye had been. But it was lost now to the weave of that beautiful cover. She let her own eyes close. She took a deep, clarifying breath.

She was still here, still alive. She had possession of *The Book*. There was still time.

Then a soft, resonant voice emerged from the pages, sweeping through the room like a gentle breeze.

"Thank you, Ember."

The hairs on her arms stood up.

The voice challenged her senses, because she didn't hear it so much as she *felt* it. She shook her head gently, knocking out the dense web of information that had built up in the course of these last hours.

Ember took another hard look at *The Book* in her hands. The eye was open now, peering intently at her. The voice sounded again.

"Would you give me just a moment, please, to stand on my own?"

Ember set *The Book* carefully down on the table. She was uninclined to speak, uncertain what she would say or how, in fact, to communicate this way. But she listened intently.

"It's easier, I've learned, for most people to think of books as objects, to touch us, move us, pack us away and pull us from our resting places at will," *The Book* seemed to say. "I have felt like this for some time— like an object. Used, as I have been, for reasons other than my own purpose.

"But you, Ember, have awakened me from my protective slumber. You have initiated a new course for us both. I thank you."

The Book speaks, Ember thought, unable to muster a real response. *The Book* seemed to hear her anyway.

"Ink and parchment, wound string and woven cloth—" *The Book* said, "These, and so much more, have shaped me."

Its voice carried as a soothing murmur. Ember could feel its resonance at every layer of her consciousness.

"I know you, dear soul. I had the honor of knowing your grandmother before you. I have heard the stories of your lineage, of generations past. You come from a line filled with clarity, wisdom, and wit.

"For a long time, your ancestors have offered quiet contributions to the turning of the universe. You are a special soul, Ember. I am lucky you have found me here."

How do you know me, my story, my lineage?

Her questions became thoughts rather than vocalizations. She found it effortless, to think with *The Book*. The real task was in keeping her mind flexible, being open to the unexpected unfolding within her.

"I hold more than I can name. Inside these pages live stories of civilizations, truth-seekers, triumphs and tragedies, rises and falls. The deep, compassionate histories of my makers form my foundations. In my lifetime, I have held precious intentions, practical spells, and powerful incantations. I have held the real source of possibility and change.

"And," *The Book*'s tone shifted precariously towards anguish, "as you have found, I now hold the essence of real people—those people who have crossed the dangerous path of my recent Keeper, Alena Voss."

Ember was losing herself now. She had let go of her distinctions, the boundaries of her consciousness. She felt as though she was *inside The Book*.

"Alena's powers mirror those of your lineage. She is a person of wit and wisdom. Her ancestors were some of the wisest among the witches.

"And yet, her path has taken her quite a different way. In truth, Alena lost her course. But it was not completely of her own accord."

Compassion resonated through them both.

"And in her distinction," *The Book* continued, "she claimed her own role. When her parents died and Alena searched for meaning, for belonging, she found power in my pages. Her parents' death left a great void in her young psyche. In those early days, it was my power that filled that void. She craved more of it, and soon the magic within her was corrupt with desire."

The Book's pages fluttered, as if it were gathering its thoughts.

"Within weeks of opening my cover, Alena was entrapped to her own altered ideals.

"I did not resist her," *The Book* said. It seemed to say, without saying, how it should have. Resisted her. What mattered now, though, was not how it had been bent around Alena's will, but where it had landed.

In Ember's hands, it did not feel awakened or transformed, only steadier, as though it had returned to a familiar orientation.

Voltaris had needed this, she realized. He needed *The Book* in the hands of someone who could reflect back its original essence. That was the only way he could be rejoined with his.

The Book needed a steward, and Voltaris needed *her* both because she was still bound to the living world *and* because she would not use her access, her understanding, to control.

Ember's heart raced. Her world was changing rapidly, but she had been longing for such pointed insight into Dr. Voss's life. It would only help to know more about her now: the story of how she came to be so serious, so committed, and so clear in her path as a physicist at the university and beyond.

"Eventually, everything she had became a tool for power," *The Book* went on. "She found ways to use what was within my pages to her advantage. She combined the ancient tools embedded here with her interests in modern science. Eventually, her ambition turned to straight hunger—hunger for power. When power won out over knowledge, my own purpose was doomed.

"She meant to employ the tools in these pages to expand her reach in the scientific realm. Her experiments took on a dark alchemy.

"With time, her ambitions grew, so that she sought to enhance her control over the forces of nature not only in experimentation but also in her relationships. Alena began to crave the minds of her peers, her competitors, and her teachers. She drew upon the knowledge of my pages, using it to fuel her ambitions.

"It worked. Her application of these spells made her stronger, but she couldn't account for what she had stolen from those around her. With every step she took, she lost a piece of herself. Alena slipped deeper into the shadows.

"As did I—"

That last, an uncomfortable admission. *The Book* had been lost to the shadows.

●

Ember's hands shook. "She is *dangerous*," the thought escaped Ember's lips.

"Indeed," *The Book* affirmed. Did its pages rustle? "Alena is consumed by her desire for control. She decided long ago that knowledge was not a gift to be shared but a weapon to be wielded. She embraced the darkness to feed her ambition.

"Her choices made her stronger, but they also isolated her. The deeper she delved, the stronger her attachments grew. She is indebted to the material world. She has paid for her life.

"She appears to the living as a youthful woman, quite a bit younger in years than the experience she embodies.

"I'll tell you that Alena has been alive, and youthful, for a *long* time. In all this time, she has forged the chains that bind her, one after the other. The same darkness her child-mind yearned to control has become her master."

Waves of empathy washed over Ember and drowned her worry. She couldn't help it. Dr. Voss was broken herself. *The Book* confirmed—

she was dangerous, to her core it seemed. But, despite the threat she posed, Ember cared for her teacher. Could she help her somehow?

"Is there some other way?" she asked, hoping that *The Book* could offer more than history, more than stories of what has been.

"I don't yet know. Her choices are far beyond our control. And what you are soon to encounter..." *The Book* trailed off. "Your attention must be on your gifts. You must protect your magic. Only then will we know how to proceed."

All the tension that had been rising through her body softened at this clarity. The outcome was uncertain, but all was not lost.

It seemed *The Book* envisioned the good possibilities, but it would not let Ember be distracted by the will and deeds of others. Its voice became low, serious, and incredibly clear as it voiced a single warning: "But be clear, Ember—knowing Alena at all puts you in danger. From here on out, you risk your soul."

Voltaris

Chapter 26: Bloodline

The Book's words hung in the air. "You risk your soul."

The crimson-bound tome lay still on the table before her. She hadn't opened it again. She wasn't sure she should.

Chills ran along Ember's spine. Voltaris had told her. Her grandmother had confirmed it. And now, *The Book* that would help Dr. Voss complete the threat had spoken the words to her directly. The danger felt profoundly real.

Ember desperately wanted *all of this* to be a dream.

She had spent so much time in the world of her dreams lately. Couldn't this be just another strange iteration? Couldn't her subconscious have worked *The Book* into reality? Yes, that was it. In a breath, she let it all go:

Ember imagined that her excursion to Dr. Voss's house, to the apothecary, had been an elaborate hallucination brought on by serious stress. She imagined that Momo's presence had been memories masquerading as a vision. She imagined that the volume on her dining room table was just an old artifact, strange and beautiful, but inert. She imagined that Voltaris was a projection of her own guilt, an attempt by her imagination to reconcile the weight of her work on her conscience. And she imagined that Dr. Voss was the same trustworthy, gracious, ingenious mentor she had known just weeks ago.

She saw herself waking up tomorrow with nothing but a headache and a strong sense of embarrassment. She would report to the lab for work and lose herself in the familiar comfort of data and calibration and error bars. She would laugh with Max and Olive about how badly the stress of her dissertation and the state of the world had shaken her but all was well now.

Her imagination did nothing to alter her circumstances. The relief she sought was nowhere to be found.

She turned the inside of her arm up and pinched her skin. The nip sent a sting across her forearm, but she didn't wake.

Instead, her chest tightened, recognition of her reality building like pressure at her sternum. She wanted it to be a dream, but she knew it wasn't. Ember had known from the start that this was real.

"No dream can hold the whole of you," *The Book* spoke again. "This is real magic."

Real magic.

●

Ember closed her eyes and pressed her hands together, grounding herself in sensation. The floor was solid beneath her feet. The air in her apartment smelled faintly of her morning coffee. Somewhere outside, a car horn sounded in friendly warning. Laughter rang out. The world was still moving.

"Ember," *The Book* said her name slowly, with consequence. "The spark. Warmth. Light. Potential."

Ember saw the words scribbled across the lined pages of an elementary school notebook. Her name. Her meaning.

The spark felt far out of her reach.

Ember had always wanted to contribute something extraordinary to the world, but, in this moment, being a person of meaning felt much more a risk than an opportunity.

The Book stole Ember away, into a memory, serving as guide to her own history.

Ember saw herself as a child again, sitting cross-legged on Momo's braided rug at the center of a spacious room. A beam of light poured through the picture window and strewed its glow across Ember's lap. She was coloring as she listened to stories, one after the other.

Thinking of them now, Ember understood that these were her lessons. Momo set the foundations for the life that would come.

"Since you were a child," *The Book* offered, "you have wielded power with your attention."

Ember and her child self swapped places, and now she watched herself in the laboratory through her child eyes. This was not as a memory— her worlds were overlapping, juxtaposed, mingling.

The familiar geometry of the lab took shape: the optical table, the lattice of mirrors and beam splitters, the careful alignment she and Max obsessed over for hours at a time. She saw the photon work in motion, pulses of light cycling through the apparatus, counted and recounted, collapsing into data on the monitors.

But threaded through that precision, she noticed something she hadn't before. The photons did not merely pass through the system; they responded. Subtle pathways of interaction shimmered through the space itself, faint channels forming between the apparatus, the air, and her own attention as she adjusted a mirror, recalibrated a delay, and held her focus steady on the readout. She could see how the light responded to her, and at times it looked like she was directing it.

She realized then that the photons didn't linger because she was doing something to them. They lingered because she wasn't. Where others intervened too soon—measuring, correcting, collapsing—she waited. And in that waiting, something held.

She realized then that hers was not a path of power over, but power with. Power through. Her power was matched in resonance with the energetics of the world around her. Ember was awash in gratitude—for years her work with photons had been preparing her for this clarity. Finally, they had shown her this truth.

Ember felt the insight settle—not as revelation, but as confirmation of something that had been quietly true all along.

Her work had never been about control.

Even in the lab, under pressure, she had resisted the instinct to force outcomes. She adjusted, observed, waited. She held the conditions steady and allowed the system to show what it was capable of without being pushed toward a predetermined result.

The Book registered that pattern immediately. It had been created to accompany minds like hers—minds that could hold complexity without collapsing it into certainty in an effort to pin "it" down. Over centuries, *The Book* had passed through hands that demanded answers and leverage to command authority. Ember asked different questions. Not what can this give me, but what is already here, and how do I listen to it clearly?

And Voltaris—Einstein—had been drawn to the same posture in his own life. Not mastery, but curiosity disciplined by humility. Not domination of nature, but conversation with it. That was the thread between them: a shared refusal to reduce the world into something small enough to own.

Together, they formed a configuration that had not existed before. *The Book* held continuity. Voltaris held insight severed too soon. And Ember—still fully human, still unfinished—was the condition that allowed those things to remain in motion without being consumed.

"Alena understands the value of your power, Ember. Without her wickedness, you are her competition, her opposition—a threat to her mission," *The Book* reminded her.

"She knows precisely who you are. She knows much of what you are capable of. And she will stop at nothing to ensure that your power is in *her* hands."

Ember felt that all of her fears were realized in this single phrase: *Her power in someone else's hands.*

The Book's words came with an unsettling clarity. Alena had not simply gone astray, and the path she had taken was not accidental—it was methodical. She had mapped a route from perception to possession, from knowledge to leverage. Ember could see the shape of the danger ahead. This was not about isolated harm or private ambition. It was about scale.

"Alena does not work alone," *The Book* reminded her.

Ember's thoughts shifted, aligning with something colder, more deliberate.

The Book went on, "Hadden does not need me the way Alena does. What he wants is application. He has been honing systems to influence populations with mechanisms that can shape belief or memory without appearing to touch it. Alena's research offers him the raw material: proof that consciousness could be isolated, redirected, preserved, or suppressed."

The realization tightened in Ember's chest. "If I am a target, I am a pivot point," she said with complete conviction. Voltaris had glimpsed this paradox in his own time, too late to stop it. The same pattern was repeating now, only faster—embedded in infrastructure and justified by fear and necessity.

Voltaris.

The thought struck her with sudden urgency. How could she have forgotten? His soul was here—present, waiting—contained within

The Book resting quietly on her table. The possibility flared through her. If the danger was accelerating, if the pattern was reforming, then perhaps the interruption had to happen now. Could she release him? Could she undo what had been done?

Before the question could fully take shape, *The Book* answered.

"Yes," it said. "Einstein's soul is here. His soul—and the others—are safe so long as I remain with you, in your hands. You must keep me from Alena. There is work for us all to do together."

●

Ember stood at the center of the room and let the noise of her thoughts drain away. She did not brace herself or reach outward. She slowly began to envision the comforting form of her grandmother and a conversation between them. Momo wasted no time. In no more than three of Ember's slow, deliberate breaths, Momo was there, materializing like a mirage beside Ember. She looked steady and familiar, her expression attentive rather than alarmed, as if she already understood exactly what Ember needed.

"Hello, dear," Momo said gently.

Relief moved through Ember so quickly that it nearly unbalanced her. This was not a vision unfolding on its own terms. This was not memory masquerading as guidance.

For a moment, Ember could not speak. The words she had been holding back pressed against her chest all at once, too many to sort. The words found her at the same moment she found her voice.

"You knew," Ember said. "Everything." Thoughts poured from her mind into her heart. The light, the magic, her capacity to hold it all, the sacrifice that would be demanded of her. Yet, somehow, the most pressing thing made its way through her lips.

"About Charles Hadden. You knew he was my grandfather. You kept this from me."

Momo did not flinch. She did not look away. "Yes," she said simply.

The admission landed harder than Ember expected. Hurt rose first— not sharp, but deep and disorienting. "You let me believe he was just... out there," Ember said. "A stranger. Unknown. Yet another man who was too independent to be bothered with a family."

For a moment, Ember thought tenderly of her mother. What it might've been like for her, to miss her father's presence. Had she known who he really was? Had that shaped the course of her life?

Momo's gaze softened, but her voice remained firm. "Because if you had known, you would have gone looking for him."

Ember opened her mouth to protest, then stopped. She could see it now—herself as a teenager, then a young woman, drawn by curiosity and unanswered questions. Had she known then, she would not have hesitated to track him down.

"And that would have been dangerous," Momo continued. "Not because you were weak, but because he was patient. And because proximity would have given him time.

"I protected you for as long as I could," Momo said. "I couldn't stop him from reaching for you. It was only a matter of time before he found you through your work." The truth of it settled into Ember's chest with quiet inevitability. "Your achievements are only part of your assets, and they were signals to Hadden."

"That's why he's here now," Ember said. "Why he's circling so close."

Silence stretched between them, dense with everything that could not be undone.

"And now?" Ember asked.

Momo took a breath, as though choosing her words carefully. "Now the danger has changed," she said. "Because he no longer needs to approach you indirectly. He doesn't want *The Book*," she said slowly. "He wants you."

The words landed with a chilling clarity. The room seemed to tilt slightly, as if Ember's body were registering the weight of that realization before her mind could fully catch up. Images surfaced unbidden—standing across from Hadden, his attention fixed on her with unsettling precision, his presence pressing not against her body but against her mind. She sensed how easily he could enter her thoughts if she allowed even the smallest opening.

"There's going to be a confrontation," Ember said quietly.

Momo nodded. "Yes, and you must maintain control of *The Book* and your mind, or you will become someone you don't recognize."

Ember exhaled, tension threading through her shoulders. "I don't know how to stand against someone like that."

Momo stepped closer and placed a steadying hand over Ember's chest. "You do, my dear. You have always known how.

"You learned it before you ever understood what it was for."

A memory rose with sudden clarity: sitting on the floor of Momo's study as a child, eyes closed, hands resting loosely in her lap while her grandmother's voice guided her inward. "Notice what belongs to you," she had said. "And what does not."

"You learned how to remain present without being open to everything that pressed against you," Momo went on. "You will need that practice again," Momo continued. "Because Hadden will not try to overpower you. He will try to persuade you that yielding is what you want."

Weariness crept into Ember's bones then, heavy and unignorable. "I thought understanding would make this easier," she admitted. "Instead, everything feels closer to the edge."

Momo smiled gently. "Understanding doesn't remove the edge," she said. "It teaches you how to stand on it without falling."

Before Ember could respond, the presence beside her began to thin, as though the room itself were reclaiming its space. Momo smiled once more, warm and resolute.

"Remember," she said. "Protect your mind. Protect *The Book*. And trust the work you've already done."

The knock came then—sharp, urgent, unmistakably real.

"Ember!" Olive's voice called. They knocked harder. "Let us in. Now."

Momo nodded to Ember as she moved on from that space.

Ember stood alone, breath steadying, the weight of what was coming settling into her bones just as she crossed the room to answer the door.

Voltaris

Chapter 27: Doorway

The knock at the door did not stop after Ember opened it.

Urgency spilled into the apartment as Max rushed past Ember. Without taking a moment to breathe, he launched into an account of the conference, spitting details faster than Ember could follow. He was pacing around the dining room and through the kitchen before Olive even crossed the threshold.

She followed more slowly, closing the door behind them and leaning back against it as if to brace herself, and the room, before speaking.

"They're working together," Max said. "Not loosely. Not coincidentally. Coordinated. We saw them—together."

Olive nodded, her expression grave. "In a storage room off the panel hall. Mid-conversation. Something is going on between them. Whatever it is, it's active."

Ember stood very still, absorbing the sounds of their voices, their words landing one by one. The apartment seemed to contract around them. The air grew thick, heavy with the convergence of truths. *Them,* she thought. *Who were they?*

She gestured toward the couch—habit more than hospitality—but neither Max nor Olive could sit.

"Start from the beginning," Ember said. She wanted to catch every detail.

They did. Max and Olive recounted their day efficiently and potently.

Max began with the panel. He described Hadden's presence first—the ease with which he commanded attention, the way his authority seemed to settle over the room without effort. He spoke about Hadden's language: the careful phrasing, the emphasis on stability and ethical intervention, the way every statement was framed as responsibility rather than control. Max admitted that, at first, he'd found himself nodding along.

"That's what scared me," he said. "It all sounded reasonable. Necessary, even."

He explained how Hadden spoke of a world growing too complex for unmediated understanding, of systems whose scale demanded guidance. He never said manipulation. He never said coercion. Instead, he spoke of stewardship—of protecting fragile structures from collapse under the weight of uninformed engagement.

"He talked like someone who genuinely believes chaos is the greatest moral failure," Max said. "Like uncertainty itself is something unethical."

Olive chimed in supportively, her serious demeanor shaping Ember's interpretation with each new detail. "Dr. Voss was there the whole time," she assured Ember. "She'd had a strange demeanor about her, eerie and unfamiliar. But it wasn't until after we heard her presentation that we understood why."

Apparently, Dr. Voss's presentation on encryption framed ambiguity as a vulnerability to be sealed rather than a condition to be studied. It wasn't at all what Ember would have expected.

"She talked about risk the way people talk about disease," Olive said. "Something to isolate. Something to eradicate."

As Ember listened, she layered their observations over her own experiences—the apothecary, *The Book*, Momo's warnings. The pattern was unmistakable now.

"And then we opened the wrong door," Max said, his pacing finally slowing for this pivotal moment. "Or the right one."

He described the storage room, unmarked and unremarkable, except for the unexpected contents. They were shocked to find Dr. Voss and Hadden there together, mid-conversation, standing close. It was clear—this wasn't a chance encounter.

"She looked surprised for about half a second," Max said. "Then you could see the change like a switch flipped. Anger, calculation, control. All of it in the space of a breath."

Olive nodded. "She introduced Hadden like it was normal. Like there was no reason for us to question why they'd be together."

"They weren't whispering," Max added. "They weren't hiding. It was like they assumed we didn't have the sense or, more likely, the context to understand what we were seeing."

"I don't think it's just a philosophical alignment," Olive said quietly. "I think they're planning something."

"And after what Hadden said today," Max added, "I doubt it's anything good."

●

Ember nodded slowly. None of this surprised her—not really. She realized the shape of things had been forming for her for days now, solidifying with each revelation.

And yet, hearing it spoken aloud—confirmed by the two people she trusted most—sent a strange current through her chest. Relief, dread, clarity. All at once.

"No, it can't be good," Ember affirmed. "I think Hadden has had his hand in this for some time now."

Max's head twisted to look Ember in the eye. "What do you mean?" he asked.

"Charles Hadden is my grandfather," Ember said.

The silence that followed was absolute. It stretched, taut and fragile, like glass under pressure.

Olive's eyes widened. Max stopped pacing, his feet frozen mid-step.

"How?" Max's question registered with a tone of defeat. But Ember knew that this would propel them deeper into their work tonight.

She didn't rush. She explained carefully—about the apothecary, about Momo's confirmation, and about *The Book*. Max wanted desperately to see its magic for himself, but she waved him off. Time felt more precious by the moment. Ember went on.

She spoke of Hadden's interest in her. She told them how, unlike Dr. Voss, Hadden didn't care about *The Book* itself but rather about Ember's ability to remain coherent under pressure, to stand inside systems that fractured others. To hold complexity.

Max ran a hand through his hair, exhaling sharply. "Goodness, Ember."

"This certainly explains certain things," Olive said softly. "Their proximity. The similarities in their presentations."

"And the danger," Ember added.

"It sounds like he has some way to use you as a weapon. But Hadden doesn't see himself as a villain," Max said, worry in his voice.

"That's the worst part," said Olive.

The words settled between them. Despite the intensity of the moment, it was grounding to have each other.

They unpacked the day in depth—moving on from the clipped urgency of discovery to measured, searching dialogue. They talked about what it meant for research to be absorbed into systems of power. They talked about how often scientific ambition had been repurposed as justification, about Einstein, Curie, the Manhattan Project. They talked about how consequences seemed to come long after the equations were solved.

"This is the part no one prepares you for," Max said quietly. "The moment where the math works, but the world doesn't."

But what did it mean for their course of action?

"What do we do?" Any of them may have asked the question. It settled in the air, stale and uncertain.

Ember turned her gaze toward the table, where *The Book* rested— quiet, heavy, aware. Even closed, she sensed its presence. It was listening without insisting, and she was grateful.

"We stop Dr. Voss in her tracks," Ember said. "We return Einstein's soul. We keep any more details of our research out of Hadden's hands. And we ensure that the world has the best possible chance at peace."

"No small task," Max chimed.

He was right. Ember still had more to tell her friends—about the threat of control and just how close she might come to losing her soul. But she wouldn't burden them with any more conflict. She needed their bravery.

"What can we do?" Olive asked.

"It's time to see what Dr. Voss has built," Ember said. "We need to get Einstein back his soul and find out exactly *what* Dr. Voss knows..."

"And what Hadden's really up to," Olive added.

"And how we can stop them."

Max's eyes flicked toward the window, then back to Ember. "The underground lab."

Ember nodded. She left the room for a moment and returned with the piece of woven cloth that lay across her altar. She wrapped it around *The Book* to protect the ancient fibers of its cover. She placed the package safely in her bookbag, securing it from outsiders' observation.

As her friends collected themselves, Ember sat, for just a moment, beside the door. She laced up her red boots. Bookbag, boots, and a deep breath. To the underground laboratory.

That was their next step, and the time had come.

●

They moved quickly after that. There was no formal plan yet, only alignment, trust, and the shared understanding that, whatever came next, they would be together.

As they crossed campus together, Ember noticed how different everything looked now—not visually, but conceptually.

The changing light stretched long shadows across the walkways. The protests had thinned, but the tension lingered, a low hum beneath the ordinary rhythms of students heading home or to class. News alerts buzzed faintly from passing phones.

The world felt precariously poised, as though its very foundations were unstable. Whether most people recognized it yet or not, change was imminent.

The physics building loomed ahead, both comfortably familiar and newly ominous.

Inside, the lab welcomed them with its usual hum. The soft glow of monitors and instrument panels cast a cool light across the space. As she entered, the familiar order of the lab settled Ember's nerves. This room had always been a refuge—a place where uncertainty could be measured, where complexity resolved into structure.

They moved through the lab quietly. Max checked the hallway before closing and locking the door behind them.

"So," he said. "How do we get in?"

Ember knew what her friends were risking as they endeavored to help her with this mission. But she appreciated their commitment. It made sense to her—it was all of their research at risk. Still, she was in no rush to put either of them in any more danger. She wanted to do these next steps well.

So she didn't answer right away. She was already moving toward Alena's desk, guided by a subtle pull she'd felt before. If ever there was a time to follow...

The desk was immaculate—papers stacked precisely, pens aligned with almost ceremonial care. She rested her hand on the surface and listened.

There.

Her fingers traced the edge of the drawer, finding the nearly invisible seam. She pressed and felt the mechanism give smoothly, soundlessly. The false bottom slid open.

Inside, she saw the small, old-fashioned key and a flat metal disc etched with the same symbols she'd seen in the apothecary. Beside them was the lock and frame that had fit so perfectly into the wall. Olive and Max had followed Ember into the office. They watched as she lifted the key and its lock from the desk.

"Will you clear those books from the second shelf?" Ember pointed to the place on the wall where they'd first found the lock. That day that everything had changed.

Max followed her instructions swiftly, taking the books from the shelf in one fell swoop.

From where she stood, Ember could just barely make out a shadow. *That must be the board Alena used to replace the lock*, she thought. A tiny seam was visible between that board and its neighbor. *The disc!* Ember realized. It was its own sort of key.

She retrieved the disc from the drawer and slid it easily into the space between boards. She tilted it to catch the edge of the wood and Ember lifted the placeholder out of the wall. There. She replaced it swiftly, positioning the lock in the hole. It clicked firmly into position, awaiting only the key.

Ember paused, unexpectedly. She was stalled. Uncertain. — finding herself in a vulnerable moment of contemplation. Somehow, she knew. *There would be no going back from here.* Watching her intently, Max paused for just a moment, then stepped forward and took the key from her hand. He fit it into the lock and turned.

They watched as the door opened once again.

Ember turned to see Max and Olive's expressions transitioning rapidly: surprise, recognition, familiarity. She had hoped this moment would spark something in their memories.

Max was clearly at a loss for words.

"Listen," Ember interrupted him before he had a chance to speak. "I'm glad you see it now. But we shouldn't spend time talking. I'm not sure we have a moment to spare."

She turned towards the screening monitor but thought better of it.

"But I want to say..." She looked at her friends. Ember was holding her breath. It all felt so tenuous. Could she bring up the magic to them now?

She had to tell them.

"We know Alena is dangerous." Ember drew from a deep well of truth within her. "It's not just the research—hers or ours. She wants my soul. She might want yours. Don't let your guard down.

"Whatever you do," she said, warning in her voice, "don't let her into your mind."

She reached behind her towards her backpack and placed a hand on *The Book*, then stepped forward to look directly into the security panel. The final door opened.

Cold air rushed out. The stairwell beyond descended into shadow. But she knew where it led.

The path was clear. *The Book of Aeons* was with her. Ember was ready.

Ember tightened the straps of her backpack, feeling the weight of *The Book* settle against her spine—not heavy in the usual sense, but insistent, as though it were aligning itself with her movement.

She led her friends back down the stairs to the underground laboratory. The three of them descended together, leaving the familiar world behind as the door closed softly above them.

Voltaris

Chapter 28: The Wall

The underground laboratory was silent.

It wasn't the hollow, expectant silence Ember remembered from that first time they had stumbled into this place, days earlier, wide-eyed, breathless, and unsure whether they had uncovered a secret or wandered somewhere they were not meant to be.

This silence felt held. Tuned with purpose. As though the room itself had been waiting for something to arrive, as though the room itself had adjusted its parameters accordingly.

It was strange. She was so confident that Dr. Voss would be here. Maybe Hadden too. But the circumstances of the space were distracting. Or compelling.

She had felt the shift immediately. She sensed the subtle resistance that permeated the space.

The light was the same unforgiving green-white it had been before, the same fluorescent panels flattening the room into sharp clarity, stripping depth from shadow and color alike. But something in the air was different. The room absorbed sounds before they could fully resonate. Their footsteps echoed, but the echoes felt muted, or blunted, returning thinner than expected.

Ember couldn't help but think the space defiant in their presence. It had an air about it. Distinction. She might have thought it meant to refuse their entry, or at least to fully acknowledge their passage tonight.

The vastness of the central chamber was active—not in any visible sense, but structured in invisible ways.

Yes, Ember understood the space was up to something, some sort of process that did not require visual evidence. It had taken on a life of its own. She could sense something potent—like important things were happening just beyond the limits of her perception.

She found it disquieting. She focused her perception on what was beneath the surface.

But right before her eyes, she could tell that even the massive screen at the center of the chamber appeared altered. The feeds they had seen before—laboratories across the world—were still there, still updating. But now, in tandem, they could see what appeared to be city centers. And in another box, they saw a rotating satellite view that seemed to reach the world over.

All of the visuals felt quieter somehow. And Ember recognized that the scrolling data no longer read as real-time information but as residue. The aftermath. She had a haunting sense that certain consequential decisions had already been made, and the screen now existed merely to confirm compliance with those determinations.

Ember turned to see Max and Olive taking in every detail.

As the three friends moved farther into the room, crossing the polished floor with cautious deliberation, Max slowed without realizing it. Ember watched as his gaze tracked across each of the eight doors spaced evenly along the curved perimeter of the chamber. Olive remained close to Ember's side, her posture alert, her attention split between the room and Ember herself.

She suspected her friends were having their own conscious experiences, integrating their lost memories with the reality they now encountered. Did they recognize how this place had changed? As Ember, Max, and Olive reached the center of the room together, it happened.

Her mind was quiet as she sensed for any other souls in the underground laboratory. Despite the dense energy in the space, she was certain. It was just her, Max, Olive, and *The Book of Aeons* and all its souls.

But it was in that powerful quiet that Ember felt it—a convergence of energies.

She recognized that the long-stretched threads of their story were finally drawing tight.

Before she could speak, before she could give voice to the weight pressing behind her sternum, a door on the far side of the room slid open with a low, deliberate sound.

Dr. Voss entered.

She moved quickly, her stride precise, controlled fury radiating from her without disrupting her composure. The sharp elegance Ember had once admired in her mentor had hardened into something severe. All unnecessary softness was stripped away.

Dr. Voss's gaze flicked first to Max and Olive, registering them with unmistakable displeasure, before locking onto Ember with an intensity that made the room feel suddenly narrower.

"You shouldn't be here," Dr. Voss said.

●

Her voice was calm. It did not rise. It did not need to.

"We know," Max replied, his tone steady despite the tension threading his spine.

Dr. Voss did not look at him. Her attention never left Ember. "You don't understand what you're interfering with."

Ember felt the words land and settle. An accusation—that was not what she'd expected. She straightened slightly and ground herself in her bones. She felt the weight of *The Book* against her back anchor her stance. She felt the courageous confidence of Max and Olive beside her.

"I understand enough," she said, gazing intently into Dr. Voss's eyes.

The silence that followed sharpened.

Another door opened.

Dr. Milton stepped into the chamber more slowly than his predecessor, his movements hesitant, uncertain. He paused just inside the doorway, eyes darting briefly across the room before dropping to the floor. He did not look at Ember. Or at Dr. Voss. Or at anyone else. Instead, he drifted toward the periphery, folding himself into the edge of the space like a man who had understood that invisibility was its own form of survival. But something about him made Ember wonder—was he under Dr. Voss's control?

A third door opened.

Ember felt it before she saw him.

The pressure in the room shifted—an unmistakable change, like a sudden drop in altitude. Something old and calculating slid into alignment, and her body reacted before her mind could name it. Her skin prickled. Her breath caught halfway in her chest. He was here.

Ember did not turn immediately. She did not need to. He entered from the side, an unmarked door. Through the back of her body, she could sense every detail of his movement.

Charles Hadden stepped into the lab.

A slow trickle of fear began to tease through her mind. How had she known he was present? It wasn't intuition but something else. Like premonition, but more certain. Entanglement.

Her awareness wrapped around Hadden the way memory wraps around a scent—long before the mind recalls the story does it recognize its family. She looked towards the stranger who, she now knew with certainty, was her biological grandfather. He smiled, cunning in his eyes.

"You felt that, didn't you?" His voice was pleasant, subdued. Why would he say that?

Ember turned to face him.

He looked exactly as he always had—immaculate, composed. His posture suggested ownership, as though he belonged here more than the others, more than Ember, more than Dr. Milton, even more than Dr. Voss. His expression carried a trace of delighted curiosity, as though this moment was unfolding precisely as he had anticipated.

His eyes lingered on her with unmistakable satisfaction. "You've grown into yourself, your gifts," he said. "That's rare."

There was nothing of compliment in his voice. Rather, he spoke with contempt and subtle intimations of hatred and fury. All of it he offered with the most pleasant expression painted across his face.

Something in Ember's chest tightened—an instinctive recoil, the kind that precedes certain pain.

She did not respond. Not with her voice, nor with her eyes or face or form. He understood her message.

"You were always perceptive," Hadden continued lightly. "Even as a child."

Max shifted beside her, tension radiating from him. It sliced through the thick air, building a barrier between Ember and Hadden's threatening tone. But he knew better than to speak.

Olive's jaw set, her fingers curling into her palm. Ember felt her ready to pounce, to protect. Ember knew she was not alone, but it was not just her friends who kept guard. She recognized another energy in the room. But she could not yet place it...

A bitter voice interrupted "Enough," Alena snapped. "This is not the time."

Hadden smiled faintly, but there was steel beneath it. "On the contrary. This is the only time."

The words hung there, charged with implication for each of them.

●

Ember inhaled slowly.

She did not brace herself. She did not push outward.

Instead, Ember turned inward, the way Momo had taught her. She was not summoning but remembering. Warmth bloomed behind her sternum, steady and anchoring, and spread outward in a quiet, controlled expansion. *The Book of Aeons* shifted against her back, and

Ember felt its weight suddenly immense. *The Book* was present, awake, and alive in the space. Magic.

The air rippled.

Voltaris materialized near the central platform—not whole, nor fragmented, but visibly incomplete. Light traced his outline, coalescing into a form that was both recognizably human and unmistakably not alive.

His presence altered the room's geometry. The space itself had recalibrated to accommodate him and so too had the people, whether they meant to or not. Ember knew Voltaris's presence was sacred here. He needed her, but she needed him too.

Hadden's breath hitched.

Ember watched as his jaw hardened and then opened into a sly smile. What was the meaning of his delight?

"Well," Hadden said softly, nodding in the direction of Voltaris. "It has been some time."

Time? Voltaris turned toward him, eyes dark with comprehension that transcended the measure of days or months or years. What was the significance of time between Hadden and Voltaris? When he spoke, Voltaris's voice resonated in poised clarity.

"You mistake continuity for control," Voltaris said.

Hadden laughed quietly. "Still idealistic, I see. It never quite landed for me—your convictions. Even when I was the child and you the elder, I found your visions simple. Mundane."

His comments were so clearly meant to wound. But much more was at stake than a scientist's pride. Voltaris didn't flinch. Ember saw him wink in her direction.

This was her opportunity. She stepped forward, leaning into the tension of the moment.

She reached back and withdrew *The Book of Aeons* from her backpack. The woven cloth fell away, and Ember clasped the ancient *Book* firmly before her heart, its presence a force uncontained.

The room responded. Hadden's face registered his recognition just as Dr. Voss's face drained of color.

"No," she whispered. "No—"

Dr. Voss could not hide her shock; she had not expected to see her precious tool in someone else's hands. She did not know it was possible for it to submit to another, after all these years under her control.

She lunged towards Ember, towards *The Book*, towards the Collection that fueled her power. But *The Book*, with its golden embroidery, its glittering eye, faced away from her, towards Dr. Voss and the others. *The Book* could see.

The movement was sharp and sudden, the restraint she had maintained until now cracking under the strain. She would not bear the loss that was so fast approaching. Dr. Voss crossed the space between them faster than Ember expected. It was not desperation or panic that moved her, but the precision of someone accustomed to acting before consequences could fully form. But before she reached Ember and *The Book*—

The Book of Aeons flared.

Light surged from Ember in a widening radius, *The Book* itself unmistakably alive. A source of energy itself. Undefinable and yet profoundly real.

Photons articulated in the open room, gathering themselves in spiraling patterns. There was no command, no instruction. They were responding not to authority but to coherence. They aligned themselves instinctively at the center of the room, collecting first around Ember and then into formations along the contours of Ember's body.

They were sketching the beginnings of a boundary. Neither shield nor armor, this boundary would not repel by force.

It refused.

Its potency was palpable. It halted Dr. Voss abruptly, and she staggered as though she had struck an invisible wall. She raised an arm to shield her eyes. Her breath caught in her throat.

"No," she said again, the word breaking as she spoke it the third time. "You don't know what you're doing."

But she was wrong.

At the center of the light, Ember stood steady on her feet. Her attention was fixed and quiet. The photons arranged themselves around her without urgency, settling into position according to some shared understanding. Ember recognized the pattern immediately—

This was the Wall.

The same Wall she had learned as a child, formed now, as then, through collaboration.

This Wall was made of light, of fundamental particles of energy, of interactive, living manifestations of fundamental reality.

This Wall did not shield her from the world. It resonated with her, responsive and perceptive, holding its shape because she did.

As it held its living form around her, Ember knew—*this* was the moment of convergence.

Voltaris sensed the transformation. Behind Ember, he shifted to reach his immaterial fingers toward *The Book*. Just as he brushed its cover, Ember opened *The Book* to him.

The pages of *The Book of Aeons* unfurled in vibrant discourse. They fluttered and turned, responding to Ember's intention as it poured forth from her hands. Though her knees shook, Ember stood steady. Holding *The Book* with fortitude, she implored that this reunion liberate Voltaris into true death, into his full expression, into this next iteration of life.

The air folded inward towards them all, compressing and releasing in a rhythm that made Ember's ears ring. The feeds on the massive screen flickered. Max would later tell her what they had done—how even time hesitated in the wake of their power.

Einstein's presence surged into fullness.

The Book did not summon his essence, nor was it extracted from the contents of *The Book*.

No. This was an immortal return.

For a fraction of a second, Ember had the disorienting sensation that she was witnessing a transformation that had already happened. It was simply that, in this moment, the truth was being acknowledged by the universe, each of them a witness. *The Book* opened a path. It was theirs to follow.

The room settled with them, then.

It was undeniable—Einstein's soul rejoined him. The fullness of his spirit, his consciousness, his imagination, his corporeal integration— all of these pieces were all now inherent to his singular being.

The transformation was immediate, visible, undeniable. Voltaris— Einstein—stood straighter, more complete.

He was still translucent, still not fully embodied, but the flicker was gone. The fragmentation that had clung to him dissolved, replaced by a density that revealed his integration. The instability that had once defined his presence resolved into something harmonious and whole.

Alena was made to confront her own loss with eyes wide open.

She screamed in horror, and the sound tore through the chamber, raw and unfiltered, stripping away the composure she had so carefully maintained. She collapsed to one knee, clutching her chest as though the most precious within her had been torn from her at a fundamental level. Her face contorted with a grief so intimate it felt almost invasive to witness.

Ember knew this was not rage. This was new rupture. This was infinite loss.

This essential being—aspects of Einstein's essence Alena had possessed for over a century—had been severed from her.

It was not just Einstein's soul she had lost, either. *The Book* had liberated them from her grasp—all of them.

For the first time in one hundred and fifty years, Alena was alone in her own mind. She lay on the floor in a heap, defeat wreaking its havoc on her solitary existence.

She looked up at Ember, terror and fury warring in her eyes. "You don't understand what you've taken from me."

"*I* didn't take it," Ember said, holding contact with Alena, revealing her own steady life force. "*You* did."

Dr. Voss surged forward again, but Hadden reached to catch her arm mid-motion.

"Enough," he said sharply. A tense anger diffused from his own eyes.

She rounded on him, her fury incandescent. "You said you would prevent this. You swore I would keep the souls."

Hadden released her without ceremony, his attention already drifting back to Ember. "I do not pretend to predict all outcomes. We adapt. We remain in motion. We *are* the control."

His dismissal was equally disquieting to Ember. She would not become his tool.

The photons around her thickened, resolving into clearer structure. The boundary that separated her from the others sharpened. She was not closed off from the world, rather the boundary clarified for her, and for the others, where she ended and everything else began.

The Wall.

●

Not solid. Not opaque. Not stagnant. Alive. Sensing. Changing. Protective. Integrative. Powerful.

Hadden's smile returned, slower now, something evaluative glinting beneath it.

"There you are," he said to Ember. "I was hoping you'd show me this."

Show him? Before Ember could react—before she could even register the shift—his presence slid effortlessly into her mind.

There was no force, no intrusion, no announcement of passage nor of violence. One moment she was standing in the underground laboratory, light humming around her; the next, she was spinning, spiraling through a crystalline tunnel, racing alongside her mind towards memories of her grandmother. She flashed through one and then another, the world around her rearranging itself without resistance. Until she was still.

She was seven years old.

She sat cross-legged on the floor of her grandmother's study, sunlight spilling through the window in warm, familiar bands. Dust motes drifted lazily in the air. Old books lined the shelves, their spines worn and comforting. She was sitting on the floor of her grandmother's study, passing thoughts back and forth. Momo's laughter filled the room, bright and unguarded. Ember was filled with delight.

She felt safe.

Curious.

Open.

Then someone else entered.

A younger Charles Hadden, at once familiar and strange.

He stood in the doorway, smiling—not with his mouth, but with his thoughts.

I'm so proud of you, his voice said, his thoughts entering Ember's mind, just as her grandmother's had. *So young*, he went on. *So smart. You'll go far.*

Confusion bloomed. Something tugged gently at the edges of her consciousness, lifting, probing, cataloging.

The sensation was wrong—not sharp, not violent, but deeply unsettling, like a hand rearranging something private under the guise of affection. His words landed differently than her grandmother's. Ember's delight began to fade.

Pain followed.

Not immediate. Not acute.

It unfurled slowly, disorienting in its intimacy, as though her thoughts were being unfolded and examined without her consent. Memories loosened. Associations blurred. She felt the first threads of herself begin to drift.

This is how it starts—a distant part of her recognized the disintegration. It was not domination but invitation that would allow the fracture.

Like an ocean swell, Momo's presence surged in Ember's mind.

Boundary, her grandmother reminded her gently. *You know this.*

The warmth behind Ember's sternum intensified, spreading outward in measured waves. The photons responded instantly.

Ember began to build.

The Wall rose precious piece by glowing piece, not with force but clarity. Each photon filed into place with deliberate intention, a primordial grace.

This was not a Wall erected in opposition. It was assembled in recognition of Ember's fullness *and* her edges. It understood and protected what belonged to her alone.

Hadden took a pause, slowing his influence. Or maybe it was Ember that slowed him.

He studied the structure with fascination, his presence pressing lightly against its forming edges. *Remarkable*, his voice uttered, like a murmur in her mind. *You are teaching me, little light.*

Get out, Ember thought, resolve fortifying her practice.

Hadden resisted.

His efforts were not of brute force but distraction. Doubt scattered through her awareness, abrupt and insidious. There were questions everywhere. *Wasn't she doing harm? Wasn't she alone? Wasn't keeping such a solid boundary a selfish choice for a child?*

Nothing stuck.

Ember was reinforced in her intention. She cleared her mind deliberately, stripping away everything extraneous until only three presences remained: herself, Momo, and Hadden.

The onslaught intensified.

She held strong, iterating photons as sustenance.

Hadden fought, clinging to fragments of thought, attempting to anchor himself to the very structure she was constructing. But the photons rejected him. They did not attack; they simply refused to align with him.

This is my mind, she thought. *You were not invited.*

With a final billow of deep clarity, Ember expelled Hadden from that luminous space.

The Wall was sealed.

Inside her mind, silence bloomed—thoughtless, present, peaceful.

●

When Ember opened her eyes, the laboratory still held its altered character.

The fluorescent lights burned steadily overhead, their greenish cast flattening the vast space into sharp relief. The massive screen at the center of the room continued its quiet surveillance of the world above: the lamps lining the lawn, students crossing the quad, the old classroom building standing unchanged. The smaller windows along the bottom edge of the display scrolled with data from laboratories across the globe.

She blinked, her balance faltering for a moment as the room snapped back into place. The light surrounding her thinned and faded, its careful structure unraveling until only the ordinary air remained, heavy and real around her.

She looked around. *Something* was different.

Max and Olive remained beside her, frozen in stunned silence. Voltaris—Einstein—stood nearby, whole and steady.

The others were gone.

All the doors were shut.

Einstein met her gaze, something like quiet approval in his eyes.

"Now," he said softly, "we begin."

Chapter 29: The Coherence

"Now," he'd said, "we begin."

Einstein's words settled, threading themselves into the quiet hum of the underground laboratory, as if they belonged there, as if the room and all who occupied it had been waiting for them.

For several seconds, no one moved.

Max was the first to break the stillness.

He exhaled slowly, the sound of his breath audible in the open space, and turned in a careful arc, his eyes tracing the sealed doors around the chamber. His posture was alert, wary, as though motion itself might invite something back into the room.

"They didn't leave," he said finally.

It wasn't a question. Their absence lacked the sense of departure. They all knew—something else had altered this space.

Olive shook her head once. "No. But what happened to them?"

"They were displaced," Einstein said, his voice calm, measured.

Dr. Voss and Hadden—persons of position and power, authorities in their fields—and Dr. Milton, too. What did it mean to *displace* bodies such as this? And what of their souls?

Max frowned, unable to reconcile the questions with Einstein's simple answer. "Should that distinction be a comfort?"

Einstein inclined his head slightly. "No, it is not meant to comfort. These are the facts." But Ember knew he was not withholding. Rather, he wanted them to see what was unfolding and how they themselves were now at the center of it. It was indescribable. And yet...

She remained still—an articulating presence standing between the others. But her attention was now divided in a way that felt new and unsettling.

Part of her was fully present in the room. She was radically aware of the polished floor beneath her feet. She could sense the faint vibration of machinery deep in the stone foundation of the building. And the steady glow of the massive screen at the center of the lab invited her attention too.

But another part of her was turned inward, aware of the Wall. She felt was learning it, this new aspect of herself. It felt integral and inherent, not a barrier she maintained but an arrangement within her. The Wall was an attentive structure of living light; it was responsive to her awareness and inseparable from it. And with the Wall, she found new dimensions of relationship with the world beyond herself.

Just now, she found, despite the alterations in the space—and in herself—Ember was not straining. She was not resisting. She was—or perhaps it was the Wall that was—just holding.

It was the first time Ember had ever felt entirely certain of where her edges were. Because they moved with her.

This was a change.

Her hand was positioned firmly against *The Book of Aeons*. She held it, tucked in at her side. Its presence was constant now. It no longer beckoned to her; no urgency required her attention. But she knew certain qualities of *The Book* had changed since it had lay dormant in Dr. Voss's possession, before their connection.

The Book was now alert, an entity of its own agency. Now, Ember sensed *The Book* intimately, almost as though they were entwined, or entangled. She felt they were collaborators. Its wisdom percolated through her own, her thoughts sifting through the layers of knowledge *The Book* held sacred.

Ember understood that the wisdom of *The Book of Aeons* was truly at her side. With just the flip of a thought in its direction, she could unwind clarity and consciousness that extended deep into the past and, perhaps, into the future.

With this access, this resource, Ember felt keenly aware of the choices unfolding around her. It wasn't her or the Wall within her that had transformed the space. Or, at least, it wasn't her alone.

She had a sense that the underground laboratory had been altered by something else. Something that was at once bigger and more defined. Something familiar and yet...

"This wasn't us," Ember spoke the words as clarity rang through her mind. "The system..." she paused. And then—

"The system did this."

Einstein's gaze shifted to her, sharper than it had been before. He recognized the integration she was experiencing—self and *Book*, Wall and witness.

"The system responded," he corrected her and explained, "to a contradiction it could no longer sustain." His clarifications landed so briefly, and yet Ember, Max, and Olive—three young scientists following in his path—understood. They were speaking of quantum dynamics.

"The system?" Olive questioned. But she realized as she spoke that this question was not meant for an answer. She crossed her arms, and lifted her head, so clearly presenting the conundrum this information seemed to require of them: being open and closed at the same time. Her expression was tight as she clarified her question. "A contradiction between what and what, exactly?"

Einstein turned toward the screen, and Ember, Max, and Olive turned their eyes to observe what was playing out now in the underground laboratory.

For the first time since they had entered this subterranean place, they noticed a shift in the nature of the display. Where before it had seemed passive—built for human observation and analysis—now it seemed autonomous. Dr. Voss and Dr. Milton were gone. Hadden was gone. There was no one here to fix its settings, to alter its positioning. The question was mysterious and yet apparent. Was the display choosing its own course?

They observed it thoughtfully. The familiar feeds were still there. Lamps glowing against the early evening through the campus quad above. Below streamed a steady procession of data from laboratories around the world.

But something had changed. It was apparent in the way the information was arranged, the organization and perhaps even the orientation of the thing.

Ember noticed that certain windows had expanded slightly, their borders now emphasized to draw her attention. Others had receded, now deprioritized. New markers—numerical sequences flickering with light—pulsed faintly along the margins. These new details were integrating themselves without fanfare or alert.

This was the system at work. It was not merely recording, not collecting data for observation. For the first time, Ember recognized that this system was more intelligent than that. It was evaluating.

It was difficult to perceive. Ember knew that too. Max and Olive would have questions.

"This infrastructure was built to seek equilibrium," Einstein offered, opening into the details for the young physicists. "When influence exceeds coherence, it adjusts."

But Max did not find these insights reassuring. His jaw tightened. "Adjusts around what?"

A new quiet permeated the space. Einstein did not answer immediately, and Ember felt the shift before he spoke.

It was a subtle and yet unmistakable sense of attention turning toward her, not just from the people in the room, but from the space itself. From the architecture. From the materials, the structure, the dimensions of this place. From the network threaded invisibly through the walls and far beyond them. All orienting towards a center. And then, as slowly as her consciousness would allow, Ember began to realize just what, or who, was at that center.

"A source," Einstein said at last, "that can remain intact under sustained pressure."

The words rocked her inner worlds, but Ember did not flinch. She had already felt the truth of them settling into place. She knew this had nothing to do with flattery. This was no complimentary elevation of her mind or person.

This was responsibility. Though Dr. Voss and Hadden both were gone from this space, the threat was not over. The infrastructure adjusted. Around a source that can remain intact under sustained pressure. If she was right, this meant *more* risk for her, not less.

As she looked to Max, she saw in her friend's eyes that he understood too. He looked intensely at Ember, so clearly reckoning with the alterations this new knowledge required of him.

"So this thing—" he said, gesturing toward the screen, "it's orienting itself around you?"

Ember lifted her eyes to Einstein, and he met her gaze, responding so she would not have to. "Yes," he said.

Olive began to speak, then stopped and cleared her throat. When she spoke again, her voice was low and clear.

"Because she can't be taken," Olive said. "She can't be controlled." Her soft voice lilted up—she was offering that last as a question to Einstein. Olive did not fully grasp the dynamics at work here, but she understood the gravity.

"No," Einstein said. "Because she cannot be made singular."

Ember's fingers curled slightly against *The Book*. She, too, was reckoning with profound change. It was not just a dance with control but a fortitude she now bore. Yes, just now, it felt like weight. Yet another responsibility she was integrating. Her internal landscape was a blank slate.

"And that makes me—what?" Ember asked. She needed to know just how deep this alteration would go. "A stabilizer?"

Einstein's expression softened, though the gravity in his eyes did not.

"In this case," he conceded, "and for Hadden's purposes, it makes you a constraint."

Silence stretched between them.

Ember absorbed Einstein's words slowly. For whatever plan that was playing out around her, Ember was an instrument—but not a key. She was a source—but not a solution. She sensed her role was one of definition. Ember had become something that would prevent collapse by refusing completion.

"This is not the same as safety," she said quietly, as though to herself, but she knew her friends could hear.

"No," Einstein agreed. "It is responsibility. But Ember—" he offered, and she felt an extension from him. A grace emanated towards her. Einstein—this newly integrated being—felt compassion for her.

"This is your magic," he said.

The hum of the laboratory deepened, almost imperceptibly. It resonated through the floor and into Ember's bones. She felt it as alignment rather than sound—a subtle pressure that made the Wall within her feel suddenly, unmistakably relevant. She had to ask.

"Am I still in danger?" a question, though she was certain of the answer.

Einstein did not hesitate. "Yes." He was unflinching. "That will not change. Not so long as Hadden is alive.

"And," he continued. "Who knows what will come beyond that."

Max swore under his breath. Olive stepped closer again. Her presence offered Ember a steady anchor at her side.

Einstein had more to say. A reminder, a comfort: "Ember, this is not danger in the way Alena intended. You cannot be collected or consumed." And then, what he really meant to say: "She cannot steal your soul."

Ember nodded once.

"It is Hadden who will try to position you now," Einstein said, "to better shape his own powers. It is no longer Alena but he who is most dangerous to you now."

At the sound of his name, the screen shifted again. How was it responding to them, to the dynamics of the room? A new feed expanded smoothly across the center display.

Ember recognized the building instantly. She had seen it featured across news media countless times over the past 24 hours. It was the chamber room of the Sovereign Nations Alliance.

Now, on the display before them, the room was empty except for the board table, the podium, and the multiplicity of flags that lined the walls. But there was a foreboding sense about it, and Ember, Max, and Olive each recognized the tone. Some sort of preparation was unfolding there.

A timestamp glowed in the corner, flashing with each second that passed: three minutes.

Max stared. "Is this *the system*? Why is it watching the SNA?"

Einstein's gaze sharpened. "Because *it* is already being consulted."

The weight of the moment overcame them then. Among Ember, Max, and Olive, there was not panic; rather, an inevitability settled over them.

The course had shifted. Their work was no longer about Dr. Voss. And though it was about Hadden, it was not about him alone.

Whatever Dr. Voss had been doing here, beneath the university, had begun to interact with the world above it. It was intersecting with technologies, individuals, and organizations far beyond these walls.

And Ember, source, reference, mode of utility to the strongest powers in the world, was standing at the point of contact.

The countdown continued at the edge of the screen. Once she forced herself to really look again, she noticed that first. The timestamp sat unobtrusively in the corner, its numbers changing with quiet regularity. The system would not center it, almost in denial of its significance.

Instead, the display continued its work—streams of data flowing, windows resizing, relationships recalculating, as though the approaching moment were simply another variable to be absorbed.

That, Ember realized, was the most unsettling part.

The system was not bracing for impact. *It was incorporating it.*

She stepped closer to the platform without quite meaning to. The air shifted subtly as she did. It was practically imperceptible, not strong enough for Max or Olive to comment on or even notice, but quite enough for her to feel it along her arms and across her sternum. It felt like pressure adjusting in a sealed room. The Wall inside her responded automatically, not by hardening, but by clarifying. She was still fully present. Still porous to sensation. But the boundary remained intact.

Einstein watched her with careful attention.

"You're feeling it now," he said.

Ember nodded. "It's... orienting."

"Yes," he said. And then after a long pause, "That is coherence."

"That word again," Max said below his breath. He seemed frustrated. Max was particularly annoyed at the circumstances unfolding and particularly their impact on his friend. He had not yet realized all the ways the impacts for himself. He looked to Einstein with an expression of sincere supplication.

But Einstein didn't smile. "Because the structure is doing more than prioritizing information," he said. "It's beginning to weigh decisions, to position them against one another, and to pursue a course of action of its own accord."

Olive stiffened in her tenuous stance. "Decisions about what?" Her mind was running rapidly, integrating what she'd comprehended from the day thus far with what she was hearing from Einstein now.

Einstein gestured toward the lower edge of the screen, where several of the laboratory feeds had dimmed slightly. As their data streams thinned, other feeds became more prominent. Ember recognized them as facilities tied to communications infrastructure, defense hubs, behavioral modeling, or large-scale predictive analysis. These new feeds had brightened subtly, their connections tightening.

"The system is reallocating its attention," Einstein said. "It will reduce its reliance on noisy or cumbersome inputs. It will elevate sources that demonstrate internal consistency under stress."

His observations were articulate and discerning. He was trying to guide them, but to what end, Ember did not yet know.

A cold clarity settled over her. "The system is learning who to trust," she said.

"Yes," Einstein replied. "And more importantly—what not to amplify; potentially, what to conceal."

Max spoke again. He was broadening his imagination. He was beginning to harness the pieces, starting to grasp the relationships. Still, the words came through under his breath: "Not oversight, but curation."

"Exactly," Einstein said.

The Book stirred faintly at Ember's side in recognition. She could feel its discomfort now more distinctly. It was not fear or resistance that disturbed *The Book*—it was strain, as though it were being pulled toward a function it had been designed to avoid. Its wisdom meandered its way through Ember's consciousness until she understood its message—daunting but not fearful.

Voltaris

"They're going to frame this as neutral," Ember said quietly. "As optimization."

How much were Hadden and his team influencing these elements? It was becoming clearer and clearer that they would use any means to meet their goal. The language was simply a way to orient other powers to their ends.

Einstein inclined his head. "Yes, we can assume as much. That is how such systems justify themselves."

The countdown ticked on. Less than two minutes.

Sensing the urgency of this new timeframe, Olive turned sharply to Einstein. "Hadden knew you would be reintegrated with your soul. He set this up... he expected you would be here with us now."

"Yes, Olive," Einstein said. "I think you're right. It does seem he anticipated the possibility. I'm not sure how..." his voice drifted for a moment, and then he brought his thoughts back to them, "he knew my intentions." But his aspirations for regaining his soul were shifting by the moment.

Ember wondered at what Einstein meant, but her thoughts were interrupted.

"So this was never about Dr. Voss. Or, at least, it was not about her alone," Max said. The wheels were turning. "Hadden's collaboration with her—was he just appeasing her?" Disgust registered through Max's body.

339

"She was a test case," Olive said, sensing in her own body what that might mean—for Dr. Voss, for them, and for their research.

"A catalyst," Einstein corrected. "Hadden needed her to initiate his design. And it seems it worked.

"Alena proved that control was more than possible; it was powerful. However, now Hadden is interested in a distinct opportunity: he wants to learn whether control can be sustained without overt force."

This was the definition of manipulation. Ember closed her eyes briefly, following the inner walls of her psyche, unraveling the visions, the dreams, and the very real experiences she had had over the past weeks. When she opened her eyes, she spoke the words like a confession:

"And I'm the proof of concept."

Einstein did not deny it. Ember was unmoved. By now, she understood that she would have to face whatever was to come. She knew that would be infinitely better off with as much understanding as possible. Every page written among them tonight was worth collecting. She was building a bank of knowledge. Who knew what would come for her from this moment on.

"But Hadden doesn't want you inside the system," Einstein said. "He's not looking for an operator nor a collaborator. He sees you as a *source*."

A source. A beginning. *Yes, this was a beginning. But...*

"But he needs you for reference," Einstein went on. "You remain, in his mind, a tool for his application."

A reference doesn't choose, Ember thought to herself. *It just... exists.*

But she was not a tool. She was not a reference, nor any sort of source, or resource, to be used as he pleased. Ember's heart warmed as the fire grew inside her. She would not succumb to the will of Hadden's influence or power.

"I can see now," Einstein continued. "Hadden has his own vision for you. And everything else adjusts around it."

And that was when the danger sharpened—not for the first time, but anew. She could no longer justify its abstraction. Ember saw it clearly: a future in which she was never invited to consent, never honored in her decision. She might be cited, or invoked. Her integrity would be used as justification for actions taken elsewhere.

She imagined the empty eyes of those who would insist they were celebrating her coherence, even as they hollowed her out.

"That's how he protects himself," Ember said. "And now it has come down on me. He has all the tools he needs for total manipulation, total control. He doesn't need my agreement. So long as I persist, he has access to me. If I lose my agency..."

Einstein's expression darkened. He knew the truth of this threat far too well.

"Yes," his voice was distant yet profoundly clear. "Persistence without agency is a form of captivity."

Ember witnessed in him the grief of his fractured existence.

She witnessed the world, its iterative crises, and the lack of true integrity and power among its leadership.

How could she protect herself *and* alter the course of Hadden—and any other villainous magicians among his accomplices?

The Book pulsed once, requesting her attention. She was not alone, nor was the magic she now claimed a solitary one. It spoke, in its way: *I cannot remain neutral if singularity is imposed. The Book* directed its meaning intently to Ember's mind. *Neutrality becomes endorsement, and I promise you, Ember—I will not persist in this way.*

Ember's fingers tightened against its cover. *The Book's* own boundaries had implications for her. Was it possible?

When she spoke, she referred to both of them—herself and *The Book*—together: "And if I refuse?"

Einstein's gaze flicked back to the screen. Ember, Max, and Olive looked up to see that the system had begun to draw faint outlines around certain data clusters—emergent shapes, provisional models. Ember recognized the similarity between the shapes and Dr. Voss's sigils, the same ones that had led them here that first night.

Finally, Einstein offered what he could to Ember's question. "If you refuse," he said. "Then the system will seek substitutes. If it finds unworthy ones, it will fracture in its attempt to resource elsewhere."

At first, fracture seemed like possibility, but then... there was more Einstein wasn't saying. It was as though the system ensured that everyone in that space knew what would happen.

If the system *were* to fracture, each of them risked disorientation beyond their imagination.

Max looked between them. "So the world either bends around Ember—or breaks trying not to."

A smile flickered in Einstein's eyes. Finally, the light.

"*That* is the false dilemma Hadden is constructing," he said. But what did he mean?

"There is always an alternative," he said.

Was that hope Ember heard in his voice now?

And finally, Einstein completed his thought: "I entreated my whole life towards undiscovered possibilities. I am, in fact, certain that no answer is entire, no course ever truly complete."

The countdown reached one minute, thirty seconds.

Olive exhaled slowly, grounding herself. "We can't let Hadden control the narrative. We can't let him control *you*, Ember. Is there not some resolution in *The Book*? Some dynamic we've yet to discover?" She looked to Einstein and then back to Ember. "How can we apply our imagination to this?"

Ember nodded. Olive's question inspired her. She could sense a path crystallizing before her, a way forward. Momo's words swept through her consciousness, pressing away the doubt and fear that flirted at its edges:

Science and wonder are the same.

It was not a solution, but it offered her a way forward—the same direction she had been craving for so long now. Ember would be true to her knowledge, her power. *And* she would be protected. "We can't let this become about me alone. We won't." It was about so much more than her. The wonder in the world required it.

Einstein studied her. Approval and then admiration flickered across his features. Finally, he could see the strength in her magic. This was what had compelled him towards her from the start. "Good," he said. "Because that is the only way." *You will survive.*

Again, Ember found within her what he didn't say.

The hum of the lab deepened again, and this time Max noticed the screen. "It's escalating."

Einstein confirmed. "The consultation is imminent."

The SNA chamber feed sharpened. Staff began to enter the room above. Assistants moved across the space with practiced efficiency, placing documents, testing microphones. The preparations were complete. The chamber was ready.

Ember felt the pull then—a new sensation. It was not physical or mental. She would later describe it as contextual. She had a sense that she was being utilized. She felt herself positioned within a larger frame, her coherence a stabilizing constant. Whether she wanted it or not, this was happening. Despite her earlier negations, she didn't know what else to do.

Boundary. Momo's voice. She was here.

Science doesn't kill magic; it reveals it.

Hadden's science, or whatever it was, was calling forth her magic. And she knew how to do this. Ember straightened. Would he stay to work with her?

"Einstein," she said. "If your reintegration means you're finite again, does that mean you can't remain like this? What—" Then Ember stammered, unexpectedly. She was surprised at the depth of this loss. "What will happen to you?"

But Einstein held promise in his eyes. "I am staying to see you through," he said, knowingly. He understood that Ember felt she was out of her depths. But he also knew that that was only a feeling. She was not out of her depths. And he would be sure she had the tools she needed. "Mabel has requested it," and there was another twinkle in his eye. "But our work will continue, Ember."

Einstein's form shimmered faintly, the edges of him now a bit softer, less defined than they had been moments earlier.

"I will not vanish," he said. "I might call it... redistribution." In her body, Ember knew what this meant.

But Max and Olive both widened their eyes in surprise.

"Into the system?" Max asked, still tenuously holding Einstein's role in this moment.

"No," Einstein replied. "Into the spaces between it."

Ember remembered Momo's story—the child and the neighbor woman who baked the delicious cookies and what happened after death. She understood then. Not disappearance... diffusion. Influence from the ethers.

"Will we be able to hear you?" she asked. *I. Will I be able to hear you?*

"You will recognize me," Einstein said gently. "But you must trust yourself. Count on yourself. Coherence is congruous, integral, whole. This is your work to do."

The words carried finality. The mission that had brought Voltaris to Ember, bridged him from the liminal realm to the living world, was complete. Einstein would move into his next reality.

No one noticed the perceptible edges of Einstein growing softer.

The countdown had slipped under one minute, and the screen above them had captured their attention. Ember, Max, and Olive watched as the first delegates took their seats. Olive stepped closer to Ember, as though standing guard. Her trust in Ember was perceptible. As was Ember's own.

Ember felt the Wall steady within her, agile and yet strong, animating her exactly, precisely and completely, where she was. She gripped one hand around *The Book*, letting her palm soften into its worn cover. The other brushed Olive's sleeve, grounding herself in what was human and present.

Fifteen seconds left. "This is it," Einstein said quietly, turning to Max.

A responsibility, Max understood. The articulation of matters at hand. He spoke, "Our studies have just breached the surface. Now..." Urgency was building in his voice, but he remained strong. "Ember, if you hold fast..."

One last look from Einstein quieted Max's forceful voice. A responsibility, to perceive. Einstein nodded to Ember as his form filtered into space. "This, you know how to do." And he was gone.

Seven seconds left. Ember was grateful for her friends' courage, for Einstein's direction, and for Momo's guidance. But no one else could hold her together now. In this moment, not one resource outside herself could keep her intact.

She took a breath, sensing the barrier of photons she had constructed, and their attunement to her intentions. For the first time, she reached her consciousness into the dimensions of energy that surrounded her now and crystallized their power. Light consumed her vision, the photonic glow transforming her perception from sensory to integrated. Waves and particles danced, and Ember, no longer the observer, danced with them. As a dynamic force grew up within them, she felt stronger, more clear and more articulate.

She felt the tragic force of consumption against her edges. But now, she was the Wall. Full of trust in her knowledge, her wonder, *and* her magic, Ember stepped forward into the light and only then did she respond. "Yes." As Ember spoke the words, they echoed through space and time. "This, we know how to do."

Epilogue

Dr. Quinn strode through the halls of the physics building, a paper-wrapped parcel clutched to her chest. She wore a long wool coat, stunning ruby lipstick, and the same red boots that had carried her through the last three years. Students described her as insanely brilliant, immeasurably kind, and profoundly quiet. A passerby might say she seemed confident and composed. On this Monday morning, inside the now-familiar Wall, she was feeling particularly content. This was a new beginning in so many ways.

She paused at the door to her old laboratory. So much of her life—so much of the world—had changed through the other side of this door. She took a beat and peered through the glass pane. Everything she could see on the inside looked just the same, but she was undeniably different.

She took a step back, gathering herself, when a glimmer of light on the gold plate beside the door caught her eye. There, to the right of the doorframe, was one crucial piece of evidence that this place was different too: "Dr. Ember Quinn," it read. "Albert Einstein Photonics Laboratory."

Memories swelled Ember's chest. It was an honor to see her name beside his.

Ember reached for the handle and crossed the threshold into *her* laboratory. She took it all in, every direction, every spot of light, every cupboard and drawer. Some things had changed, she had to admit. Dr. Voss's unusual antique cabinets had been retired from the laboratory. In their place, the university had restored the fine cabinetry. A simple gift to account for her massive undertaking. But Edmondston University hadn't had to do any convincing to get Ember to stay. She longed for continuity. At the same time, she appreciated this fresh start.

She could tell someone had already been here, though. Because positioned across the walls were photos of guides, her mentors, and her inspirations. It meant everything, to know that so many brilliant minds had influenced her knowledge. She felt as though the room was full of friends. The place sparkled with charm, a laboratory through time.

She wondered what kind of future would be made inside these four walls.

"Well, hello! Max poked his head in the door. He must've been passing by on the way to or from his laboratory down the hall. His space was a bit smaller than this one but an ideal spot for his solitary approach.

"If it isn't the coherence, right here in our building?" he whispered, teasingly. He smiled genuinely at Ember. They'd been through so much to get here. Max knew—more than most ever would—what it had taken for Ember to survive the last year, let alone choose to be a teacher of quantum physics, after all of that.

"It's a new page," she said. It was. Nothing was finished, not in the global context, but she saw a way through. Ember knew, it was time to look ahead.

"More like a new stage," Max responded. "We're the big dogs now. Lots of responsibility," he nodded.

A passerby might misinterpret his quippy statements, but these two understood the responsibility that came with their knowledge.

"You know Olive's really proud of you," he said, and Ember could see the tenderness in his eyes. Then, after a moment, he was the same ol' Max. "Back to it, then," he said, and trotted towards his spot just a few doors over.

Alone again, Ember turned towards the only room inside the laboratory: her new office. It was sparse, undecorated, waiting to be arranged to her liking. She'd asked for only a single piece of furniture.

The new desk took up the bulk of the space. It was still wrapped in the shipping material, at her request. She released her grip on the parcel to run a finger over the bubble wrap, following the contours with her mind. Imagining the photons taking the same amorphous organization around her. The bubble wrap was also at her request— she hadn't wanted to have any doubts that this room was untouched. She trusted her friends, but she wouldn't say her confidence in others extended very far beyond that.

She reached towards a hole in the plastic at the corner and pulled the wrapping across the surface until it fell in a pile on the floor beside her; then she laid her package on the open surface and unfolded the paper.

Inside was no instrument, no book of secrets, not even a letter from someone important in her life. No, it was just a photo. Well, maybe *just* wasn't an accurate descriptor.

She walked around to the chair behind the desk and sat down on the bubble-wrapped cushion. She stood the frame at the corner of her desk, like a forcefield between her and the outside world. These were her most essential guides. It would be unwise to neglect their influence inside this laboratory.

The picture showed three people pressed together—friends, Ember knew now—dressed in their nicest. Her grandmother's smile shone. She was so clearly delighted to stand between two of the most inquisitive, impactful scientists the world would ever know and call them her friends. In hindsight, Ember recognized the complexity of these dynamics and the unexpected roles each would take in the others' lives as time went on. But it was extraordinary to see them all together:

Mabel Quinn, Alena Voss, and Albert Einstein.

A treasure.

As she admired her grandmother's smile, she thought of all that had transpired since the moment that photo was taken. Even what had come to light since the photo first entered her memory on the cobblestone street.

If Ember could bring just one thing from recent months into this next stage of her work, it would be the wisdom she'd garnered from these three.

Her grandmother's guidance resonated within her often. Though Momo's voice was not as clear as it had been during those early days of the coherence, she trusted her beloved grandmother would be there in just the right moment. Dr. Alena Voss's influence was undeniable. It was in her laboratory—this laboratory—that Ember unwound the unexpected truth of her magic. Dr. Voss's photon research had been the window into a world of communication and integration: photon sentience. And finally, Dr. Einstein. Voltaris—that's what he had called himself in those transformative days. He had guided her into the fortified clarity she needed to wield her power with integrity. Einstein understood Ember's magic, reminded her of her knowledge, and illustrated, in what had been the most intense moment of her life, how to braid the two together, all in the service of peace.

These three—their brilliance, their achievements, and the cautionary tales born of their choices—had provided Ember with everything she needed to move deeper into her work. But Ember knew, with all her mind, heart, and *intact* soul, now more than ever, what came next was up to her.

Voltaris

About the Author

Corrina Westfall is a producer, director, and author. She has built a career on her passion for sharing stories that resonate. Moved by real world stories, Corrina works to create elements of visual and literary storytelling to weave the practical with the possible.

Her writing is inspired by creative forces like Tim Burton and Stephen King. The story of *Voltaris* was born out of Corrina's passion for photography and thus her admiration for Albert Einstein, whose imagination and, especially, his explanation of the photoelectric effect have made possible the evolution of modern photography. *Voltaris* celebrates Einstein's passion for peace and hopes to bridge his insight to guide modern generations as we navigate the uncertain and important questions of our time.

This first book marks Corrina's heart-led venture into authorship. With *Voltaris* as her guide, she knows the possibilities are endless.

www.ingramcontent.com/pod-product-compliance
Lightning Source LLC
Chambersburg PA
CBHW070319030726
47505CB00004B/1026